THE BELTANE FIRES

Janet MacLeod Trotter

Published by MacLeod Trotter Books

paperback edition: March 2011

ISBN 978-0-9566426-9-1

www.janetmacleodtrotter.com

Janet MacLeod Trotter was brought up in the North East of England with her four brothers, by Scottish parents. She is a best-selling author of 15 novels, including the hugely popular Jarrow Trilogy, and a childhood memoir, BEATLES & CHIEFS, which was featured on BBC Radio Four. Her novel, THE HUNGRY HILLS, gained her a place on the shortlist of The Sunday Times' Young Writers' Award, and the TEA PLANTER'S LASS was longlisted for the RNA Romantic Novel Award. A graduate of Edinburgh University, she has been editor of the Clan MacLeod Magazine, a columnist on the Newcastle Journal and has had numerous short stories published in women's magazines. She lives in the North of England with her husband, daughter and son. Find out more about Janet and her other popular novels at: www.janetmacleodtrotter.com

Also by Janet MacLeod Trotter

Historical:

The Hungry Hills
The Darkening Skies
The Suffragette
Never Stand Alone
Chasing the Dream
For Love & Glory
The Jarrow Lass
Child of Jarrow
Return to Jarrow
A Crimson Dawn
A Handful of Stars
The Tea Planter's Lass

Mystery:

The Vanishing of Ruth

Teenage:

Love Games

Non Fiction:

Beatles & Chiefs

CHAPTER ONE

Mairi threw back her head and laughed as she spun recklessly in the reel. Her red hair lit like heated copper as the crackling flames from the bonfire threw warm light onto the revellers.

'Faster!' The word caught in her throat as she threw herself against her partner and forced him to swing harder. Mairi danced bare foot like the village girls, her heavy gown tucked up into her girdle. Lost in the heady music of drums and pipes, the cries of the dancers as they swirled in the smoke of sweet birchwood, she was unaware of the eyes watching her. The music stopped.

'More Rory, please,' the young redhead smiled breathlessly at the old itinerate piper, her green eyes alive with mischief. 'It's a sad day when a Highlander like you has not the puff for a second tune.'

His craggy face split in a grin and he spat into the fire.

'And 'tis a sad day when a daughter of Lismore is not chosen as Queen of the May,' he teased back in Gaelic.

Mairi flushed a deeper crimson in the flickering light and tossed the tangled mane of hair over her shoulder. 'The tastes of these Sassenachs are too tame,' she pouted back in mock offence, the amusement pulling at her full lips. Rory struck up his pipes in agreement.

As two young local boys moved towards her, Mairi felt a cold bony grip seize her arm. 'It's time you came home,' the thin sharp face of her stepsister was suddenly close.

'Isabel,' Mairi smiled in surprise, 'I thought you hadn't come. Don't tell me the Kirk has allowed you to indulge in dancing for one night? How sinful.'

The fingers dug painfully into the younger girl's bare arm, making her eyes water. 'Don't blaspheme you little fool,' Isabel's black eyes narrowed and her mouth tightened. 'You've made enough of a spectacle of yourself tonight. Look at your mud-stained ankles. And where's your caul? Only harlots go bareheaded.'

Mairi winced at the savagery of her words and involuntarily wiped the flecks of spittle that had landed on her cheek.

'It's only in fun. We always danced at the Beltane fires at home.' Mairi tried to worm her arm free from the iron-fisted hold. 'It will ensure a good harvest. Anyway, there's little enough to celebrate around here these days and if your ministers get their way, there won't be anything left to dance about.'

She did not see the slap coming; Isabel struck like an adder. Mairi reeled back, the shock registering before the stinging flesh.

'This debauchery should never have been allowed! Father will have to answer to the presbytery before long.' Isabel pointed a menacing finger at her stepsister. 'And you are no longer a little Highland savage; you're a daughter of Duntorin and will behave like one.'

1

'Never!' Mairi felt the quick spark of temper flush her blood. 'I'm here by force, not choice.' Her green eyes blazed back in defiance, taunting further punishment. 'I'll never be a Roskill of Duntorin, no matter that my mother chose to marry one. My veins are thick with the red blood of Lismore and always will be.'

Isabel looked about her and saw some of the local people taking an interest in the quarrel; the ones who were neither yet befuddled with drink nor had slipped off into the woods hand in hand. She felt at once out of place in her sober black dress and prim white ruff, her black hair imprisoned in an all-embracing coif.

'Mairi,' she controlled her voice with difficulty, 'please come with me. There will be trouble.'

Something in the urgency of her voice checked Mairi's brusque reply. What did she mean by trouble? If it was the amorous advances of some ale-smelling youth, she could cope with that. But a sudden chill went through her; there was something more dangerous afoot. Perhaps she should follow meekly and leave the dance to die with the fire?

'I'll take care of our sweet wee "sister",' a deep amused voice cut into the silence between the two girls. Mairi swung about, peering through the twilight for the joker. No one here called her sister.

A tall broad-shouldered figure walked leisurely forward from the deep shadow of a nearby tree. She could smell the leather of a rider's breeches and jerkin, warm and male, though she could not make out his face. Mairi could feel his amusement and it left her at a loss for words.

'Well, do I get no greeting?' The man threw open his arms in question.

'Douglas?' Isabel faltered, the surprise softening her voice. 'Is it really you?' The rider laughed in reply, stepping forward and enfolding the thin young woman in a bear-hug.

'You didn't think I'd miss the crowning of the May Queen did you?' he chuckled and kissed her again affectionately on the forehead. Isabel stifled a giggle at her elder brother, the hard frost of minutes before, thawing under his warm attention.

'How long have you been here? Have you seen father yet? How was Denmark? Tell me!' she cried in excitement.

'Plenty of time for questions later, dear sister,' he squeezed her shoulders, 'I have much to tell. And Mairi, so quiet?' he turned to her. 'I remember you as such a chattering child.'

The young Highland girl felt her cheeks begin to burn, annoyance releasing a string of words from her hitherto speechless mouth.

'No longer a child, "brother",' she stressed the term with disdain, 'and I prefer to choose to whom I chatter.'

To her fury Douglas roared with laughter and came forward to greet her. Mairi stiffened and he thought better of a welcome like the one he had given Isabel. Instead he seized her hand and brought it up to his lips. At that moment, a sappy branch caught fire at last and set off a fizz of white flame, lighting the darkened face of the newcomer. Mairi found herself looking into the black-violet eyes of her stepbrother, filled with merriment. His raven dark hair was swept back from his forehead in unruly waves and she would not have recognised him with the closely cut beard that brushed her hand. No longer the dare-devil youth who had delighted in teasing her and then gone abroad in search of more dangerous sport.

She could not break her gaze from the eyes embracing her, like the deep velvet of a night sky, larger and more alive than the cold black of Isabel's.

'I stand rebuked,' he murmured in a low infuriating voice, 'I can see you are no child, sweet sister.'

'No sister of yours,' Mairi pulled her hand away from his warm hold and glared. 'I see before me my father's executioner.'

She had not meant to greet him with these words, but he had deliberately provoked her and they were out before she could stop them. His eyes clouded like a night storm, black and forbidding, the amusement dying from the corners of his mouth.

Isabel cut in sharply, 'how dare you accuse my brother of such a thing, you know it is not true, you wicked child.'

She tried to move her thin tall frame between Douglas and Mairi, protecting her brother from the temper of their stepsister, disturbed by the effect the glowing red hair and piquant face appeared to have on him. She had not realised it, but in the last year Mairi's small stripling body had begun to take on the fullness and bloom of a young woman in her sixteenth year. And Douglas, who had been away for the last three, was aware of the change.

'All I know is that Douglas was there at his death,' Mairi raised her chin, trying to fend off the retort.

Douglas towered like a dark tree, his face hidden again in the twilight shadow. 'I was there, Mairi. Your father died in my arms but not at my hand. I do not know what villain took his life so near Duntorin. I'm sad your childish imagination has conjured up such fantastic ideas, but then it was a long time ago and I don't wish to talk about it.'

The quiet words of iron cut to her heart like a knife. What if Douglas had not been party to her father's murder? It was a terrible thing of which to be accused. But she could not believe he was ignorant of the crime. Even if he had not actually held the dagger, it must have been an accomplice as hot-headed as Douglas and acting under his father's, Duntorin's orders. For had not Duntorin then kidnapped her mother and herself, travelling with the party on their way back from cattle trading in the Lowlands and visiting her mother's kin?

Yes, her mother had grieved for Lismore, but she was soft and eventually succumbed to the attentions of widower Duntorin. Within a year they were lovers, within five she agreed to marry and she, Mairi, was a child far from home, landlocked among strangers and Lowlanders.

'It does not matter what she thinks,' Isabel said coldly, putting a hand on Douglas's chest to stay him, taking advantage of Mairi's sudden silence. 'Let us go home brother, I have no wish to see more of these pitiful pagan rites - they are the work of the Devil himself, Reverend Black says so.'

Douglas looked at Isabel with surprise. She had changed far more than Mairi, her lustre of black hair completely hidden in a nun-like headdress, her face pale and drawn with tight lines about the mouth and eyes. And what was all this talk about the Devil and the Reverend Black? Surely Isabel had not been lured by the all-condemning new religion of the Reformed Kirk? She was only eighteen but she dressed and talked like a middle-aged matron. He would talk to their father about marriage for his sister; it might put the sparkle back in the dark haunted eyes.

He glanced back at Mairi, standing mute but defiant, a ring of wilting flowers clinging to the wild red hair, echoing the simple embroidery of flowers on her bodice. But the green eyes and pink face lit by the bonfire looked reflective and sad and he did not want to quarrel with her now.

'Sister,' he squeezed the hand resting on his arm, 'you return as you wish and warn them of my coming. Take my horse. Sam will go with you for it is growing dark - and we don't want you falling into the hands of the Beltane witches do we?' Douglas said the words in his boyish teasing fashion that Mairi remembered so well, but the effect on Isabel was like lightning striking. She began to shake, clutching furiously at Douglas.

'Don't say such things,' her voice rasped, 'there is evil abroad tonight, make no joke about it.'

'Sam!' Douglas put a reassuring arm about his sister. 'Escort the daughter of Duntorin to the castle. And then come back and rescue me from the May Queen and her fairies.'

The miller's son detached himself from a group of young men and came over. He too had grown into a man, Mairi thought, taking in the brown bushy beard and long hair that belied the young dancing hazel eyes. The two had been inseparable comrades-in-arms since Mairi had been at Duntorin and it was natural that Sam should have followed Douglas across the seas to Denmark to fight for fortune in the Scottish regiment at the disposal of the Danish King Christian.

Sam made a small gallant bow and held out his arm for Isabel. To Mairi's surprise the older girl accepted without protest and gave a weak smile. At the last moment she turned as if remembering suddenly the presence of their awkward step-relation. 'Are you coming too, Mairi?'

'I hope she will do me the honour of dancing the jig she was so keen Rory should play,' Douglas intercepted quickly, as if challenging them both

4

to thwart him. Mairi blushed to think Douglas had been watching her all this while. She knew Isabel would accept anything her adored older brother suggested; but she was not so easily swayed. It was a choice between returning to the gloomy boredom of Duntorin Castle with Isabel or staying and losing herself in the dance, even if it meant doing so with her teasing, overbearing stepbrother. Her hesitation was taken by both of them as acquiescence.

'Good,' Douglas smiled, stepping towards Mairi and into the light of the fire, holding out a hand. Reluctantly taking it, she at once felt the vital warmth flowing from him. Their eyes met briefly.

Mairi felt the colour flooding to her neck and cheeks, her heart beginning to pound at the nearness of this half stranger. It could not be from excitement, just the embarrassment of having to dance before the villagers with the young master of Duntorin. She was aware of eyes upon them and whispers drowned by the crackle of branches and Rory warming up his bagpipes.

'I do this only to avoid the scolding of your bossy sister,' Mairi said between gritted teeth, loud enough for only Douglas to hear. Her stomach lurched as she felt him grip her hand tighter, pressing it to the leather of his breeches.

'Of course, sweet sister,' he smiled and murmured back. 'I realise I must be keeping you from your boy admirers, with their newly shaved chins and their slavering kisses.'

The words came as such a shock that Mairi's mouth dropped open, her breath caught in her throat. His taunts were insufferable. What would her mother say to hear her being spoken to in such an easy manner? He would not get away with this barefaced cheek! She tried to free herself of his grasp, but his fingers fixed more tightly about hers like a gauntlet.

'Come sweet Mairi, we must not disappoint our people,' he pulled her forward; 'they wish to see us dance.'

'Your people,' she returned, flinging him a warning look.

The music swirled up with the smoke and Mairi felt it taking hold of her, commanding her movements, lightening her senses. The dancers weaved and spun, changing hands and partners, then came back to their chosen ones. Mairi let herself go in a vortex of speed with Douglas; the more she pulled away from him, the faster they turned. They came to a breathless stop at the call of Rory's pipes.

'Where did you learn to dance like a Highlander?' Mairi panted, hands on hips, her flowered bodice heaving. Douglas chuckled, breathing in gulps of air.

'From you, I take that as a compliment. But even us Lowland chieftains learn to dance with the village maidens as part of our education.'

She might have known he would turn the jibe back at her. Mairi tossed her hair back and turned away from him. He had had his fun with her, but he need not think he could continue.

'Andrew,' she called to one of her earlier partners and beamed a generous smile. The youth strode over, practising a swagger, his dagger strapped to his slim-hipped long doublet. Mairi tried not to giggle, remembering Douglas's unkind description.

'Mairi,' he took her hand boldly in front of young Roskill of Duntorin, 'will you do me the honour of the next dance please?' He left a wet kiss on her hand. Mairi nodded in acceptance, ignoring the amused look on Douglas's face. Dancing with Andrew she was in command; with this mercenary soldier she had sensed a loss of control, the heady feeling that anything could happen. Certainly she was not going to allow him to disrupt her self-contained world.

'With pleasure, Andrew,' Mairi smiled, her sea-green eyes flashing wickedly as she placed a hand on his arm.

Her triumph was short-lived, as with a prick of annoyance she saw Douglas turn from them with a bow and walk straight up to the Queen of the May. She was the daughter of the local blacksmith with pretty large blue eyes and dark curling tresses uncapped for the festival, and she gave her hand willingly.

Mairi felt an unaccountable stab of irritation seeing them dance together, Douglas's attention rapt on her attractive rival. But how ridiculous to think of her in competition. The May Queen was welcome to his, no doubt, amorous intent. She had heard it was the soldier's Mairi preoccupation and why should the lusty Roskill be any different? His own father had shown no scruples in widowing her mother in order to gain her for himself.

Suddenly she was tired; the heat had gone out of the fire and also the evening. Mairi raised a hand to stifle a yawn at Andrew's boastful prattling.

'Sorry Andrew, I am weary,' she apologised truthfully.

'Allow me to escort you home,' he insisted eagerly, his eyes sliding sideways to see if Roskill was within earshot. But he seemed quite absorbed in conversation with the young Queen.

'Thank you,' Mairi accepted the offer, pulling her cloak about her shoulders. As they made for the clearing in the rocks which led down from the promontory to the wooded lochside, a voice stopped them.

'Going home, Mairi?' Douglas stood close behind her.

'Yes, brother,' Mairi bowed her head in mock modesty, a feeling of exultation that he had noticed her departure in spite of the May Queen.

'Then I'll accompany you through the woods,' he swept a short cloak over his shoulder.

'There's no need, Roskill,' Andrew butted in, emboldened by drink, 'the lady has agreed to my protection.'

Impatience flashed momentarily in the dark eyes and Douglas seemed about to say something. Then the moment passed and he smiled disarmingly.

'She is in good hands then,' he put forward a strong stockinged leg and bowed elaborately. 'Return her to her mother,' he added, his eyes meeting hers mockingly. Mairi pulled her hood over her hair and left without a word, Andrew following quickly.

A strong breeze hit them as they left the shelter of the natural amphitheatre of rock on the hillside and descended to the loch. Clouds rushed like outriders past a bright moon, hurrying them on their way. Mairi felt drained after the emotion of the evening and Andrew had fallen sullenly quiet after she had unlinked his arm from her waist. An owl hooted their arrival into the woods and Mairi felt unusually ill at ease at the restless rustling of the trees. Douglas's words about Beltane witches and Isabel's urgings about trouble echoed in her mind and she quickened their pace. Briefly she regretted having allowed Andrew to dismiss Roskill's offer of company.

Her young suitor stumbled after her. 'Not so quickly, my sweet,' he grabbed at her billowing cloak, 'I can hardly keep up and we're in no hurry.' He laughed and hiccupped as she pulled her cloak tightly about her.

'I do not wish to linger in these woods,' she threw the words over her shoulder at him, 'please Andrew.'

The shadowy path was hardly lit by the moon and the trees about them moaned with the wind whipped off the loch. At least Mairi knew the path well from her visits to old Agnes, Douglas and Isabel's nurse, who had retired to her family home in the woods. It was she who had befriended the frightened young Mairi who spoke no Lowland Scots and cried at night for her old life, when her mother was still too shocked at Lismore's death to be of comfort.

Kind Agnes, with soft words and lullabies, had sung her to sleep, even neglecting Isabel to make the young lass feel at home. Mairi often came to visit her in her woodland turf hut, surrounded by the company of animals she befriended and which were now her only family.

'Come on, Mairi,' Andrew began to sober up in the bracing air, 'walk close to me.' He caught up with her and pulled her to him. The warmth of her body against him was reassuring, for he too was growing nervous at the sinister atmosphere of the woods.

He put it down to too much ale and walking in the woods with a fanciful attractive young woman now in his care. 'Just one kiss,' he whispered at the pale face so close to his, the feel of her breath on his chin. Andrew bent and clumsily fixed his mouth on Mairi's parted lips, cutting off her ready retort, feeling the desire rising in him as he did so.

'No,' she gasped with annoyance and pushed him away with unexpected strength, 'you're just a drunken oaf! I'll see myself home.'

'Mairi,' Andrew gained his balance and looked at her in surprise, 'don't leave me. You can't walk through these woods on your own.'

Mairi turned and began to run. She was tired of Andrew's company and his unwelcome attentions; she just wanted to be home.

'Mairi!' she heard him call her back, but did not hear him follow. There would be no reason to tell anyone of Andrew's advances; she knew he would regret it in the morning. She wondered if Douglas would have been brushed aside so easily and then felt herself go hot for having entertained the idea.

She was almost at the cliff edge that dropped down to Agnes's clearing by the loch. It must be a trick of the moon, but Mairi was sure she saw the flicker of light from below. Impossible, Agnes would be asleep now and she continued along the higher ground, skirting the tree-hidden enclosure.

Mairi stopped dead in her tracks at the piercing scream coming from below and behind. She whipped round, her hood flying off the untamed hair, which shimmered silver in the moonlight.'

'No, please God, no,' the words of panic caught in her throat as her sharp eyes searched the clearing in the trees beneath the cliff. What she saw froze the blood in her veins and rooted her to the spot like a lithe young tree.

'Have mercy, I beg you!' the high-pitched wail of the old woman stabbed at Mairi's beating heart. 'I've done nothing, nothing . . .' Then again the screech of pain above an eruption of noise. There were men pushing and jabbing her with sharp pricking instruments, illuminated by lurid torch light. The cap was torn from her head.

Agnes the nurse who had befriended Mairi when she had first come to Duntorin Castle as hostage, miserable and afraid, stood now like a broken ragdoll, her sparse white hair straggling about her terrified face.

'Daughter of Satan!' a burly black-bearded man shouted in the old woman's face. Mairi gasped to sec it was the blacksmith. 'We know you're in league with the Devil, you old hag.'

'You gave my child the fever you wicked witch, took him from me with your evil potions!' This time it was a woman who spoke, one Mairi recognised as a local farmer's wife who had used Agnes's herbal remedies for years.

For these were no band of vagabonds setting about a frail old woman, they were the respectable cottars and farm-workers of Duntorin's lands. Only that morning she had left milk and oatmeal at Agnes's hearth and laughed at her friend's predictions of a lover before the year was out.

'I must go to her rescue,' Mairi whispered to herself, a sudden outrage at their cruelty fanning through her like flames, setting her green eyes ablaze with anger. She ran barefoot down the stony track forgetting her first moments of dread, knowing only that she must save her old friend.

Mairi tore out of the dark into the green dell in front of Agnes's turf cottage, screeching like a wildcat. Her bronze coloured hair seemed to catch alight in the torch flame, pale limbs flying as she ran.

'Stop,' she cried, 'stop this now, you've made a mistake!'

Mairi halted breathless in front of the score of villagers, arrested by this noisy arrival. The hubbub of the crowd for a moment died down, but the mood was still hostile. The young girl dropped her underskirts, managing to control her breath and spoke.

'You all know Agnes as a kind person. For years she has tended to our sickness and wounds and saved many a life.' She looked tenderly at the frightened woman sobbing quietly, her shoulders caved in under the burden of their abuse. 'What are you doing? How can a faithful servant of Duntorin be a witch?'

Mairi appealed to their stony faces, the eyes of the farmer's wife sliding away from hers. She could feel their indecision at her mention of Duntorin. Surely they would listen to common sense? As she moved forward to comfort Agnes a figure in black stepped out of the crowd and barred her way.

'Oh no you don't,' the icily calm words cut like a blade through the hushed suspense of the dark woods; even the night owls appeared to be silenced, waiting.

Mairi looked up into the harsh pointed features of the young local minister, glowering above her like a dark pine, his words the needles ready to prick her. She felt his grey narrow- eyed look boring into her, sweeping over her small body hatefully. Not until this moment had she realised his presence or the authority behind this witch hunt.

'This woman you seek to protect is an instrument of Satan. It is our duty to root out this evil and bring her to justice on this night of witchery and debauchery.'

Again the eyes scanned her from her bare feet, taking in the gown hitched into her girdle and up to her tousled hair, challenging her to defy him.

For a moment Mairi hesitated, stepping backwards from the cold eyes, aware of her vulnerable position for the first time, alone in these black woods against a hostile crowd. She had felt so angry before and acted, as usual, on an impulse. Believing these people her friends, it did not seem possible that they could be so easily roused to ugly hysteria over one harmless old woman. Mairi had visited their houses and helped tend their animals in busy harvest time, feeling more at home with their simple country hospitality than the boredom of ordered life at the Castle. Her mother had not scolded her for constantly wandering off, for she understood it as her daughter's way of forgetting the past traumatic wrench from the old life.

Now these villagers stood stubbornly hostile behind the rigid back of Reverend Zechariah Black, the new Presbyterian minister. Mairi felt her heart begin to beat painfully, realising he was gaining the upper hand. Fear quickened her breathing and she was uncomfortably aware that Zechariah Black could see it, his eyes glinting with triumph at her rising panic.

'Please sir, let Agnes be,' she managed to control her voice, looking beseechingly at the unblinking minister in his severe black coat and breeches.

He looked at her down his thin pointed nose and a flicker of a smile twitched at the thin purple lips. Mairi took this as a sign that he was about to relent and she smiled her open, full-lipped smile that lit her pretty face like sunshine and set the green eyes sparkling.

Something changed for a brief moment in his look, so that the dark grey eyes of the Reverend Black seemed to dilate like pools, as if they would draw her in and drown her. Mairi could not break from their hold, her heart beating in a slow thud that was visible, her skin beginning to crawl with goose-pimples. If there was evil in this place, she thought, it was embodied in this man's look. It made her shiver and the smile die on her lips.

He turned to face the crowd. 'Let not Satan win the day!' he shouted in a harsh voice. 'We are here as God's instrument to seek out evil and eliminate. Seize this sorceress,' his voice rose to fever pitch, as he spat out the vitriolic words, 'she will confess to her sins and name her confederates!' At this he spun around and stabbed a look at Mairi that made her blood run cold as ice water.

The villagers grabbed hold of Agnes with cries and jeers, spurred on by the words of their leader, drunk with fear and the scent of blood to be spilled.

Mairi returned the look of satisfaction and self-righteousness on the minister's face with a haughty tilt of her chin and a defiant glare. She stood her ground, her cheeks burning with frustration at Agnes's plight.

He leaned forward smiling and under cover of the din, whispered, 'I will deal with you later, you Highland minx. I'll teach you for not coming to hear my words on the Sabbath, daughter of Jezebel.'

So quietly hissed, Mairi flinched from the insult. How dare a man of the cloth speak to her like that and slander her own mother in this shameless way! She knew her gentle parent was disliked by some for adhering to the Old Faith and for living as Duntorin's mistress for several years before she would consent to marriage. But it had taken her a long time to recover from the death of Lismore, Mairi's father, and a long time to grow to love her rugged captor Duntorin.

'Call yourself a man of God?' Mairi raised her voice in rebuke. 'You're nothing but a hater of women who preys on the defenceless and lonely. A common dog has more learning than you!'

The words were out before she could think and her mouth curled in disdain. There were shocked cries from the mob. Zechariah Black raised his arm to strike her, his face creased and distorted with wrath. 'Wait 'til Duntorin hears of this!' Mairi threw the words at him as his hand came down and struck her on the side of the head. Her ear exploded in pain and she felt herself falling as the scene in front blurred into flashes of light.

'The witch's friend,' the Reverend Black's voice swam somewhere above, 'must be punished too!'

From the ground Mairi could make out a surge of feet towards her. Someone kicked her while another tore at her clothes. She felt hands pulling at her arm as if to raise her in help and then drop her again. As the frenzied crowd dragged her forward her head hit a stone and the noise and ghastly procession began to recede.

She must have been mistaken, but the cry that drowned all, on the point of unconsciousness, sounded more like a man's than Agnes's screaming.

CHAPTER TWO

Sam and Isabel returned expecting to find the Castle asleep. It was a scene of mayhem. Horses were being saddled and shouts echoed around the enclosed courtyard. They saw the grey-haired Duntorin striding around like a sore-headed bear, calling his retainers with purple words. Douglas's pack-horses stood patiently by the stables, still bearing their loads.

Mairi's mother rushed forward when she saw Isabel enter with Sam.

'Sam!' she cried with unhidden delight. 'I'm so glad you and Douglas have returned.'

'Madam,' Sam kissed her hand quickly. 'But what in God's name is going on?'

Isabel threw him a disapproving look but let the exclamation pass.

'Oh, I'm relieved to see you home, Isabel,' she put a hand on the young woman's arm and felt it tense. 'But where is Mairi?' Florence Roskill's soft-lined face creased into worry.

'She would not return with me,' Isabel answered stiffly.

'She is safe with Douglas,' Sam assured her hurriedly, intending no irony. 'But please tell us what is happening.'

The older woman's voice quavered as she replied. 'I fear my husband's kin - my first husband's kin - are raiding to the north of our lands. Mairi's cousin has been seen lifting cattle and has set at least two villages on fire.'

'Stealing and slaughtering you mean, stepmother,' Isabel said levelly, 'like the savages that they are.'

Florence Roskill seemed hardly to hear her as she looked distractedly towards her husband.

'Sam Scott!' the voice of Duntorin thundered from the mounting block as he spotted Sam. 'Where's my worthless son?'

It was hardly the greeting Sam had expected for either of them after three years away, but he knew the bluster was not malicious, it betrayed the concern the laird felt for his besieged people.

'He is at the Beltane dance, my lord,' Sam bowed and stepped back, his body alert for action. 'I was to return to meet him.'

'Ha!' Duntorin barked, his weather-beaten features trying to hide the trace of amusement, 'well you'd better fetch him quickly from the arms of whichever maiden. Now he's going to see some real fighting; we'll leave before daylight and cut off Lismore of Glen Garroch's retreat. Go, damn you!'

Sam turned on his heels and leapt into his saddle, throwing the reins of Douglas's steed to another of Duntorin's men and beckoning him to follow.

Isabel had seen Florence blush at Duntorin's words, knowing that the maiden with Douglas was Mairi.

'These Lismores seem to bring nothing but trouble and misery,' her stepdaughter commented haughtily. 'Of course, I do not mean you stepmother. You were just unfortunate enough to marry into such a lawless rabble.'

Florence turned her eyes on the pinched scornful face, wondering at the waspishness of the words. Her pale blue-green eyes filled up with sadness. Isabel had been such a spirited open child when they had first come; mature beyond her eleven years since the tragic death of her mother in childbirth.

At first it had seemed that she and the eight-year-old Mairi would be friends, but Isabel had been stung with jealousy over the young quicksilver Lismore on whom Agnes, her nurse, openly doted. An uneasy sister relationship had developed, with the Roskill children sometimes ranging against Mairi, Douglas's natural boisterousness egged on to cruelty by Isabel.

Still Florence could not dislike her tall stepdaughter, for she had been a mother to her as much as Mairi for nigh on eight years. And it did not stop her worrying about Isabel's latest obsession with Zechariah Black and his censorious teachings. The thought of him sent a chill through her like a cloud blocking out the sun.

'Come Isabel,' she smiled quietly and took her arm, 'let's go and see if we can help them prepare.'

Her stepdaughter flushed slightly and allowed herself to be led.

Sam and Duntorin's guard rode back along the cliffs, skirting the edge of the woods. The sky had almost cleared of ghostly clouds and the night stars were bright. At this time of year it was never completely dark, as if the night spirits kept the sky awake with eerie lights.

One such patch of light illuminated the trees below them. Surely there was no revelling going on so near Agnes's house and the freshwater loch? It was the spine chilling wail that made Sam pull his horse down the cliffside without further thought and brought him to the horrible scene in the clearing.

It took a few moments to realise what was going on amid the chaos of jostling bodies, blazing torches, cries and screams. Agnes had her hands tied down to her sides, another rope tied like a leash around her neck. She was staring glazed-eyed at something else and sobbing out loud.

Sam dismounted and pushed his way past the outside circle of cottars. At his feet he saw with horror, a girl's unconscious body, the face smeared with blood and the dress torn. It was Mairi.

'Stand back!' Sam roared with blind rage. 'What in God's name do you think you're doing?'

The blacksmith made as if to punch him, but Sam countered the blow swiftly and answered him with a bloody nose. Sam drew his sword.

'Back I said.'

The farmer's wife recognised him at last. 'It's Sam Scott, young Roskill's man,' she gasped, feeling sudden shame at her half-hearted attempt to raise Mairi from the feet of the mob, 'so Master Douglas will be home too.'

The jeering subsided as the crowd made way for Sam's mounted companion. Sam bent to see the damage done to Mairi and saw her eyelids flicker in half consciousness. How had she come to be so astray, when he had last seen her in the company of Douglas? Headstrong she was, but finding her here was a mystery and it was not like Douglas to let her walk alone in the dark woods.

'How could you?' he said with tightening jaw at the senseless brutality. 'And she the foster daughter of Duntorin.'

'It is God's work to attack black magic, whatever its guise,' Zechariah Black stood forward, staring down at them with hatred.

'Man, she's a young girl not a witch,' Sam answered angrily.

'She consorts with witches and dances with the Devil,' the minister spat out the words, maddened at the thwarting of his purge. 'Why else would she walk abroad on her own in these woods on such a night?'

Sam ignored him, gently picking up the limp body of Mairi. She stirred and groaned in pain; he had arrived just in time. He lifted her up on to Douglas's horse.

'Hold her tightly, she is barely conscious,' he cautioned the guard. 'Take her straight to the Castle while I go on to warn Douglas. We will return at once to ride with his father.'

'What news is this?' the minister asked with sudden interest, sensing trouble. Sam gave him a scornful look.

'The Lismores are raiding to the north and west, so Duntorin will not sit and twiddle his thumbs while it goes on.' He swung up into the saddle. 'We could have done without nonsense like this, Black. Let Agnes free at once, else Duntorin will slap you into your own stocks - the rest of you had better hurry home.'

With that he spurred his horse forward up the sandy bank after the disappearing hooves of Douglas's horse and into the darkness. The silence told of the villagers' indecision; there was fear of reprisal from their laird and dread at the news of raiding. Black sensed it. He was not going to be told what to do by any nobleman's lackey.

'Are you to be frightened from your duty by that sinful young buck and his godless masters?' his voice cracked harshly. 'They are already damned. But you are not. You must win your salvation by bringing this witch to trial. Then God will decide.' He swept a stern look over his shifting flock. One or two voiced their agreement. 'Duntorin can do nothing to stop us,' Black gave them a verbal whiplash. 'You answer only to the Kirk and woe betide those who incur its wrath!'

Their mania soon rekindled with his ravings and dire warnings. They were his again to lead. Agnes was pushed forward too stunned to protest, her body wracked with tearless sobs, part in fear, part in relief that Mairi had been rescued.

Sam found Douglas in the middle of a mellow band of men, regaling them with stories of Denmark. The May Queen sat on his knee, the young lord's arm linked comfortably round her waist, his cloak keeping her shoulders warm.

'And the drinking lasted for four days after the hunting trip. King Christian, our own fair Queen's brother, leading the way I may add.'

Douglas's man broke into the merry group and drowned the laughter. 'Sir - Duntorin calls for you - and any man who will ride with him,' Sam blurted out breathlessly. 'There is serious trouble at the foot of Glen Breacin - Cailean Lismore and his reivers.'

The easy smile vanished from his master's face as he jumped to his feet. The blacksmith's daughter nearly toppled with surprise, but he caught her firmly at the hips.

'Do we ride by moonlight?' Douglas asked, already strapping on his sword belt.

Sam nodded. 'Aye, Duntorin intends to cut off their retreat. They'll be slower with the stolen cattle.'

Several of the group said they would march and be there to fight the next day. They would put the word out that Duntorin was calling on his men for support.

Douglas turned to the blue-eyed Queen of the Beltane and kissed her hand lightly. 'You must return with the others to the safety of your home. Speed prevents me from accompanying you myself.'

Sam noticed the pink tinge of her cheeks and the returned smile and for a moment wished they were for him. If the evening's events had gone differently he had intended to make his mark with Mary Bain, the blacksmith's daughter. She was obviously flattered by the attentions of his good-looking lord, though Douglas seemed unaware of his affect, being used to the gallantry of court life.

'How bad is the news?' Douglas shouted to Sam as they dipped their horses down the slope.

'One of your father's guards says two villages are on fire and pillaged,' Sam replied grimly. 'And Cailean of Glen Garroch is becoming bolder; these townships are across the river and well into the plain, not far from here.'

'They come out of the hills like wildcats,' Douglas's voice cracked angrily, 'will they never live at peace with us?'

A memory flared like a spark and in spite of their haste, his mouth twitched with wry amusement. 'I suppose Mairi finally returned to the

Castle, did you see her Sam?'

Sam jerked his horse's bridle at the unexpected enquiry and the beast whinnied its objection. There was no point in troubling his friend with the macabre witch hunt yet. Mairi was safe and Douglas was needed elsewhere.

'Yes, she is at home,' was all he said.

Douglas grunted and his mouth set in hard purposeful lines as he spurred on his horse.

They found a group of Duntorin's gentry amassed by the gateway, the atmosphere charged with nervous impatience. Douglas saw his father by the thick wooden door of the tall keep with Mairi's mother. She looked older than he remembered, her pretty oval face lined with time, the dark hair streaked with snails' trails of silver. The eyes, a pale echo of Mairi's green, looked deeply troubled. As Douglas approached he caught the end of their conversation.

'Do not fret my dearest Florence,' his father's voice was unusually soft, 'we will return soon and seek out those other scoundrels.'

'Take care my love,' came the barely audible reply, 'we need you.'

They embraced quickly and then Florence caught sight of her stepson. Douglas's ready smile died as he saw the moist green eyes harden. It was not the look of the kind, motherly woman who had delighted in his company before he left three years ago. But perhaps she felt awkward meeting again under such circumstances.

'Mother,' he kissed her check which she neither proffered nor withdrew, 'I'm glad to see you well and still so beautiful.'

Her lips fluttered with the beginnings of a smile and then retracted. 'Your father has need of you Douglas. I hope Denmark has not totally rid you of responsibility to your family.'

Douglas's eyes widened in surprise at the tartness of her words and was about to ask her meaning.

'Come Douglas,' Duntorin embraced his son in an encouraging grip, 'we can speak of this later.'

The young Duntorin threw Florence an enquiring look and her eyes dropped with embarrassment at her churlish greeting. Then the men were mounting and joining the thud of hooves across the trampled earthen yard. There was no time to discover what he could have done to upset his stepmother; it could only be that he had stayed away from home for four winters without much correspondence.

Florence watched the stable boys heave back the outer gate and bar it from the inside. She listened to the beat of hooves grow distant until it just tickled the ear. Silence followed, falling on the tall lean tower of Duntorin like a smothering blanket. A light in the corbelled tower on the fourth floor glowed as a watching eye and she wondered if Mairi slept. Florence turned and went in, a sense of foreboding niggling like an itch inside her.

Mairi lay still under the covers, the cuts to her ear and cheekbone bathed of their blood, her rich gold-red hair spread across the pillow as if blown by the wind. Her eyes moved rapidly under their lids and soft moans left her colourless lips.

Her mother bent and kissed her pale brow, wishing she could erase the frightened dreaming. How could Douglas have let her walk back through those woods on her own? In the past he had often teased her daughter, who rose to his taunts with her flashes of temper and spirited replies. Sometimes she had to admit Mairi was the provoker of Douglas's easy-going nature.

But the Douglas she remembered would never have put her in danger, quite the opposite. He had shown a protectiveness towards her that was touching, such as the time when Isabel persuaded a group of travellers to take Mairi with them. The spiteful girl had assured Mairi they would deliver her to the shores of her homeland and the child had gone eagerly. When Douglas learned she was missing he caught up with the tinkers as they were crossing the river into the mountains and gave them his silver dagger in return for Mairi.

Florence remembered the hurt on the youth's face when Mairi told Douglas she hated him for bringing her back to Duntorin.

But perhaps he had changed? Douglas had certainly grown into a powerfully built man, his strong handsome jaw now darkened by a fashionably short beard. Had his feelings been trained to harden along with his body, she wondered? If so, she feared for Mairi and her fiery pride, as she had once feared for her own feelings against the weight of Duntorin's will.

Florence left the candle burning and tiptoed out of the rounded chamber.

Mairi woke with the grey light of morning filtering in through the narrow window on to her boxed-in bed. The candle at her side had long since spluttered and melted into its dish, a burnt waxy smell pervading the cold room.

She felt the tenderness at the side of her head and struggled to remember how it had come about. Had she fallen? How had she got home? A picture danced in front of her of swinging with Douglas, his black eyes lit by the firelight, consuming her in his look.

But no, a feeling of unease stirred her as the fog lifted from her mind. There was Andrew and the dark woodland path. Surely he had not. . . ? No, she had run away from him and into a greater danger. Mairi shuddered at the memory of Reverend Zechariah Black's evil look and stinging words and she pulled the covers to her chin. He had inspired fear in her that she could only ward off with words. The minister had struck her for her audacity and then the mob had all come at her with their hands and their cruel faces.

'Stop!' Mairi cried aloud to banish the nightmare. The throbbing at her temple reminded her that it was reality and no dream. And what of poor Agnes? The last glimpse she recalled was of people seizing her and

17

binding her with coarse rope like an animal.

Mairi threw back the sheet and homespun blankets and swung her feet on to a stool by the side of the high bed. For a moment the walls moved sideways and her vision blurred. She steadied herself on the tall aumbry that held her dresses and reached for her bedgown which she threw over her nightdress.

Her mother stopped her at the door.

'Where do you think you're going, young madam?' Florence steered her back into the room.

'No mother, I must -'

'You must rest,' the older woman interrupted the protest. 'For once you will do as you're told.'

Mairi bit her lip in frustration, but her knees buckled and the light-headedness returned. She allowed her mother to take off her gown and put her back to bed.

'It's Agnes, mother,' Mairi struggled with the words, 'they think she's a witch.'

'Nonsense,' Florence replied, smoothing back the red hair from her brow, 'no one could think that.'

Mairi tried to raise herself in her panic. 'But they do! That's how I was attacked trying to stop them. They were like a pack of dogs. It was horrible, horrible!' She covered her face to block out the sights that haunted her.

Florence felt a familiar flutter of alarm. There had not been time to hear Sam's explanation of the attack, only that a group had set upon her in the woods. She put her arm around the slim shoulders and rocked her daughter gently. 'What do you mean, Mairi? Who were they?'

'It was that terrible man, he was leading them,' Mairi tried to control her voice. 'He said Agnes was in league with the Devil and they believed him. He even called you . . .' she broke off unable to repeat the hurtful slander.

'Who did?' Florence pressed gently.

'Reverend Black,' Mairi whispered the name as if it might conjure him up.

She looked up at the sound of rustling by the door. Isabel stood watching them, her face set like white marble. Mairi wondered how long she had been there listening.

She had not meant to shock her with the news of Agnes's arrest. But Isabel's first words took Mairi's breath away.

'You should not speak so wickedly about our minister, stepsister,' Isabel's voice sounded taught. 'He is a good man who sets an example to us all in the words that he speaks. And yet you would sinfully discredit him with your fanciful tongue.'

Spots of pink came to Mairi's pallid cheeks.

'Fanciful!' the bones in her slim neck showed as she strained forward.

'There's nothing fanciful in these bruises on my head and arms Isabel. Your precious minister is so godly he terrorises an old woman - your old nurse - and strikes at me for trying to defend her!'

Her pulse raced at the thought. Florence, seeing beads of sweat breaking out on Mairi's brow, steadied her with a hand on her arm.

'Wheesht daughter, there's no need for shouting.'

'Mother, you don't understand, Agnes is -'

'Agnes must be possessed by the Devil in her dotage if our minister believes so,' Isabel's steely voice silenced them both. 'Did she not give a potion to the son of farmer Johnson last month and did he not die of a strange sickness within the week?'

Florence looked dumbstruck at the calm crude logic of her stepdaughter's words. The only movement in the white face was that of the dark eyes that seemed to burn with a zealous light as she spoke. Mairi realised with creeping horror that Isabel must at least have suspected the hunt, worse even, known about it. For had she not warned Mairi to hurry home from the dance as there would be trouble?

'Agnes was our nurse, Isabel,' Mairi said hoarsely, 'she showed us nothing but love. When did she ever hurt you?'

Isabel's face flushed a plum purple, her brows gathering like storm clouds.

'Oh, Agnes had so much love for me she spent all her time tending to the whims of my selfish little stepsister, didn't she?' Isabel trembled with suppressed rage.

'That's not true,' Florence remonstrated. 'Agnes was kind to you all, only Mairi was younger and needed more looking after.'

'She's always had all the attention,' Isabel cried like a petulant child, 'and you have encouraged it. Even my own father loves her more than me.'

'No Isabel,' Florence instinctively moved towards her to reassure, 'you will always be his favourite.'

The older woman went to put her arms about Isabel to stem the hurtful tirade, but she backed away. With deep breaths Isabel controlled herself. Mairi had gone silent with shock at the display of jealousy, pent up for years until this moment. It explained so much; the disagreements, the petty bickering and downright spitefulness.

'Sister,' she spoke quietly, trying not to provoke her further. 'The minister respects you for your church-going and the example you set. Surely you could say something in Agnes's defence?'

Isabel's black eyes looked at her in triumph, she seemed pleased with the compliment and her mouth twitched with the beginnings of a smile.

'I will see what I can do for Agnes, though I will not go against the judgment of the Kirk,' she agreed tersely.

'Thank you,' Florence laid a tentative hand on her arm. 'If only the men had not been called away at such a time,' she added distractedly.

19

She looked at Mairi, forgetting until now to ask how she had come to be in the woods on her own. 'And why were you walking abroad alone child, Sam said you were last seen with Douglas?'

Mairi coloured as they both looked at her keenly.

'I - er - I was accompanied home by Andrew Ramsay,' she faltered.

'So he was there at the attack?' Florence asked sharply.

'I - I don't remember.' Mairi recalled the strong man's voice above the din as she passed out. 'The man who came to help me - was it Douglas who saved me?'

'Hardly,' Isabel gave a dry harsh laugh. 'The talk among the servants in the Great Hall is that Douglas had to be prised away from the May Queen to ride with his father.'

Mairi's face was on fire with embarrassment and confusion. Florence came over and placed a hand on her forehead.

'You are still feverish, child.'

'So who brought me home?' Mairi asked stiffly.

'Sam Scott saved you,' Florence sighed, 'on his way to collect Douglas.'

'So where are D-Douglas and his father?' Mairi felt awkward asking, but she wanted to know.

Her mother explained about the attack by the Lismores.

'My brothers?' Mairi breathed the question.

'No, your cousin Cailean from Glen Garroch, as far as we know,' Florence answered.

'They're all as bad as each other,' Isabel said with disdain. 'I will go now to see our minister. Perhaps this episode will make you both think again about how you neglect your duties to the Kirk.'

'I will come with you Isabel,' Florence insisted, 'I want to make sure Agnes is not being harmed.'

She kissed Mairi quickly and bade her stay in bed until she returned. Mairi watched her mother and Isabel leave the room in silence.

As she lay there, her mind still reeling from Isabel's hateful words, she almost believed her stepsister had taken relish in telling her of Douglas and the May Queen. It might not be true; she may have invented the story to hurt her. But then Douglas had been with Mary Bain when she left with Andrew and her mother had said Sam had returned to fetch him. Of all the things Isabel had said, ridiculous thought it seemed, it was this that pricked her the most.

'I cannot be right in the head after the lynching,' Mairi chided herself out loud.

And now Douglas and kind Sam and Duntorin were far from here, perhaps already engaged in a violent and bloody clash with her cousin and his kin. She remembered Cailean as a wild young man with flames of long red hair and unkempt red beard.

As a child she had harboured a feeling that her father had no patience for his reckless nephew, though he had always been slow to anger and Mairi never recalled a public disagreement. If only her father had lived, he could have exercised control over the wayward Cailean, whose own father had been killed in a feud on Roskill land.

But why fret over these Roskills? Would it not only be revenge for her father's brutal murder to have them slain in some northern pass and rolled into a nameless dyke by her kinsman? Mairi shivered at the gruesome thought. Her imagination was too vivid; she could not wish such a fate even on her mocking stepbrother.

Mairi came out of her doze with a start. There was no sound, just an eerie quiet ringing in the ancient stones of the Castle. Something was wrong and despite her light-headedness, she could not lie there torturing herself with the unknown; she must act.

Mairi climbed out of bed for a second time and with no one to stop her, dressed hurriedly. She still felt weak and dizzy, but she had to know what was going on both in the village and to Agnes. Her mother might be glad of her support against the hard-line clergyman.

The Castle was disturbingly quiet, emptied of its able-bodied men; no shout of male voices or hounds barking in the courtyard. Mairi descended from the living quarters into the Great Hall without attracting attention. The high beamed room was deserted. Mairi found some ale left over on a trestle table and drank. It tasted bitter but she felt some strength seep into her limbs. Pulling her blue woollen cloak about her, Mairi made her way down the stone steps to the ground floor and pushed open the heavy outer door.

Her heart lifted to see she was not alone; a figure hovered in the gateway, head covered in a cloak to keep off the spitting cold drizzle. Mairi, used to the driving squalls of the west coast, hardly felt it as she hurried across the muddy courtyard.

Her heart missed a beat as she recognised Douglas's cloak of black velvet with the sable lining fringing the head of the wearer. The cloak lifted and Mairi gasped.

'Mary!'

The blue eyes looked at her half-quizzically, half-warily.

'Miss Mairi,' she began with fear in her voice, 'I came to find you.'

Mairi's cheekbones showed red at the unexpected encounter. This girl, her own age, had indeed been favoured with Douglas's attentions, she had kept his cloak. She wondered in what compromising position Sam must have found them for Douglas to leave her wrapped in his expensive cape? If Mary had come to talk about him she was not in the mood.

'Why should you want me?' Mairi bristled momentarily. Surprise registered for an instant in the large eyes and then Mary remembered her errand.

'You must come quickly, Miss,' she urged, 'they have taken Mistress

Florence. I fear she may be put on trial too.'

The words did not register at first.

'Taken? What do you mean Mary?' Mairi asked blankly. Her body felt frozen and immobile.

Mary promptly burst into tears. It made Mairi take command.

'Please don't cry,' she put an arm about the girl's shaking shoulders, 'just tell me what's happened.'

'Everyone is there,' Mary tried to talk coherently. 'They have made Agnes say some terrible things - I think she has gone quite mad with the pain.'

'Oh dear Lord,' Mairi whispered.

'Your mother was so angry when she saw Agnes standing by the Kirk wall with the iron ring about her neck,' Mary sniffed, 'I've never seen her so furious.'

'Go on,' Mairi coaxed gently.

'So the Minister had Mistress Florence arrested as one of Agnes's coven. They were taking them to the lochside, so I came at once. Oh Miss, what can we do?'

Tears sprung to the red-haired girl's eyes. How dare he treat her own mother in such a way? And why did the Roskills have to be far from home when they were needed here? But of course, Black was taking advantage of their absence to bring unspeakable humiliation to her mother, for daring to remain a Catholic.

She looked at Mary's trusting face; it was brave of her to come to warn her, she could so easily be named an accomplice for doing so.

'But surely my sister Isabel will stop them?' Mairi looked for reassurance. Mary's eyes dropped and her hands grasped Douglas's cloak more tightly.

'She has given evidence against Agnes,' Mary's voice was almost a whisper, 'she dare not go against the Minister now.'

Mairi felt cold fingers of dread squeezing her chest. Surely Isabel would not stoop to this treachery just to win the praise of Zechariah Black? She must indeed be eaten up with jealousy to treat poor Agnes so.

'We must stall the trial somehow,' Mairi spoke her thoughts. 'The men will not be back before nightfall at the earliest, so we must take action ourselves.'

'Tell me and I will help,' Mary wiped her eyes with the back of her hand.

'Why have you put yourself at risk like this?' Mairi asked suddenly.

Mary tinged pink.

'My father was one of those who arrested Agnes. And because I danced with Master Douglas and took part in the rituals, he thinks I have been under her spell.' Mairi watched her keenly. 'But I danced of my own free will,' Mary pouted her pretty mouth and Mairi felt her heart lurch.

'And I think my father is mistaken in calling Agnes a witch, although I do believe in the power of the Devil.'

Mairi thought of the cruel eyes of Black and nodded, keeping her thoughts to herself.

'Come then Mary, I have an idea,' Mairi steered her back to the Castle.

Douglas winced with pain as Sam bound the strip of torn sleeve around his head. A crimson stain spread like spilt wine into the bandage.

'We'll need another sleeve Douglas,' Sam said in the familiar way that he addressed his friend when they were alone.

'Ah, take mine this time,' Douglas grimaced, holding up his arm in surrender. 'We gave those Lismore boys a beating though, didn't we Sam?' His companion smiled and nodded as he ripped the material. Douglas grinned weakly. 'I'd fain have chased them all the way home,' he joked.

'Your father thought you foolhardy enough, going into the pass after them,' Sam commented wryly.

'I wish I'd caught that mad fox Cailean,' Douglas gritted his teeth as the second bandage was applied. 'He has plagued us for long enough. There will be no trust between Roskills and Lismores while he breathes.'

For the first time since they had set out Sam remembered about Mairi and the witch hunt.

'Douglas, I must tell you now, you may be needed to do some score settling at home.' His friend twisted round to look at Sam.

'What's that supposed to mean?'

Sam took a deep breath and told him all he knew about the attack.

'God's truth!' Douglas clutched Sam's arm trying to rise. 'Why have you said nothing until now?'

'Because we were needed for this,' Sam sounded defensive.

'I shouldn't have trusted her to that mewling boy, Andrew.' Douglas cursed himself, 'what a fool I am.'

He pulled himself to his feet and reached for his discarded sword belt and pistols.

'We must return at once, I don't trust this viper of a man who calls himself a minister of the Kirk. From what I hear his appetites are not wholly spiritual.'

'But your father expects us to join him on the western border to help round up the cattle. Anyway Mairi is quite safe now,' Sam tried to reassure Douglas.

'She might still be in danger without Duntorin's protection,' Douglas jerked his belt tight. 'You can chase after cattle if you wish Sam Scott, but I'm returning now.'

Sam kicked over the traces of the fire and followed.

Two heads bent over the smouldering pile of cut reeds, the dark and the auburn, waiting tensely for the fire to catch. The reeds were dry but the surrounding grass and gathered twigs were damp in the entrance of the old bothy. It had been deserted for years, once a cowherd's summer hut, but Duntorin had allowed it to fall into disrepair.

It was ideally placed on the northern edge of the village, hidden by a small rise in the land that would show only the sinister smoke rising behind it. Mairi had never liked to play there as a child, somehow the derelict forlorn building frightened her; she was sure it was haunted by mountain spirits.

'You must get back to the lochside quickly, Mary,' Mairi insisted, 'before they start asking where you've gone. Don't mention anything about coming to the Castle or seeing me, you've done enough to help us already.'

'And you, Mairi?' Mary said as if to a friend.

'When the fire's underway, I'll ride in and break up the trial with the story about a raid on the village.' Mairi tried to sound more confident than she felt. It would only be a small diversion before they discovered there were no attackers, but anything was better than no action and it would take time to put out the fire.

With Mary gone, Mairi waited until the remains of the turf roof started to smoke and then she mounted her mare and galloped for the lochside.

Considering how many men must have gone with Duntorin, there was still a large crowd of onlookers.

The minister was conducting the trial with the aid of members of the Kirk Session, upright figures of the community like Sam's father, the miller. The crowd was largely of village women dressed in their long woollen skirts and huddled in shawls and chin-cloths against the stiff breeze. The bile rose in Mairi's throat to see Isabel standing close to her leader, assuming a look of detached piety.

Even from across the outfields, Mairi could see their victim Agnes and her stomach turned. She was strapped to a chair, her thumbs red with the torture of the barbarous screws. As the young rider spurred forward she could see that the expression on the woman's face was crazed.

Charging into the makeshift court she caught sight of her mother tied to the ducking chair and stripped to her undergarments, her grey hair tumbling about her shoulders. Still she held her chin high. Mairi wheeled the mare in front of the judges.

'Reivers have reached the outskirts of the village!' Mairi did not have to put the nervous fright into her voice, 'They are plundering the animals from the high ground.'

She watched the look of disbelief and triumph light the stony features of Zechariah Black.

'Look how our other witness has been delivered into our hands, riding like a man,' he cried and pointed at the intruder. 'No doubt you will find she bears the growth that is the witch's mark, just like her mother!'

24

Mairi had not looked directly at her mother yet and did not dare for fear of fainting. Her head felt light and detached as she insisted to the crowd, 'You must go at once and protect your cattle.'

Their murmurings buzzed in her ears like loud flies and Mairi clutched the reins tightly, knowing to dismount now would mean the end of all resistance.

'She lies!' Black shouted at the worried whisperers. 'It is a vile attempt to thwart the course of justice, to save her fellow confederates. Has not Agnes already condemned her as an accomplice in wicked charms and diabolical remedies? Seize her!'

'I have seen the fires,' Mairi's shrill voice kept them back, 'go and see for yourselves!'

All at once, Scott the miller rose from his wooden stool. He seemed disconcerted by her entrance, perhaps he already knew of his son's intervention to save her in the woods.

'If it is true, we must go with what strength we have and protect our village.'

Mairi closed her eyes with relief; he was not above self interest at least. Agreement rose from the assembled people and the gathering began to break up, the cottars calling at the older women and children to stay here by the loch where it would be safer.

Black's face was livid with rage, the grey eyes narrowed in pure hatred of the young woman defying him from her horse. But he knew he had lost control of the others and must go with them.

'Do not let these sorceresses out of your sight,' he ordered, 'they must not escape punishment.'

A tense silence fell on the group as the men left for the village. Mairi steeled herself for one last effort, catching the anxious face of Mary as she did so.

She pulled out one of Duntorin's pistols which had been tucked into her girdle and hidden by her cloak. It was so heavy that it shook in her hands. She had no idea how to use it or whether it was loaded. There was a gasp from those nearest to her. Naked fear registered on Isabel's pale face.

'Untie Lady Roskill,' Mairi commanded in a strained level voice. No one moved. 'Now!' Mairi shook the pistol at Isabel and the woman beside her. Mistress Johnson, the farmer's wife broke the spell and moved forward quickly to unstrap Florence. Isabel quickly followed.

For the first time Mairi met her mother's gaze and nearly passed out at the harrowed face that had aged years in the past horrible hours. But a quiet dignity still shone in the green eyes. She stood up and walked unsteadily to the horse.

'And now release Agnes,' Mairi waved the gun carelessly at the crowd, seeing heads duck.

Mary stepped forward and tore at Agnes's bonds, though the old widow seemed unaware of what was happening to her. Mairi bade her mother lead Agnes in front of the horse. When they reached the tree line, a spit of sand between them and the women, she dismounted.

'You must take Agnes on the horse, mother,' Mairi ordered quietly, fighting down the waves of nausea, 'and I will run behind.'

To her amazement, Florence obeyed and both struggled to lift the old nurse on to the back of the horse. She was as light as a sheaf of dry reeds, but a lifeless weight. They lay her across the horse like a bundle of cloth.

'Run my brave one,' her mother brushed her cheek with a kiss, 'they will not dare to follow.' She mounted the mare.

Mairi glanced at the huddle of people, watching warily at a distance. Isabel stood like a stone statue, a stranger to her.

Mairi sensed that most of the villagers were relieved to see Duntorin's wife released, in spite of their palpable fear of Black and his authority. It was fragile shifting ground between the accused and the accusers and every woman there knew it. Still there were half-hearted comments shouted after her as she headed into the woods.

'Only a witch would play with the weapons of the Devil,' it was the blacksmith's wife, Mary's mother.

'Aye, and ride like a soldier,' another agreed. But no one followed.

Mairi tucked the pistol into her waistband, bent her head and ran. They would soon be within the welcome walls of the Castle. The thud of the horse's hooves grew away from her, as Florence took Agnes to safety. Her own footsteps pounded in her ears like hammers, the trees around merging into a blur of colour.

Nearly home, nearly home, she urged under her breath.

As the woods opened into fields, with the Castle looming on the cultivated rise, Mairi thought she saw someone waiting for her. Was it her mother returning? No it was a man's figure that swam ahead. Could it be Douglas watching out for her coming home, as he used to do when she was a child and he was already a grown man in her eyes?

Her vision broke up into strange darting lights; Mairi tripped on a root and fell. Footsteps ran to catch her. She was lying on her back and the hands on her shoulders were rough. Opening her eyes for a moment, Mairi saw the ghastly grey face of Zechariah Black hovering over hers.

'Don't call out, there is no one to hear you,' he grunted. 'Do you think I would let you escape me, you young temptress?' he breathed heavily in her face. 'I will find the witch's mark on you, my beauty,' he leered, the snake's eyes consuming the pale flesh in his hands. 'You will be punished for your collusion.'

Black pulled her up from the ground, dragging her back in the direction of the loch. With the strength fading rapidly from her, Mairi fought off his bony clutch, frightened to lose consciousness to this tormentor. Digging her nails into his face she heard him yelp and then a hand cracked across her cheek and she slumped against him.

CHAPTER THREE

Douglas did not spare his horse on the journey home and Sam found it difficult to keep up. They arrived outside Duntorin's walls, their steeds foaming at the mouth with white spittle. At that moment Douglas saw Mairi's chestnut mare galloping out of the woods below them.

Narrowing his eyes he could see it was a distressed Florence who rode, her hair flying about her shoulders as Douglas had never seen it before. Horror gripped him at the sight of a body straddling the horse's flanks. It was Agnes and she appeared lifeless. The young men spurred their horses down to meet Florence.

'What wickedness has befallen you, dearest mother?' Douglas's voice rasped with anger, taking in her state of undress.

'Oh, Douglas,' Florence sobbed with relief at seeing him, 'you must rescue Mairi quickly. She runs behind.'

Waiting for no explanation, save that of knowing his stepsister was in danger, Douglas kicked his horse into a gallop.

He was unaware if Sam followed, acting with the lightning swiftness of a soldier going into combat.

Even in the darkness of the dense trees he saw someone wrestling with a dead weight and heard a muffled cry. He leaned down from the saddle and with the butt of his pistol, smote the minister on the back of his head, sending his black hat toppling. He groaned and keeled over, knocking Mairi to the ground as he did so. Douglas jumped down and kicked the heavy body from the small one pinned beneath.

'Oh my sweet,' Douglas leant close to assure himself she still breathed. Her breath came in low short gasps, her eyes staring fixedly ahead, wide and terrified. Mairi lay rigid and shaking and Douglas's head throbbed at the sight of her dishevelled hair and the scratches to her flesh. He thought he would burst with anger at the brutality and turned on the stirring body beside her. His hands went for Black's throat. He wanted to squeeze and squeeze until the life went out of him for ever.

Sam arrived in time to pull his friend off the purple gasping face of Black before he strangled him.

'You'll solve nothing by killing him,' Sam shouted, trying to break through Douglas's blind rage. 'We must get Mairi home before the others find her.'

The mention of her name triggered something in Douglas's mind and his hands fell to his sides.

'Yes,' he murmured and bent down to lift her trembling body to him. Sam helped him lift her up into the saddle and Douglas cradled her to him as he rode back to Duntorin.

What madness had overtaken the place in the short time he had been away? And how long had it been festering like a sore in the breast of the community? There certainly had been evil about on the night of the Beltane fires. Strange things were happening; this was the first witch hunt to erupt at Duntorin and there was the unexplained fire blazing at the small bothy as they had ridden in from the north.

Mairi was in shock. She drifted in and out of a feverish, fitful sleep for several days, while her mother and Sarah, the cook, fed her sips of potions and cooled the sweating brow. Duntorin and the rest of the band returned and the sickness that had possessed the village subsided. An uneasy truce appeared to be drawn between the lord's household and the minister and his supporters.

Duntorin acceded the Kirk was too powerful to provoke at the moment and Black and his elders did not relish the wrath of Duntorin about their heads. Zechariah Black was ambitious; better to use what temporal power offered itself, as well as the spiritual.

Mairi awoke weak and dazed, the butterflies on her embroidered bedspread dancing in the shafts of May sunshine piercing the window. Her mother served Mairi with a favourite Highland dish of carrageen moss boiled in milk to make a jelly flavoured with fruit juices. It was easy to swallow and with each mouthful her appetite returned.

'Is that better my love?' Florence asked anxiously like a fussing mother hen. 'It is bringing colour back to those pale cheeks, I can see already.' Mairi smiled and nodded, the soft words bringing tears to her green eyes.

'Did it really happen?' she whispered croakily. 'Are you all right mother?' Their arms went around each other in a fierce hug, nearly spilling the remains of the jelly on the bedclothes.

'Yes, my dearest child,' Florence squeezed the frail body to her as if she could protect her from the evil of others for ever. 'My brave, brave daughter. Duntorin is so proud of you.'

Mairi cried into her mother's soft shoulder, turning the velvet of her dress damp. She noticed for the first time that her mother was dressed in one of her best robes, her hair neatly brushed back and crowned with a French hood. Gone was any trace of the humiliating state of disarray at the trial.

'And Agnes,' Mairi sniffed, 'is she recovered?' Her mother hesitated.

'She is quite safe here at the Castle - and comfortable,' Florence said gently. 'But she is old and you cannot expect her to be unaffected by her ordeal.'

Mairi bit her lip, trying to keep back the tears that came so easily. How cruel life could be, she thought. They talked about the Highlands being unruly, but she had never seen such cruel savagery as here among these soft rolling Lowlands. The picture of Isabel's hard face came into Mairi's mind.

'Isabel betrayed us, didn't she?' the young redhead's lips set in a tight line. Florence sighed.

'She cannot wholly be to blame, daughter. She was so under the influence of Zechariah Black and believed what she did was right in God's eyes, even if it meant bearing witness against her family.' Mairi looked keenly at her mother and said nothing. 'I can't say I understand her,' Florence admitted, 'but she does seem contrite about the way things turned out. She has wept in her father's arms and asked his forgiveness.'

'I cannot forgive,' Mairi muttered and shook back her red-gold hair.

'You must,' Florence squeezed her hands in hers, 'she is your stepsister and you both have to live together.' Florence's heart ached at the subdued look on the young transparent face. Mairi showed her feelings so easily, she would have to learn to mask them in this world of deceit and intrigue. She kissed the small tilted nose. 'Come, it will not be so bad. You can get up today and sit in the antechamber. There is someone else who wishes to see you.'

Mairi looked up enquiringly into her mother's smiling face. 'Your rescuer, of course,' Florence's eyes twinkled. 'He has been pacing the gallery and the Great Hall and the courtyards, getting in everyone's way for the past five days.'

'Five days?' Mairi exclaimed. She had not realised how long she had been detached from the world. A healthy rose-pink blush stole to her cheeks. 'You - you mean Douglas?' Mairi whispered.

His face had recurred in her dreams, close to hers; angry, laughing, gentle, mocking, sad. Her mother nodded and smiled with surprise to see the effect the name had on the peaky features. At least Mairi had not fallen into disagreement with her other stepsibling.

Florence had misjudged him herself and had long since apologised to Douglas for her frosty greeting. He had made up for any apparent neglect of his duties the other night. Not only had he saved Mairi from the clutches of the monster Black, but he had risked his own life seeing off Cailean's unruly band and sustained a blow to his head.

'So I will send in Margaret to help you dress, shall I?' Florence rose.

'Yes. I would like that,' Mairi said coyly.

Margaret, Mairi's favourite young maid, helped her wash and perfume her body, fastening her into a gown of green damask, slashed to reveal the gold lining. The bodice was scattered with embroidered birds of many colours and she wore her ruff open with a thin gold chain around her neck. Margaret combed back the luxurious copper hair and bound it up in a criss-cross net with golden flowers.

'How do I look, Margaret?' Mairi asked nervously. Her maid gave her an encouraging grin.

'As beautiful as a May day in sunshine,' her eyes twinkled. The compliment brought tinges of colour to the thin cheeks and a spirited light to the dulled eyes. She would soon be herself again, Margaret thought as she left.

Douglas found her sitting in an armchair flooded in sunlight, an open book lying unread in Mairi's lap as she gazed out of the casement window to the fields beyond. It was a favourite corner of the Castle and Mairi hummed quietly to herself, with her back to the door. Douglas stood for a few seconds watching the sun play on her hair, bringing it to life with auburn lights. He could have drunk in the sight for ages, but she sensed him and turned.

Their eyes met and held for a long moment, Mairi's heart lurching at the tender unguarded look in the deep violet eyes, the cut of his handsome bearded face. But he was hurt; the clean bandage told of his head wound. She had been so wrapped up in her own troubles that it had not occurred to her Douglas might have also taken risks.

Douglas recovered himself and smiled at the pretty piquant face turned up towards his.

'You look rested and quite beautiful,' he came forward and kissed her on the pale naked brow. Mairi flushed with pleasure but found she could think of nothing to say.

Before her stood a man dressed in the leisurely garb of a gentleman not a rough soldier. He wore a black velvet jerkin over white silk doublet sleeves, short trunk hose and white silk garters fastened at the knees over tight-fitting stockings that pronounced his muscular legs. Douglas wore them with the ease of a courtier, but then he had lived as one at the Danish court for three years. She found his manliness and the attentive gleam in his dark eyes quite disconcerting.

It was a new Douglas she was going to have to get to know afresh, almost like receiving a stranger to her small chamber. The thought made her pulse quicken, not altogether uncomfortably.

'Thank you for what you did, Douglas,' Mairi gulped and lowered her eyes from his intent gaze. 'Your injury - I hope it was not because of me - because of that horrible man . . .?' Her voice trailed off.

'It depends to which horrible man you refer,' Douglas gave a wry laugh. 'It was one of Cailean's lackeys gave me a parting blow.' There was an awkward silence. 'And what I did was little enough compared with your brave act,' Douglas's voice was quiet and deep, the joking gone.

Mairi looked up through her long fair lashes. 'It was nothing really.' He raised an eyebrow.

'So setting fire to Duntorin's property and galloping about like a wild clansman, brandishing pistols and saving witches from a burning, is nothing?' She heard the familiar amusement and flushed deeper at his description.

'Not witches,' Mairi flashed back, raising her chin, 'and it was all I could think of to do. After all, you men were chasing your tails looking for elusive Lismores, were you not?'

Douglas moved forward quickly and laughingly planted a surprise kiss on her lips.

'My dear, sweet Mairi, now I know you are better!'

She looked in amazement at the man bent on one knee at her feet, holding her hand in his as if it were the natural thing to do.

Her lips felt on fire where he had touched her, not a brotherly kiss at all and her heart was knocking so loudly she felt he must hear it.

Douglas saw the soft skin emerging from the flowered bodice, turning pink, setting her chest and neck alight. She was like a flower opening to the sun, responding to the slightest touch of warmth. He found it exciting, resisting with difficulty the urge to run his finger along the soft flesh of her breasts cut by the neck of the dress. He saw a pulse throbbing in her throat and wondered if she felt the same arousal?

At the dance he had found her wild barefoot defiance of him strangely irresistible. He had to admit his interest in her was more than that of protective older brother and it had galled him to see Mairi being escorted off by that insufferable youth, Andrew Ramsay. Now the young woman in her was more apparent in the grown up cut of her green dress that set off the vivid green shining eyes. Tendrils of hair had already escaped, caressing her face. Mairi licked her dry lips and smiled shyly, pulling her hand away gently.

Douglas drew back. 'I'm sorry, I have embarrassed you,' he guessed correctly. Mairi's gaze fell to her lap. She did not know what to think. Part of her wanted him to touch her again, part was frightened of the strong reaction it provoked in her. It reminded her of the time they had danced together and she had briefly felt his strength in the heady reel.

'So what news do you bring?' Mairi looked up, trying to return the conversation to normal. Douglas stood up and walked to the window.

'Well your cousin was persuaded not to make a present to himself of father's cattle and fled home. And now that things have calmed down in the village, Sam has gone home to taste some of his mother's delicious bread and cakes.'

Mairi smiled, 'I'm sure he deserves fattening up after all his exertions, kind Sam.'

Douglas laughed. 'Looks as if you could do with some feeding up too. Will you be rested enough to dine with us all tonight?'

'It takes a lot to make me miss a meal, as you well remember,' Mairi giggled. 'I shall look forward to that, though I may draw the line at dancing afterwards.'

'Then you can tap your feel to the music instead, milady,' Douglas put on the querulous accent of the physician Bethune. 'You will be excused the dancing just this once.' Mairi tipped back her head and laughed. She had forgotten Douglas's gift for impersonation. 'In the meantime you must live on green slime from the bottom of the loch, made up into a disgusting milk jelly,' he wagged a stern finger at her, 'consumed six times daily until the next full moon.'

'Stop!' Mairi cried, nearly choking with delight. 'I promise, I promise.' Douglas crept round the room, holding his bent back like the creaking old doctor, mumbling to himself. 'You'll make me ill with laughing,' Mairi protested and he stood up, hands on hips and chuckled with her.

Mairi wiped the tears from her eyes. 'Oh, you do me good,' she admitted.

'That reminds me,' Douglas suddenly pulled at the pouch on his silver buckled belt. 'I have a small trinket from Denmark. I quite forgot you had not received it.'

Mairi watched him fumble with a small packet, the childish excitement at an unopened present seizing her. He solemnly handed it over and stood waiting for her opinion. She undid the leather tie and unfolded the protective cloth. Inside lay a necklace of pearls suspending a delicate silver filigree pendant. It was a ship in full sail with three pearl drops falling from its curved underside.

'Do you like it?' Douglas asked anxiously, fearing disappointment.

'It's beautiful,' Mairi whispered, her eyes pricking with emotion. 'It must have cost you much.'

'It was worth it to see the pleasure it brings to your fair face, Mairi.' Though spoken quietly the words seemed to fill the room between them. She looked up, seeing his dark figure through a blur of tears.

'Please would you fasten it for me Douglas?' She rose from her chair. Douglas came to her and took the necklace, feeling her hands tremble. He placed it about her slim neck, the ship lying flat on her chest and walked around to fasten the silver clasp. He lifted the coil of red hair and gold net, seeing the vulnerable pearly skin beneath, bent trustingly before his fingers.

He could not guess at the exquisite small shocks tingling down Mairi's neck and arms at his touch. They reached right down to her lower body in delightful waves. Douglas stooped and kissed the nape of her neck and something exploded like a charge inside her. She had never experienced a feeling like it. The breath stopped in her throat, the colour flooding up from her chest to her brow.

Douglas felt Mairi jump at his kiss and he gently swung her about to face him. Her lips were slightly parted, the sea green eyes moist with tears.

'Douglas, I was so frightened,' her whisper was scarcely audible. 'I thought you would never come in time.' And then she was crying and he was pulling her to him in a tender embrace, encircling her in strong secure arms, kissing away the tears from her eyelids, her cheeks, her mouth.

'If anything had happened to you I would never have forgiven myself,' he murmured in her ear, his breath sending new shivers down her spine.

Mairi did not recognise herself in this weak and weepy mood she felt, but she was enjoying these new emotions Douglas evoked in her. His mouth found hers again and she responded to his kiss with a desire that made her light-headed. She wanted it to last and last as she pressed her body against his.

'Oh Mairi,' Douglas's voice was a low rasp, 'I can never call you sister again.'

Mairi smiled, tracing an exploratory finger along his bearded jaw. He nibbled her fingertip.

Ever so gently she reached up and touched his bandaged wound. His eyes were deep pools mirroring his desire. If she were not careful they would completely hypnotise her.

'So you will not tease me as a child again?' Mairi said making a half-hearted attempt to pull away, a laugh catching in her throat.

Douglas pulled her to him more strongly and groaned, 'Not while you tease me like a woman.'

Suddenly Mairi was frightened by the situation, of forces she could unleash but not control. She felt Douglas' urgency in his next kisses, the demanding passion of a man, unlike any of the village boys who had stolen the odd kiss before.

'No. Douglas,' Mairi pushed him away and turned her face from him, 'we must not.' He was breathing more heavily but he allowed her to escape his arms. Her heart still pounded as she tried to explain. 'We have to live here as family, even if we may find that difficult.' Mairi went crimson at his amused smile. She knew things would never be the same between them again.

Perhaps such feelings were commonplace to Douglas, but he was the first man for whom she had felt such longing.

'I intend us to be much more to each other than that,' his bearded mouth curved sensuously as the dark eyes swept over her and Mairi feared her resistance melting.

A knock at the door made her spring away from Douglas. Isabel came in. Mairi noticed at once that she wore a becoming dress of dark red with an embroidered stomacher and lace ruff. Her hair was still bound tightly over a wire frame, but her cap did not hide all the black tresses from view. Isabel looked quickly from one to the other, her sharp eyes missing nothing, but she made no comment.

'Sister,' Mairi's voice was hoarse, 'what do you want?' Isabel twisted a ring about her thin finger and spoke in a strained voice.

'I have come to apologise for any harm I may have caused you, stepsister,' she said stiffly. 'I'm glad to see you looking so much better.'

Mairi searched her face for any trace of irony, but the tight expression gave nothing away. 'Thank you,' Mairi replied with dignity, 'let us put these unhappy events behind us.'

Douglas put an arm round each, pleased that they were making up. He did not want to be caught between two strong wills and forced to take sides.

'What a lovely pendant,' Isabel's eyes alighted with interest on Mairi's neck. 'A present from Denmark, I'm sure?'

'Yes,' Mairi smiled with pleasure, 'the ship is my favourite symbol; it reminds me of the sea at Lismore.'

Isabel almost smirked, 'And of your marauding Viking ancestors, no doubt.' She had not lost the sharp edge to her tongue, Mairi thought to herself, ignoring the jibe. 'Douglas chose mine well too,' Isabel smiled coyly at her brother.

She fingered the gold brooch worn on her puffed sleeve. It was a bird of paradise swinging between two chains from a gold clasp.

'Isabel, it's really beautiful,' Mairi gasped at the craftsmanship. 'We have been spoilt indeed.' Isabel's pale face lit with a smile that showed how attractive she could be when the scornful lines were banished.

'Perhaps brother, you could accompany us on a walk this afternoon? The fresh air would do Mairi good.' Surprise raised the younger girl's eyebrows. Was Isabel really going to turn over a new leaf?

'I would like that very much,' Mairi agreed, smiling shyly at Douglas. He patted Isabel's hand linked through his arm.

'Nothing would give me more pleasure than to walk with my two favourite women,' he assured them with a grin. 'But first I must exercise my horse, Elsinore. Till later then,' he bowed gallantly and left.

Mairi was glad he was gone, she was aware that Isabel had felt something in the atmosphere between them. Knowing how jealous she could be, Mairi would have to tread carefully and keep her feelings to herself.

'Where would you like to go?' Isabel asked her, walking to the window, her hand playing with the heavy drape covering the stone wall.

'Away from the woods that's for sure,' Mairi pulled a face and sank into the wooden chair again, feeling spent from the encounter with Douglas. There was a long pause and Mairi was about to begin reading when Isabel spoke softly.

'Nothing happened between you and the minister did it?' The book dropped with a thud onto the rush strewn floor. She looked in horror at the back of Isabel's head, unable to believe she would ask such a question. At her silence Isabel turned slowly. The look on her face was hard to fathom, but it was deadly serious.

'If you mean being dragged through the woods and the breath knocked out of me was nothing, then, yes, nothing happened,' Mairi shook at the thought. 'Thanks to Douglas that's as far as he got, though for me it was repulsive and terrifying and I hope I never see him again!'

Isabel let out a long breath and the ghost of a smile flickered at the corners of her mouth.

'That's as I thought,' she said, watching her stepsister with black eagle eyes. 'By the way,' she added, feeling the brooch, 'why did you set alight to the old bothy?'

Mairi could not follow her line of questioning; it was starting to agitate her. 'I - I don't know. I suppose because it was out of the village - and the smoke could be seen from a distance but not the hut.'

'Oh,' Isabel said lightly, 'I thought it might have been because it was the place your father died, a sort of revenge on your part.'

Mairi was winded by the verbal punch. She had never known that chilling, haunted place held such a personal tragedy for her. She could not speak, tears springing afresh to her eyes, as her throat constricted. Isabel was looking out of the window again.

'Well, well,' she crowed as if she had mentioned nothing more harmful than the weather, 'my brother wastes no time in pursuing what he desires. That maid is a bold one.' She turned to Mairi, her eyes glinting hard with triumph.

Picking up her skirts, Isabel swept towards the door. 'Oh, dear, I quite forgot.' She looked over her shoulder. 'I have a prayer meeting this afternoon. What a pity I won't be able to walk with you and Douglas.' Then she was gone.

Mairi rose unsteadily from her chair and dragged her steps to the window, not wanting to believe Isabel's veiled taunts.

Below in the courtyard she saw Douglas laughing with someone. That someone was handing over a velvet and sable coat and laughing back. It was too far to make out the dancing blue eyes, but Mairi had no difficulty in recognising Mary Bain, the May Queen of Douglas's choosing.

She clutched at her stomach as if she would be sick. How could he rush from her arms, having made her dizzy with his kisses and his touch and moments later be calmly flirting with the village girl? Mairi felt quick anger at the thought. She had been stupid to believe that Douglas, now a man of the world, could feel any real passion for an innocent like herself, barely out of childish skirts. He had been feeling sorry for her, that was all, carried away for a brief moment. Douglas had taken advantage of her weak and weepy state which Mairi now despised. Even at this moment he must be regretting it as she did. He and Mary were already lovers and she had behaved like a fool by letting her feelings for Douglas be known.

They were no doubt joking about her, calling her a silly headstrong child, who could not even handle boys like Andrew Ramsay. He was walking Mary to the stables, making no secret of their relationship to the stable lads. How brazen they were! Mairi watched unhappily, unable to tear herself away, punishing herself for believing there might be something special between her and her handsome thoughtless stepbrother.

A few minutes later they emerged leading Elsinore. Douglas helped

Mary mount the horse and then climbed up behind her. They were shameless! Mairi hated him for it. She would never let him near her again, as long as she lived.

Leaving the window, Mairi sank down among the rushes clutching her new pendant and cried bitter tears. She hated them all, these Roskills, they brought her nothing but pain. Mairi cried for her father dying among hateful strangers in that crude little herdsman's hut. No wonder the guilty Duntorin did not allow it to be used. It should have been burnt down many moons ago. Isabel was as spiteful as a viper for telling her like that.

And Mairi wept tears for the way Douglas had manipulated her to feel love for him. She had so easily put from her mind the part he had played in her father's death, but she would not forget so easily again. She would steel herself against him in future, so that he could never make her feel such emotions as she had when cradled in his warm embrace.

She would thwart them all and go out for a walk by herself. No longer did she want the company of either stepsibling. Isabel had had no intention of going through with the plan anyway; it had just been suggested to impress Douglas with her attempts to be friendly.

Mairi returned to her bedchamber and changed into comfortable woollen skirts and straight sleeved bodice. In spite of the warm sunshine, she put on a cloak and hood to make herself anonymous to passing glances. If her mother caught her slipping out on her own instead of resting, there would be trouble.

Looking out of the narrow window to see who was about in the courtyard, Mairi glimpsed a tall figure disappearing out of the gateway. The flash of red velvet under the black cloak confirmed it as Isabel. Let her go to her prayer meeting at the Kirk and drink in more words of the hateful Zechariah Black, if she so wished. Mairi would have none of their false piety. How different it was from the gentle loving guidance she had received from the old priest at Lismore. She missed the comforting familiarity of the Old Religion.

Mairi yearned to be out in the fresh air once more, to feel sunlight on her face and smell the summer flowers in the hedgerows and dykes. She took the back stairway which led from the private apartments down past the Great Hall. In her haste, Mairi nearly crashed into Sarah, the cook, panting up the stairs from the kitchens below.

'Oh mercy me,' Sarah gasped, clutching her enormous aproned bosom in fright, 'I thought you were a wee ghostie, Miss Mairi.'

Mairi stifled a laugh and put a reassuring hand on Sarah's floury arm. 'Sorry Sarah, I was just sneaking down for something to eat.'

Sarah eyed her in the gloom of the stairwell. 'Aye, dressed in your outdoor clothes as well?' Sarah queried disbelievingly. Mairi gave her a pleading look and the plump woman sighed. She knew Mairi would do exactly as she pleased, no one could tame her strong Highland will.

'Oh, away you go!' Sarah blustered affectionately. 'But you just take care young Miss, do you hear?'

Mairi gave her a swift kiss on her soft fleshy cheek and hurried down the stone steps. Sarah shook her head with a smile. Mairi was quite a favourite of the kitchen staff. She had often sought their company in the early days, gaining comfort from the smoky intimacy of the kitchens, regaling them with stories of the goings on below stairs at Lismore Castle.

Mairi picked up a bannock from the kitchen table, still warm from the oven and pushed it inside her cloak. Out in the courtyard she bent her head and hurried for the gate. No one called her back. Beyond the walls she started to run, her legs stiff at first and then loosening to the movement.

Heading up the old drovers' track at the edge of the outfields, Mairi made for the top of the loch, throwing back her hood and embracing the sun. At the lochside she settled herself on a sandy ledge and ate her bannock.

Above her a skylark sang a trill happy song and she lay back sleepy in the warm sunshine, emptying her mind of troubled thoughts.

Mairi woke with a chill breeze stiffening her neck. The sun had gone behind clouds and by the strength of the light in the sky, she must have lain there for some time. It was late afternoon and she should return. Too late for a walk now with Douglas, she thought stubbornly and wondered if she had been missed.

Gathering her cloak about her and brushing off the damp sand, Mairi pulled her hood up against the wind. The quickest way to return would be to cut across the fields and over the ridge to Duntorin from the north side. It meant passing the burnt out bothy but she would have to face it sometime. In a strange way it comforted her to think the ghost that fretted there was her father and no one sinister.

Yet it seemed to approach like a blackened creature as she toiled up the hill towards the hut, her strength easily sapped after her ordeal. Still, she had an irresistible urge to be near it, to explore its scorched shell, to see what was left. Mairi could have skirted it, but decided to pause on her journey home. The east wall was largely intact with even a solid piece of turf protecting the inside.

Mairi leaned up against its side out of the wind and regained her breath. Strange thoughts conjured up like spirits out of the bothy, filling her mind. Why had her father stopped here? And why had he gone on ahead without the rest of the family? It seemed foolhardy that he should have rested almost within sight of the Roskill stronghold with only a couple of retainers, who were murdered along with him.

How many had come to cut him off with Douglas at their head? How could he have left his wife and daughter in such a vulnerable position, leaving them to the mercy of the Roskill baron?

Mairi's imagination played such tricks; she believed she heard a cry from the very bothy itself. She must hurry from this unhappy place. Then her heart froze as the cry came again, louder and more urgent. Impossible though it seemed, the noise came from the other side of the wall.

The wind was blowing towards her, carrying the sound of muffled voices and someone groaning. Mairi felt a slow pounding beginning in her breast; they were not the sounds of a quarrel or a fight, but the intimate cries of a man and woman. She must leave immediately before she was discovered; Mairi had no wish to pry on a pair of lovers. But what a strange place to choose for love-making, this charred and forlorn outpost. Still, it was isolated and there was no fear of being discovered in a spot the village shunned.

Her heart suddenly constricted painfully in her chest. Could it be that this was Douglas and Mary's love-nest? It was not far from the promontory where the Beltane dance had been held and perhaps Sam had had to seek them out here? The thought of Douglas in intimacy on the site of her father's murder was more than she could bear. Waves of nausea swept up inside and she breathed deeply to control them.

Mairi had to know once and for all if her suspicions were true. She hated herself for spying, but at least it would be easy to smother any affection for Douglas if she knew he could behave so callously.

She eased her way along the back wall to where the rough stones and turf had crumbled or been burnt away. With her hood well pulled over to hide her red hair, she peered in. The sight stunned her.

They moved and grunted like animals under a familiar cloak, not at all how she imagined the act of love to be. This was base and frightening and yet in a horrible way it excited Mairi. But the shock of the actions was not as great as the shock of who lay there among the freshly laid straw.

The long frame of Zechariah Black was moving over someone. Mairi shuddered with disgust. But the woman with him was no unwilling victim.

As Mairi ran from the bothy, her retreat muffled by the wind, the sound of the woman's moaning and the sight of the loose dark hair spread on the floor, followed her. Even as she shut her eyes, the flushed face of Isabel penetrated her eyelids.

Mairi ran until her insides caved in for lack of breath, unable to comprehend what she had seen. She burst into the courtyard, her legs shaking from running as much as shock. Douglas was standing by the open Castle door looking out. As soon as he saw her he strode across to meet the exhausted runner.

'Where the devil have you been?' he sounded harsh in his concern. 'I've been frantic with worry.' She pouted her reply.

'Out walking on my own because neither my stepbrother nor sister were there to accompany me.' Her green eyes darkened like a stormy sea and she flashed him a hateful look.

'I'm sorry.' Douglas was taken aback by the savageness of her words. 'I said I had to exercise Elsinore and then I came straight back for you. Isabel remembered she had a meeting at the Kirk and I was looking forward to us strolling on our own.' Douglas drew nearer to her and looked down at Mairi with a tender look.

He could see she was agitated but thought she was over reacting. He noticed with regret Mairi had changed from her becoming gown and no longer wore the pearl and silver pendant.

'What a pity you rushed back from your ride for nothing then,' Mairi tossed back her tangled burnished mane. 'You could have spent more time with that May Queen of yours instead.'

Douglas flushed red at the edges of his beard, she must have watched from her window. He found Mary attractive, it was true. But he felt only friendly affection for her, she did not stir him in the way Mairi did. His stepsister gave him a withering look and made to pass. Gripping her by the arm he held her still.

'Let go!' she seethed with anger and confusion.

'Listen to me you wildcat,' Douglas said between gritted teeth. 'I have nothing to explain to you, but as you seem to have got yourself into such a tantrum about nothing, I will tell you. Mary came to return my cloak from the dance - and to compliment you on your courageous action - though small thanks she gets from you for her part.' Douglas saw Mairi flush a deeper scarlet. 'I gave her a ride home on Elsinore to save her the journey and if it pleases you to hear it, Sam was there at her door.'

Douglas went on. 'It seems he was making amends with Bain her father, for striking him in defence of you,' Douglas felt Mairi's resisting arm untense slightly. 'And it appeared to my eyes, both Sam and Mary were equally pleased to see each other.'

Mairi dropped her gaze, staring hard at the leather slippers on her feet. She did not know what to believe. She desperately wanted his words to be true. But then he was a Roskill like Isabel and she pretended a holier-than-thou attitude, while coupling with a hypocritical minister. It was sickening.

'Mairi?' Douglas pushed her chin up gently with his free hand, so she found herself looking into his warm dark eyes. Her heart missed a beat at the fiery tenderness that consumed her. 'Say something.' There was an tense pause.

'I'm sorry I went off on my own,' she answered very quietly, 'and I don't mean Mary any spite. I like her, but I just thought -'

'You think too much, my fanciful Highland maid,' Douglas smiled down at her, pulling her closer. Mairi's insides churned like buttermilk, she had an overwhelming impression that he was going to kiss her right there in the courtyard in full view of the Castle household.

'No, Douglas,' she breathed, 'not here please, you mustn't.' He chuckled at the look of consternation on her pretty face.

'I will desist now, if you agree to kiss me later then?' Douglas teased.

Mairi felt waves of excited warmth ripple through her at the invitation and in spite of misgivings she nodded, a smile creeping unbidden to her full lips.

'Then I must be content with that,' Douglas released the grip on her arm. 'Come Mairi, you must rest and be fresh for the banquet tonight. Father is in a good mood and has ordered the fiddlers to play.' He steered her towards the Castle entrance.

As they reached it together, Mairi heard rapid footsteps behind. Turning she saw Isabel approaching flushed and breathless.

'Sister,' Douglas's manner was friendly, 'how was your meeting? Margaret gave me your message.'

'Most beneficial to the spirit,' Isabel answered with a pious face. Mairi turned a gasp into a cough and nearly choked. Isabel regarded her with wary eyes. 'Something wrong stepsister?' her voice was hard. 'I can see by your dress you managed a stroll. No doubt it was pleasant?'

Why did Isabel always have to assume things for other people, Mairi wondered in irritation? 'Yes, it was,' she pulled herself together with difficulty. 'Douglas and I had a very pleasant walk around the farm, just a short way, isn't that so Douglas?'

Mairi shot him a warning smile and his puzzled brows assumed their normal poise. 'Quite so,' he nodded, not knowing what game she was playing now. Mairi let out a small breath of relief; she did not want Isabel to suspect she had been anywhere near the bothy. Isabel and Black were far too dangerous a combination with which to tangle.

She wanted nothing to do with their illicit affair. Let them burn in hell together, Mairi thought viciously.

'Ladies,' Douglas made way for them both to proceed, following baffled by the guarded parrying of the two young women. He must try harder to bring them together in future.

Mairi noticed nervously that her mother hurried towards them down the stairs. Scolding words in front of Isabel would expose her tale as a lie. 'You go ahead with Isabel, Douglas,' she pushed him towards the next flight; 'I wish to speak with mother.' Douglas complied and took his sister's arm without querying the request. They were out of earshot when Florence reached her daughter.

'Mairi,' she began crossly, 'you're a wilful, selfish child. Douglas told me you had disappeared off on your own and you, hardly out of your bed and still weak from your ordeal.'

Mairi let her mother have her say, and then took her arm.

'Sorry mother,' Mairi smiled at the dear worried face. She seemed to be doing a lot of apologising lately. 'I needed the fresh air and no one else was around. I didn't go far.'

'Oh no?' her mother still looked stern. 'You were spotted by two of the kitchen boys, lying by the lochside like a cat in the sun. Sarah sent them to keep an eye on you while catching fish for dinner.'

Mairi went pale with fright. 'Please don't tell anyone else, mother, please,' she stammered, instinctively looking over her shoulder. Florence was taken aback by her daughter's panic.

'Mairi what is the matter?' she put a hand on her arm. 'What are you frightened of?'

'Nothing,' Mairi tried to smile. 'It's just I don't want Isabel to know I was there by myself when I'd promised to go for a walk with her. She might be cross.'

Her mother looked into the green eyes which shifted under her gaze. She was not taken in by this explanation, but she could see how the subject upset Mairi and did not press her. 'Go to your room then daughter,' Florence bade her; 'you must rest now if you wish to attend the banquet tonight.'

She hesitated, wondering whether to break the news now to Mairi. It was not something that pleased her in the least, but Duntorin had insisted that for the peace of the community they must go through with it. Florence dreaded the effect the order must have on her young redheaded daughter walking beside her.

'Mairi,' she slipped an arm through hers, 'there's one thing I better tell you about tonight and I don't want you to be upset.' Mairi felt a queasiness churn her insides at the words, she let her mother continue. 'I'm afraid your stepfather has seen fit to invite a certain person for the meal - as a sort of olive branch.'

Mairi stopped, the blood draining out of her face and neck. Her feelings went numb. 'Not the minister surely?' She scarcely whispered the words, not even able to speak his name.

Florence turned Mairi gently towards her and nodded.

'It's not my wish, believe me, but Duntorin says it is the only way to prevent such witch hunts against any of the community in the future. We cannot be seen to be defiant of the Kirk. Even King James has to bow to their pressure, acknowledging their Assembly. These are dangerous times in which we live Mairi.'

The young girl hardly heard the explanations, the picture of Zechariah Black's lecherous face springing to her mind so clearly it was as if he were there taunting her.

'How can he?' Mairi suddenly exploded with anger. 'How can Duntorin bear to have that beast under his roof? He is no representative of the Kirk, he's a charlatan. My father would never have allowed such a thing and I never thought Duntorin would give in so easily to his threats.'

Florence gripped her shoulders. 'Do you think he likes the man for trying to convict us of witchcraft?' Her voice was quietly severe. 'Of course, he doesn't. It will be just as hard for Duntorin to keep his temper as for you. But for all our sakes you will behave civilly and go through with this.'

Tears of fury and hurt sprang into the vivid green eyes. Mairi struggled from her mother's grasp, picked up her skirts and ran up the stone stairs, her footsteps ringing accusingly in Florence's ears.

CHAPTER FOUR

Florence Roskill felt hot tears of pain pricking her eyes as she made ready in her chamber. She hated herself for having to hurt Mairi. Why was her daughter so impetuous and defiant? Neither she nor Lismore had had such a fiery spirit and it would come to no good. Mairi was imbued with the Viking blood of her Lismore ancestors, who enjoyed everything from fighting to music with equal passion.

Florence dreaded the evening as much as her daughter; she feared Zechariah Black too. The only person who seemed pleased with the arrangement was Isabel. She had glowed with a warmth Florence had not seen in her for years, when her father agreed to the invitation that morning. Florence was sure it was Isabel's own idea, for Duntorin was soft when it came to dealing with her. He still seemed to feel guilt at leaving his young daughter motherless and then forcing her to share his attentions with two other women.

Florence sighed. Maybe she had been wrong to play down Black's threats towards Mairi in the wood, when her husband had asked. She had done so to avoid further recriminations and now she felt responsible.

She would go along with this charade tonight because of her love for Duntorin and because she knew that he did it only because he loved them dearly too.

Mairi did not know for how long she lay numbed on her bed, but her room was dark and shadowed and she heard noises below in the Great Hall. Tables were being assembled and plates and knives and jugs of claret set for dinner. She could hear the fiddlers testing their strings in the overhanging gallery and the sound lifted her spirits in spite of her jaded feelings.

She had decided she would not attend the banquet; she would plead tiredness and exhaustion. They could not force her to meet Black. Mairi slipped out of her skirts and bodice and pulled on a loose bedgown. She lay under the embroidered bedcover and waited for the confrontation.

Duntorin strode about the Hall directing servants and shouting to the musicians.

'We want music even the hounds will tap their feet to!' he cried, waving his silver decorated mazer in the air so that red drops of wine spilled onto the rushes. A dog snuffled at the spillage.

Douglas watched his father sullenly. He had only now been told of their controversial dinner guest and was not pleased. He felt if he saw the lascivious cruel face again he would want to strangle him once and for all. And no expense was being spared to entertain Zechariah Black. Douglas noticed silver plates, salt-cellars and quaiches had been brought out and a rich carpet covered the top table.

The smell of succulent wild fowl and venison had been tempting him for hours as it wafted up from the kitchens, mixing with the salty smell of fresh fish.

Duntorin poured himself another cupful of claret and drank deeply.

'We will show him, Douglas, how the Roskills entertain,' his father laughed. 'And he will see exactly who is lord around here,' Duntorin lowered his voice just for his son.

So that was his game, Douglas raised his eyebrows and smiled in understanding. He was going to overwhelm the minister with the sumptuous richness of Duntorin Castle and thereby show him the power that lay behind it. It was to teach Black a lesson as much as sign a truce with him. Douglas chuckled to think how disapproving the representative of the Kirk would be at the devilish feasting and music. Perhaps it would be an enjoyable evening after all.

Florence swept in with a rustle of satin skirts. She looked beautiful in crimson and silver, her stomacher studded with pearls and sequins that threw off dazzling firelight as she moved. He saw his father's eyes deepen and a smile of welcome come easily to his mouth.

The look of worry momentarily lifted from her face, and then she began. 'Mairi will not come down, John.' The smile instantly died and his craggy face puckered with annoyance.

'She must come down,' he answered tersely, 'else she will spoil everything.' Douglas knew the signs. There would soon be shouting and storming about if nothing was done. He would not be surprised if his father was considering dragging Mairi down personally.

'I've coaxed and chided,' Florence looked close to tears, 'but she refuses to get dressed.'

At that moment Isabel entered and stopped the conversation. She was stunningly dressed in a white velvet gown with gauze oversleeves patterned in silver leaves. The same gauze hid the bareness of her chest. Her swept up hair was decorated with pearls and her cheeks glowed. Douglas's gold brooch was pinned to the dress, gleaming on the white background.

'Daughter, you look quite beautiful,' Duntorin enthused forgetting the crisis for a moment.

'So you do, sister,' Douglas kissed her cheek. She smiled, her dark eyes dancing in the light thrown by the silver candlesticks.

'Thank you both.'

Florence smiled distractedly at the girl and turned back to her husband. 'John, there is nothing I can do.'

His face set grimly.

'What is the matter?' Isabel asked assuming an innocent demeanour.

'Your stepsister's the matter,' Duntorin barked, 'she refuses to be present at our banquet.'

'Perhaps I can persuade her,' Isabel's voice sounded sweet as honey, but Douglas caught the anxious look on his stepmother's face.

'Let me talk to her,' Douglas suggested quickly, 'you should be here to greet the minister, Isabel.' She blushed at this and he felt a stab of unease. Was this radiance in his sister really inspired by her loyalty to the Kirk or deeper feelings towards Black himself? He had no time to dwell on it.

'Go then,' Duntorin said gruffly and took another swig of wine.

'Thank you,' Florence touched his arm as he passed and smiled somewhat wistfully.

Mairi was standing at the window looking out at the now drizzly twilight, swallowing up the fields and the thick walls of the courtyard. She spun round at the gentle knock, as the door creaked open. The room was unlit and practically in darkness. She strained to see the unwelcome guest.

'Mairi?' her heart jumped at Douglas's familiar tone.

'I'm here,' she answered quietly, clutching her white bedgown about her. She could make out the cut of his trunk hose and doublet, the white ruff and his bandage standing out in the gloom. He was dressed richly for their monstrous minister. Had he so soon forgotten what Black had tried to do to her? It seemed only she cared about the way he had treated them and tried to destroy the family. 'What do you want?' Mairi's voice hardened.

Douglas attempted to speak, but the words caught in his throat. It had taken a moment for his eyes to accustom themselves to the dark. Now he saw Mairi ghost-like in her white shift, silhouetted at the window, her red hair cascading about her shoulders and the loose gown. The grey light fell on half her face, lighting the cheekbone and small tilted nose and defiant chin. Mairi was more desirable to him now than he had ever seen her before and he almost forgot his mission. Douglas cleared his throat.

'I have come to persuade you to be present at the feast, Mairi,' he answered deeply.

'What makes them think you have any influence over me?' she replied haughtily. 'I've told mother I am too tired.'

Douglas took a step nearer. 'So tired that you stand like a naughty inquisitive child, peering out of the window to see who comes to the Castle?'

Mairi heard the mocking amusement in his voice and it made her colour. She was glad it was too dark for him to see his point had gone home.

'I just needed some air,' she faltered. To her dismay she saw him move closer, she wanted to keep Douglas well at arm's length, so her will would not be broken.

'Mairi,' his voice reverberated low around her, 'we need you to be there tonight - I need you.' She felt her heart somersault at the words that disturbed the air between them.

'Why?' she whispered, twisting a strand of long hair between her fingers.

'Father wants to show this man that we are a powerful family and will not be mistreated again.' Douglas continued in a persuasive, coaxing tone. 'You must be there to show that you are not frightened by what happened; that he cannot hurt you.' He paused. 'And if you are there beside me,' Douglas added very low, 'I will be too happy to think about seizing the wretch by his neck.'

He was jesting but Mairi felt a tingling frisson of pleasure ripple down her back. Douglas saw a smile creep to the corners of her full lips. He came closer and stroked her cheek with a finger.

Mairi jolted at his touch. When he was near she felt nothing else mattered, it filled her with a strange excitement.

'But I am afraid of him,' her breath was warm on his bearded chin. Douglas's arms went about the slim body, feeling the bones of her shoulder blades beneath his hands. He gripped her to him, hot desire lighting within at the feel of her firm young body unbound in the nightdress, pressing against his silk shirt. He had never been so close to the woman in her and it made the blood in his temples throb.

Mairi lifted her face to his, not caring that she stood scantily dressed alone with a man who was half stranger to her. Douglas's mouth came down on hers, his eyes flashing with warmth. She felt her insides melt at the contact, her lips opening at his exploring tongue. His kiss was insistent and she responded hungrily.

Douglas broke away, kissing urgently down her neck, burrowing his dark head in at the opening of her gown. She shuddered at the touch of his lips on the crevice between her breasts, running her fingers through his wavy hair. It was exquisite.

Then the picture of Isabel and Zechariah Black sprung like a nightmare to her mind. If that was what passion resulted in, then she should stop now.

What she was doing must be wrong; she did not want to inspire the darkness of lust in Douglas that had so frightened her in Black. If she let him continue much longer she would have no strength to resist.

'No, Douglas,' with a great effort, she pushed his head away with her hands. 'Please don't take advantage of me like this.' She backed away breathing heavily, her heart racing. She heard him groan.

'Mairi, I think you must have secret powers,' he laughed softly; 'you have quite bewitched me!' The joke was too sharp and full of reminders of the past awful days for Mairi to enjoy.

'Don't jest about such things,' she quietly rebuked.

Douglas withdrew, trying to control the thumping in his own breast. He must not allow his feelings to take over so quickly; it could be dangerous for both of them. He sensed the fear in Mairi and vowed he would do nothing more to upset her. His behaviour was quite irrational towards this girl who was so vulnerable and unsophisticated. This passion had taken him completely by surprise and he must curb it.

'You will come downstairs then?' his voice was matter of fact. Mairi let out a long sigh.

'I will do as you all wish,' then added more forcefully, 'but don't expect me to sit beside the snake.' Douglas laughed and turned to go.

'You must hurry, my love, everything is now ready.'

As he left, Mairi flushed to realise the intimate endearment he had spoken to her. It had sounded quite natural. He was right when he said that they could never again be like brother and sister; it was unthinkable. To her, Douglas had never been a brother even when she had first come to Duntorin.

Mairi had three brothers of her own at Lismore and Douglas had never behaved in the same way towards her as they had. Perhaps for the first time she realised the teasing of old had always had the stimulation and excitement of the opposite sex to Douglas's games. Could it be true, she had for years fought against her attraction towards him? Mairi called for Margaret who had been waiting outside for ages in case her wilful mistress changed her mind about dressing for dinner. The young maid brought in candles to light the dark room, making no comment about Douglas's energetic retreat or the pink face of the one he left.

Zechariah Black looked about him in awe at the Great Hall with its tapestries of hunting scenes warming the stone walls. The table silver glittered in the candlelight and the large room was warm from the blazing fire, Duntorin's coat of arms painted boldly on the wood panel above the mantelpiece.

'Come and sit beside my daughter!' Duntorin ordered the man who had tried to convict his wife of witchcraft. 'You will take claret?' Black nearly lost his balance at the powerful thump on his back.

'Well, thank you, just a drop perhaps,' he licked his dry lips, his eyes resting on Isabel. He had never seen her quite so delectable, with her neck bare and her tight bodice accentuating her tiny waist. He must keep himself in check for he had no wish to antagonise Duntorin on this special night.

A quaich full of wine later he found himself relaxing in the cheerful Hall, alert to the bustle of a large household, his mouth watering at the sight of groaning ashets of meat and vegetables. He had never seen such food; boiled mutton and spinach, roast hare, sorrel tarts and a huge pike stuffed with shellfish. Florence Roskill, witch or no witch was indeed an expert housekeeper and Duntorin's wine was far superior to the ale he was used to drinking.

'I am most honoured to sit at your table, my lord,' Black raised his quaich in Duntorin's direction.

'And we are pleased to entertain our minister,' Isabel replied quickly, smiling at her neighbour. Florence and Duntorin exchanged a look of surprise but said nothing. The master of the house was well fired with French claret and was dulled to any subtleties of speech.

Douglas began to grow edgy. Perhaps Mairi had had second thoughts, unnerved by his forwardness; though he felt sure she experienced the same eagerness as himself. She was on the verge of womanhood and smouldered with a passion he had not come across in the fully matured women he had met.

He was about to push back his chair and go to seek her when Mairi appeared, dressed in a simple yellow gown delicately stitched with jade and white flowers. Her red hair was swept off her face in a modest cap the colour of buttercups, the green eyes looking like huge coral pools in their pale setting.

Douglas caught his breath at the effect. The sweet girl obviously thought it would make her look younger and less obtrusive than the finery of the other women. In fact it was enchanting, the soft gown hugging her figure, the hair pulled away from her face accentuating the sensuous mouth and eyes. He noticed with pleasure she wore his Danish pendant once more.

Douglas met her gaze and smiled encouragingly, rising to greet her. Mairi shot Black a fierce look with the briefest of nods ignoring the flash of interest in his grey eyes as his gaze slipped over her. It made the blood drain from her face. Douglas inwardly fumed; he had better keep his lecherous eyes off her or he would never see with them again! He moved swiftly to her side and steered Mairi to the other end of the table.

Isabel threw her a hateful look. She had seen the naked desire in her lover's eyes too and it made her bubble with jealousy. This was one area she would entertain no rivalry from her stepsister, however unwilling. Mairi caught the scowl and noticed how lavishly Isabel was dressed. If anyone around this table could guess what she knew, Black would be thrown straight in the dungeon.

Douglas pressed food on her and filled her mazer with wine.

'Take this to give you strength,' he urged in a deep smiling voice. Mairi swigged at the drink, feeling its richness warm her throat as it slipped down. Florence noticed how Douglas sat close to her daughter, attentive and easy in his gestures. There was a new expression lighting Mairi's eyes when she looked at her stepbrother.

Florence shifted with disquiet and wondered with what charm Douglas had persuaded the stubborn Mairi to descend? It had worried her increasingly since Douglas's return from Denmark that he and Mairi might feel more than family affection for each other. He was undeniably handsome and she was all but full grown. They were not blood relations, so she should not object to their attraction, but Mairi was still considered a

Catholic among this strongly Protestant household. Besides, Duntorin would not approve of such a match. He expected his only son to capture a wealthier prize, someone of sophisticated noble Lowland blood who could swell the coffers of Duntorin to maintain their lavish lifestyle and bring it heirs.

Mairi deserved a happy union too, after her dark childhood. She would talk more to her husband about his idea of sending Mairi to Court as a maid for the young Queen Anne from Denmark. She had heard life was lively at the Court of King James VI and there she would meet new people.

The noise grew louder in the Great Hall, rising up to the dark beams. Mairi saw with relief that Zechariah Black was occupied in conversation with Isabel. Duntorin strode about between the lower tables in jocular mood, chatting with his retainers and household. Mairi began to relax, her pulse beating with a slow hard thud at Douglas's closeness. She looked into the violet eyes gleaming in the candlelight and held his gaze. Almost without thinking, she slipped a hand under cover of the table, into his. It closed around her fingers, warm and strong and she blushed at her own boldness.

'Play musicians!' Duntorin threw up his arms at the gallery. 'We will have dancing.' Servants bustled about clearing tables and benches for dancing space and dogs scrapped for the leavings among the rushes. The orchestra of fiddles, timbrels and drums burst into life, drowning the laughter and chatter of the assembled diners below.

'Dance with me,' Douglas squeezed Mairi's hand that he had not allowed her to withdraw. She agreed, unaware of her mother's watchful gaze as Duntorin came to claim her for the dance.

'John, I must speak to you about Mairi and Douglas,' she murmured, 'they grow too fond of each other.' Duntorin grunted in disbelief.

'They are just affectionate brother and sister, dear wife, do not fret.' Then he added with a suspicious growl, 'I'm more concerned about the influence that thin-nosed minister has on my Isabel. Look how he leans over her. 'Tis not theology they discuss, I'll warrant you.'

Florence glanced over to see the two of them sitting close in hushed conversation.

'Black!' Duntorin called across to him, ignoring Florence's clenched hand on his arm. 'Will you dance with us?' The minister looked up, a flicker of disdain lighting the grey eyes before the smile.

'I think not, sir, dancing can arouse unwanted emotions which must not be encouraged by the Kirk.' His host pulled a face at his wife, but allowed the remark to go. Isabel too, sat doucely and would not join in, her thin hands entwined piously in her lap.

Mairi threw herself into the dance, not caring for her stepsister's hypocrisy, only aware that she danced with a tall bearded man with dark searching eyes and an infectious energy. Exhausted by the one dance Mairi allowed Douglas to steer her to a lower table where Sam sat and recounted stories of their life in Denmark.

'King Christian wanted Douglas to stay so he could teach him to hunt and drink like a Dane. Do you know the King could tire twelve horses on a day's hunting?' Sam's eyes twinkled at Mairi's incredulity.

'But I wanted to live a few more years,' Douglas laughed, 'so I came home to the tame pursuits of chasing Highlanders.'

Mairi blushed a fiery red, wondering if he meant her wild cousin Cailean or herself? A guffaw from Sam did not cool her cheeks and she speculated as to whether the two men discussed their conquests and matters of the heart together. She hoped Mary Bain was the name on Sam's lips and not Douglas's.

There was a loud banging on the top table as Duntorin brought order to the deafening throng. 'Open the casks of whisky,' their lord ordered. A loud cheer greeted the order and the hubbub resumed. Mairi noticed the glower of disapproval of Black's face at this deliberate incitement to drink the Devil's water. She could see the suppressed annoyance as he and Isabel stood up.

Mairi gripped Douglas's arm, nodding towards the minister who was approaching Duntorin. They exchanged a few words and Duntorin pointed to the curtained off gallery that led out to the battlements. Douglas and Mairi looked in silent agreement and went over to join Florence.

'What is going on, Mother?' Douglas asked. 'Is Black going to cause trouble?'

'I - I do not think so, Douglas,' Florence did not sound convinced, 'perhaps he disapproves of the whisky drinking. It was foolhardy of your father, but he would not be told.'

'He should be allowed to do as he wishes in his own home,' Douglas answered quickly. 'I'll follow in case he needs help.' He disappeared behind the curtain after them, leaving Mairi and Florence waiting edgily.

'Let's just listen,' Mairi urged her mother.

'Mairi we mustn't,' Florence protested, but her daughter was already heading for the gallery. They crept into the long passageway, lined with familiar portraits. The heavy door to the outside terrace was wide open and raised voices came in with the chill air.

'I forbid it!' Duntorin's voice thundered like canon fire. 'How dare you misuse my hospitality, you scoundrel.'

'Father, do not speak to the minister so!' It was Isabel's distraught plea.

'Your daughter feels the same calling as myself, Lord Duntorin,' Black's calm, level voice was like cold water thrown on a fire. 'She feels it is God's will that we marry.'

'God's will!' Duntorin exploded again. 'I'll give you God's will. You can get out now or I'll have you thrown over these battlements into the horse muck as you deserve. My daughter will never marry a common creature who terrorises my own family. Now get out!'

Mairi and Florence stood rooted to the spot in amazed horror. They could not believe their ears. Zechariah Black had asked for Isabel's hand in marriage and this was the response. He had badly misread the hospitality of the night, Mairi thought, with an ungenerous stab of satisfaction. She would like nothing better than to see him sent packing like a whimpering hound out of their lives. Isabel sobbed loudly and Mairi heard Douglas's voice trying to soothe her.

'You will regret this unseemly response to my serious marriage proposal.' Mairi could hear the cold anger in the minister's voice. 'I am destined for great things in the Kirk; I will be chosen to lead many people and would offer Isabel a happy and secure life.'

The sobs rose higher at his words. 'I will go - go with you Zechariah -'

'Zechariah!' Duntorin boomed. Mairi felt a twinge of pity for her stepsister at the savagery of her father's tone. 'You dare to be so familiar with this man? Get out of my sight you shameless girl.'

'No father!' It was Douglas's commanding voice, 'you shall not strike her.' There was a sound of scuffling and a muffled curse as Douglas stood his ground. 'You had better leave now, Black,' young Duntorin sounded calm, 'if you don't want a taste of your own lynching.'

Mairi and Florence pressed back against the wall of the gallery as the minister stormed from the terrace without another word.

Mairi froze as he passed, pausing only momentarily to give her a vengeful stare. Passing on, Mairi felt the breath gushing up her throat, her chest pumping like bellows with relief. Moments after him, Duntorin strode back into the gallery and spotted the two eavesdroppers.

He snorted, 'As you heard everything, there is nothing to explain. Come wife, you will accompany me back to the dance as if nothing has happened.' Florence too stunned to utter a word, followed him, forgetting about her daughter still frozen to the wall.

Mairi was left alone listening to the quite words of comfort Douglas gave to Isabel.

'He is not right for you, sister,' he spoke so low Mairi had to creep forward to listen to them. 'You could not expect Father to allow such a marriage.'

'Why not?' Isabel's voice bubbled with tears. 'He is a man of learning and he is ambitious.'

'But he has no wealth Isabel, what can he offer you? A draughty house and a few pigs and hens? Come, you could not live in such a manner.'

'I love him,' she answered defiantly. Douglas did not reply. 'It's not fair,' her voice rose petulantly, 'you can have whoever you wish. Father turned a blind eye to you and that common girl Mary at the dance. Why is it different for me?'

At that moment Mairi wished she could have been anywhere but standing in the gallery, overhearing this conversation not meant for her ears.

Isabel's reference to Douglas and Mary made her heart burn painfully. Could he really still be seeing her and playing with her own affections at the same time? It was not fair on either of them to pretend to both. And where did that leave Sam? Perhaps Douglas had invented the whole story of Sam and Mary to cover his own affair? Mairi heard Douglas laugh shortly. She could not bear to hear any more.

Mairi moved with the speed of lightning, galvanised by the hurtful realisation that Douglas was merely whiling away his time here, using her as a welcome diversion, just as he used Mary. She was back in the glow of the Great Hall before Douglas answered his sister.

'There was nothing for Father to turn a blind eye to,' he sounded amused. 'But maybe there will be soon,' Douglas murmured more to himself.

They walked out of the cold air and into the empty gallery.

'If that stupid interfering stepsister of ours had never intervened in the witch hunt, Father would never have held a bad opinion of Zech - of the minister.' Isabel's words rang like metal on stone in the echoing room.

'You can't blame Mairi for the kind of man Black is,' Douglas defended her quickly. 'She was brave to try and save Agnes, you cannot deny that Isabel?' She rounded on him.

'Oh, you would take her side and not mine, wouldn't you?' she hissed.

Douglas was taken aback by her sudden change of mood. Her emotions were too volatile after the traumatic evening.

'I will not take sides,' Douglas tried to keep calm, 'but you cannot expect me to condone the way Black tried to force Mairi back to his trumped up trial. It was unforgiveable.'

'She bewitched him, it's obvious,' Isabel's voice spiralled dangerously. 'He was not responsible for his actions, he told me so!' Douglas was aghast at the near hysteria. 'Mairi poisoned Father against the minister and me; now he will never grant us our dearest wish,' Isabel shook as she spoke. 'I hate her, I do. She will always bring unhappiness to this family, you mark my words!'

'Isabel, stop this,' Douglas tried to grab her arm but she wriggled free and ran from him up the dark stairs. His head reeled from the viciousness of her words; it hurt him greatly to hear her speak of Mairi in such a callous way. But he could not rid his mind of the wicked accusation that Mairi had bewitched Black. It was nonsense, of course, but had he not also jokingly accused her of the same thing? What sort of country had he come back to that so readily conjured up charges of black magic and devilry and sought to exorcise them by picking on innocent outsiders like Agnes and Mairi?

Even King James VI had taken part in a vindictive witch trial, convinced that the poor tortured victims had tried to wreck the ship that carried him and his new bride, Anne, home from Denmark.

No one was safe from this darkness; he would have to be close at hand to protect Mairi from such evil again. Thinking of her made Douglas turn back eagerly to the dance.

Isabel's ridiculous outburst was not going to spoil their evening together. Later he would snatch a brief moment alone with her, when the household was drowsy and full of drink. He had enjoyed the gay company of several Danish beauties, but none had stirred feelings within him as Mairi had. His thoughts were far from brotherly.

Disappointment met him as he searched for her among the dispersing dancers to no avail. Sam nodded towards the stair. Douglas took them in twos excited that she had slipped away to wait for him. With his knock unanswered, he tried her chamber door.

Once inside, Douglas saw Mairi lying face down on the bed, a candle sending flickers of light over her loosened red hair. She was still fully dressed. He closed the door behind and she turned her face towards him. Even in the dim light he could see the dull hardness in the green eyes and no smile greeted him on her rosy lips.

'How dare you come in unbidden,' Mairi whispered harshly. Douglas checked himself, perplexed by her mood. What had upset her now?

'I hoped you might have been pleased to see me,' Douglas answered wryly.

'Yes, I'm sure you did,' Mairi mocked back. 'I'm sure all your other conquests greet you with open arms.' The amusement died on his face. She was behaving childishly; it must be the wine speaking.

'Why are you angry?' he kept his voice level.

'What do you care how I feel?' Mairi rose onto her elbows, 'as long as I give in to your wishes. No doubt Mary Bain was given the same caring concern before you seduced her.'

Mairi knew she had gone too far, but she could not help the raw words that had been pounding relentlessly in her head. She wanted to cocoon herself from being hurt again and the only way to do it was to lash out at Douglas once and for all.

The words were like a smack on his cheek and he bounded forward and seized her arms.

'Don't speak of Mary in that way,' Douglas hissed, 'she's done nothing to deserve your scorn or slanderous tongue.'

So he did care for the dark-haired girl, Mairi thought with sore triumph. She glared at him silently, not flinching under his grip. 'What has got into you, Mairi?' Douglas asked desperately. 'I've told you there's nothing between Mary and myself. Why can't you believe me?'

'So you tell the truth while your precious sister lies through her teeth about you and that "common village girl"?' Douglas suddenly let go. Mairi felt miserable knowing it was true, his guilt written into the angry lines around the dark eyes and tight mouth.

'You were listening to all that?' Douglas' voice was hoarse. 'How much did you hear?'

'Enough,' Mairi's eyes smarted as she looked at the bearded face.

'Isabel said some foolish things that she did not mean,' Douglas spoke more evenly. 'She was just upset. She seems to blame you for her problems because of Black's unhealthy attraction towards you.'

Mairi sat up straight. What was Douglas saying now? She had not heard everything it seemed.

'Attraction for me!' she stuttered. 'That's rich indeed coming from her.' Mairi was dismissive.

'What do you mean?' Douglas sat on the edge of the bed wearily. Mairi considered him. Perhaps she should not tell Douglas of what she had witnessed at the hut? But she felt so needled by Isabel's spite.

'I mean that it would have been better for your father to allow them to marry,' she watched him warily.

Douglas was alert again. He leaned close to her, his voice deadly calm. 'Explain what you say.'

Mairi bit her lip wishing she had kept quiet. Douglas's fingers closed around her arm, bruising the flesh. Well she would tell him what he did not want to hear, she thought bitterly.

'When I was out walking,' her heart began to thud at the memory, 'I saw them in the old bothy, the burnt one that my father died in.' She waited to see the shock of her knowing register in his dark eyes, then continued in a strained voice. 'They were together - lying in the hay.' Mairi's look dropped from his as she coloured at her own words.

Douglas was winded with shock. 'You lie!' he jerked her head up by pulling her long hair. 'You have a wicked imagination; Isabel was right.'

Mairi flinched from the white rage in Douglas's taut features. His reaction astounded her. 'I do not lie!' she shouted back not caring if she was heard. 'That disgusting man was coupling with your sister.'

Douglas struck her hard on the cheek and Mairi gasped, and then hit him back before he could recover. Her eyes flashed dangerously, defying him to strike again.

'It's not my fault if you don't like what you hear. But why should you believe Isabel before you believe me? Ask any of the household, there was no prayer meeting at the Kirk this afternoon.'

Douglas blazed back at Mairi. 'I can understand your hatred for Black, but Isabel has tried to be friends with you since the witchcraft trial. You made up fantasies about me killing your father and now you have this obscene delusion about my poor sister.' Mairi let out a gasp of frustration but Douglas silenced her with his cold anger. 'Just because you may be capable of such thoughts - even deeds,' his eyes bore into hers, harsh and mocking, 'there is no need to suspect Isabel of such base behaviour.'

Mairi dug her nails into her fists, her cheeks red with indignation. It had never occurred to her that she might not be believed. 'Get out!' she spat the words at him. 'I was a fool to trust my confidences to a Roskill; you have the honour of the pigsty.'

Douglas's face clenched tightly, he did not trust himself to speak anymore. She aroused more fury in him than any other man or woman. He would gladly leave her to stew in her own suspicions. He rose from the bed and strode to the door.

At that moment it opened and Duntorin stood blocking the low doorway.

'So it's as Florence suspected,' he growled. 'You can hear your horseplay halfway down the Castle. I'll deal with you both in the morning.'

'It's not as it seems - ' Douglas spoke with strangled wrath.

'I don't want your excuses, you oversexed young buck.' He pointed for Douglas to leave. 'There is going to be some discipline about this place from now on. You will all do as your parents say!' His voice boomed into the bedchamber and Mairi blushed crimson in the candlelight.

Douglas went without a backward glance and she listened as Duntorin's footsteps echoed away. Mairi smashed a fist angrily into her pillow. How dare Duntorin assume something had happened between her and Douglas? These Roskills were all the same. But he had mentioned her mother's name too, so even she must have mistrusted them and spoken of her fears.

It seemed she had no one to whom she could turn. Mairi buried her head in the soft pillow and let the hot tears ooze into the feathers.

CHAPTER FIVE

Sometime during the restless night Mairi must have fallen into a fitful sleep, for she woke in the grey dawn still fully dressed and shivering on top of the bed. At first her mind was blank and then the memory of her terrible argument with Douglas came flooding back. She could not believe their relationship had plummeted so quickly, like a seabird on to the harsh rocks of their temper and hurt pride.

She felt a dull ache at the thought of his black eyes filled with scorn for her, the soft light of love erased so quickly as if it had never been. But perhaps it never had? She was unused to men and had misread the momentary desire as something more. Mairi resolved not to be so easily taken in again.

There was already movement in the courtyard below. Mairi got up and decided to change her dress at once; she would sleep no more. In spite of her unhappiness, she could not help a dry smile at the picture of an indignant Duntorin in her doorway and a speechless Douglas sent packing like a boy.

What would he do with them and with Isabel, who had equally attracted his wrath? How would they be punished? Mairi decided she did not care, nothing they did could hurt her after the trauma of the last week. She dressed in simple country clothes of wool skirt and bodice and tied her hair back under a white lace cap. She would not cower in her room until she was summoned.

Mairi found Duntorin and Florence having breakfast in the small parlour on the same floor as the living quarters. It had a larger window than most of the rooms, hewn out of the stone that filled the chamber with light.

'Good morning,' Mairi smiled calmly at them.

'Come and have some bread and ale,' Florence answered nervously, pulling out the chair beside her. Duntorin silently tore at a fresh piece of bread and dunked it in a watery porridge.

They ate without a word, until Duntorin threw back his chair and stood up.

'Where are the others?' he asked gruffly.

'It's early yet,' Florence said soothingly.

'They should he here. I want to tell them all together of the plans we have for them.' Her mother avoided Mairi's look.

They did not have long to wait. Douglas strolled in, his head unbandaged, the newly washed hair still wet and close combed to his scalp. The scar at his temple gave him a rakish, piratical air and Mairi quickly looked away. Isabel slid in behind him like a pale ghost, her black eyes dark-ringed with a night of crying.

Duntorin marched to the window and stood with his broad back to them, hands clasped behind him and legs apart. Douglas reached for an apple and crunched in the silence.

'You have all behaved like the Devil's own children since Douglas's return,' Duntorin swung round to glare at them. Isabel gave a shocked exhalation of breath. 'There's no need to act the pious Kirk-goer with me, daughter,' he gave Isabel a warning look, 'you will not be attending Zechariah Black's sermons for some time.'

Isabel's face turned grey at the pronouncement, her thin lips trembling but silent.

'Your mother and I have decided it is time for you and Mairi to be introduced at Court where you will learn to behave like gentlewomen and serve your Queen in whatever manner she sees fit.'

The two girls stared at him open-mouthed.

'Perhaps there you will learn the manners and discipline fit for two daughters of Duntorin.'

Mairi flushed with annoyance at the description. She was no daughter of his! Florence saw the quickfire anger and placed a cautionary hand over hers.

'As for you, Douglas, younger of Duntorin,' his father paused and Mairi held her breath. 'You will stay and learn how to run the estate with me. Perhaps some simple farming will knock the wildness of the Danish Court out of you.'

Mairi glanced over at Douglas and saw a muscle working hard in his cheek; though he restrained himself from answering back. They all took the humiliating lecture without a murmur.

Douglas caught Mairi's look and held her eyes for a moment. Mairi felt her heart jolt as she tried to read his face, but no emotion showed. Was he vexed that he was not to join them at Court? He was not the kind of man who liked to be left out of things. She found herself smirking at the thought of Douglas pent up with frustration at being the soldier turned farmer.

He scowled at her amused face. He would bide his time and somehow pay her back for this. But for her, he would not have been treated ignominiously like some rebellious youth. Mairi stood up.

'Is that all?' she asked with a smile. Duntorin looked puzzled by her calmness; of all three he had expected trouble from Mairi. 'Thank you for your kind offer, Father,' she replied sweetly, 'I have long wished to travel to the Court in Edinburgh and get away from the tediousness of life here. The sooner we go the better.'

She kissed her mother's cheek and stepped lightly from the room, Douglas and Isabel looking thunderstruck as she left. Duntorin cursed under his breath at the way she had turned her punishment into an advantage.

'Ride with me in an hour, Douglas,' he ordered as he strode from the room, 'we will be out all day.'

Mairi sat lost in thought in her antechamber, her sampler untouched on her knee. She may have put on a good act of wanting to leave, but the thought really frightened her. She knew no one in the big remote town and she heard it was a dangerous place to live even for the monarch.

There was always news filtering back of kidnappings and ambushes and brawling in the streets by bored nobles and fortune-seekers. And by all accounts it was a dirty place, with refuse piled high in front of doors, a place cursed with lepers and outbreaks of plague.

Still, life at the Court with young Queen Anne was said to be fun. Douglas had delighted in telling her how the Queen had provoked the wrath of the local ministers with her frivolous ways.

And what of Douglas? Would he be sad to see her go or mightily relieved she was off his hands? Mairi blocked out the tender thoughts that stirred in her at the image of his wavy dark hair and bearded smile. He had not been like that at the solemn breakfast party. She had been left with the impression he regarded her with unveiled dislike.

In her reverie, she did not hear the door open and close. Mairi was so startled to see Isabel standing beside her that she pricked her finger.

'How unlucky to draw blood,' Isabel said with a dry lifeless voice.

Mairi sucked hard on the oozing finger.

'As unlucky as our banishment, Isabel?' Mairi looked up challengingly.

'You may find it amusing,' her black eyes narrowed, 'but I do not. It will take more than that to keep me apart from my love.' Mairi felt sick at the thought of Zechariah Black being anyone's love.

'There is nothing you can do about it,' Mairi bent her head again and picked up the sewing, wishing Isabel would leave her alone.

'You underestimate the way we feel about each other,' Isabel's face gleamed strangely. 'You may have thought you could break us apart, you've tried so hard, but it won't work.'

Mairi felt a chill at the cold words spoken so matter-of-factly, delivered with a mirthless smile.

'I really don't care what you and that minister do,' Mairi sparked back, 'it's not me who's refusing you marriage, it's your beloved father.'

Isabel trembled as she spoke. 'I know you went to the loch yesterday. Why did you lie about walking with Douglas?'

Mairi hesitated, needle poised. 'Does it matter?' she tried to sound disinterested.

'Oh yes, I think you know it does,' Isabel's voice was full of menace. 'I think you saw things you shouldn't have seen and told tales to your mother. How else would my father have been so against our marriage?'

Mairi was amazed at the staring-eyed thin woman before her. Isabel's distorted mind could not comprehend that Duntorin's real loathing of Black was because of the way she and her mother had been endangered by his trumped-up trial and his base behaviour. To Isabel it was just part of Black's divine work. It was no good arguing with such a closed mind. Mairi stood up, convinced Isabel was about to launch a physical attack.

Her stepsister was shaking with some dangerous inner anger, her black eyes crazed.

'But you can't stop us, Zechariah will be waiting for me,' she raised her head proudly; 'I will not be coming with you to Court, not ever!' With that, Isabel swept from the room.

For the first time Mairi wondered if the affair had unhinged her stepsister. If she was planning to run away, then she was worried for her safety. Black would never risk his career for Isabel; it was another of her delusions. But was she putting herself in danger by meeting him secretly and tempting further wrath from Duntorin? Part of her felt Isabel deserved everything she got, but an inner voice persisted that they had all suffered enough hurt and Isabel should be stopped.

Mairi's mouth set grimly, she knew there was only one person to turn to for help. She caught Douglas saddling up Elsinore. He hesitated as he saw her come in and then carried on with his task.

'Douglas,' Mairi gulped, trying to sound civil, 'can I speak with you in confidence?' Douglas looked up slowly and considered her. Then he nodded and came over.

'What is it?' His voice and face were neutral as if she were some tiresome servant. The distant look squeezed her heart.

'It's Isabel,' Mairi began with difficulty. She saw his mouth tighten with annoyance. He was obviously in no mood for more of their jealous squabbling. Mairi ploughed on. 'I'm afraid she is going to do something reckless, something that will bring further trouble.'

Douglas stepped closer and looked down into the worried green eyes.

'What?' he demanded, his hands coming automatically to touch her shoulders and then stopping in mid air.

'She says she is going to meet Black. I fear Isabel thinks he will run away with her, though I don't believe he would ever make such a sacrifice, but they may have arranged to meet,' Mairi added stiffly. Douglas's look bore into hers as if he would find the truth in her eyes. She could not look away. 'I have nothing to gain by making up such a story,' she challenged him impatiently.

Douglas considered the determined upturned face. 'No,' his features were impassive. 'Where has she gone?'

'I have a good idea,' Mairi lifted her chin mockingly, 'though I shan't speak the name for fear of being struck.' Douglas flashed a quick look.

'The bothy; I'll go after her,' he answered tightly, turning swiftly.

Mairi appeared to have been dismissed. Let the Roskills sort out their own problems, she thought, returning to the hazy sunshine of the courtyard; they were no concern of hers now. Still, Mairi was relieved to see Douglas canter out on Elsinore to find Isabel before Black did. She did not trust the minister, even with her malicious stepsister. She had shown herself easily led.

Douglas found Isabel waiting by the broken bothy, her dark figure almost part of the scorched ruin. She did not try to run from him, but stood erect, her face white and tear-stained.

'He has not come,' she spoke normally as if talking of the seasons. 'He has not come for me.'

'I've come to take you home Isabel,' Douglas said gently as if to a lost child. Her calmness and distant gleam in the dark eyes unnerved him. Inwardly he cursed Black for the way he had callously manipulated her feelings for him, making a play for the Duntorin dowry and failing. He would have no further use for her and now she was the casualty of his despicable lust. Then with a stab of guilt, Douglas realised Mairi had been too. He had not believed his young stepsister and in doing so had battered her feelings as surely as Black had bruised her body. He was no better than the minister he despised and now, because of them both, Mairi was being sent beyond his reach.

Mairi, watching from her bedroom window, saw them return. She wondered gloomily if there had been a scene, any opposition, and had she been cast as the evil stepsister again? She decided on the spur of the moment to visit Agnes. The thought of leaving soon made her realise there were people she would miss. If she was as frail as her mother had intimated, Agnes might not see out the winter.

Mairi ran down to the kitchen quarters and the small room beyond the store rooms where her old nurse sheltered. With a nod from Sarah to say it was all right, she let herself in quietly. Agnes was propped up in a box-bed next to the slit window. The room reeked of a pungent smell Mairi associated with old age; like that of grandfather Lismore, a shadow lingering on as a peculiar scent in her memory.

'Agnes,' Mairi peered at the shrivelled head on the stacked cushions, 'it's Mairi.' The old woman's rheumy blue eyes focused with difficulty on her visitor.

'Mairi?' she whispered vacantly, her mouth sucking in as she spoke.

'Remember your Highland friend?' the girl came forward and took the crinkled hand that lay uselessly on top of the wool blankets. Mairi cringed with horror at the mangled thumb but held on. The hand fluttered in her fingers, but no recognition registered on the grey tired face. Tears stung the back of Mairi's eyelids to think a life had been destroyed in just a few days. Agnes did not remember her.

'I will be leaving soon,' Mairi spoke gently, hoping something would jog the old woman's memory. 'Isabel and I are going to be maids-in-waiting at the Court of King James and Queen Anne.'

Agnes seemed to struggle through a fog in her mind, her eyes widening in recognition. The cold hand responded under the warm young hold and tried to clutch the fingers.

'You must be careful Mairi,' Agnes croaked, 'I can see danger for you there.'

Mairi laughed nervously. 'Danger at the Scottish Court is nothing new.' But Agnes's eyes did not twinkle with accustomed merriment and no cackle of laughter left her throat.

'Trust no one,' Agnes tried to lean forward, her voice growing querulous, 'promise me you will trust no one, Mairi.' To stop her agitation Mairi agreed. She thought it better to change the subject.

'And what about that lover you spoke of for me, Agnes, am I still to meet him? Or am I to be given nothing but trouble?' Mairi smiled and squeezed the bony hand.

Agnes's face softened into a toothless grin, life returning to the once pretty blue eyes. 'Ah, your man. Yes, Mairi, I still see him.'

Mairi flushed under the sudden sharp appraisal of Agnes's gaze. 'You will meet him at Court and there will be laughter besides the danger.'

Mairi did not know why, but she felt a stab of disappointment at the prediction. It seemed impossible, but maybe her feelings for Douglas were just a passing phase, to be eclipsed by some greater passion among the revelries at the Palace of Holyroodhouse. The royal carousing of the young King and Queen were legendary in the countryside. For the first time she experienced excitement at the prospect of living in a new place and meeting with famous nobility. She would soon get over her bout of lovesickness for Douglas and it was plain he would not waste a day moping over her departure.

'Then I shall have to practise the more sedate dancing steps you taught me as a child, Agnes,' Mairi felt devilment bubbling up inside. Agnes laughed like a cackling hen.

'Don't you go showing them any of your Highland ways, Mairi,' she twinkled, 'the King thinks you are all barbarians anyway.'

'Then the King is in for a pleasant surprise, Agnes,' Mairi lifted her head in mock pride and laughed.

Mairi stayed with Agnes until she thought the elderly nurse had drifted off to sleep again. She sung the Gaelic lullaby her old friend had been fond of hearing. As she left, Mairi bent and pressed a kiss on the becapped head and tip-toed out.

If she had paused at the door she might have seen the slow solitary tear trickling its way down Agnes's rutted face like a dried up burn in summer and heard the whispered words, 'Goodbye Mairi, my dearest one.'

On a May morning, the stepsisters awaited a vessel to convey them and their servant Margaret across the Firth of Forth and on to the unknown Royal Burgh of Edinburgh. Mairi glanced at Isabel, mute and expressionless, wrapped in a fur-lined cape as if it were winter. She had hardly spoken a word since they left Duntorin and was depressing company for her redheaded companion, nervous with anticipation.

They had ridden long hours on their horses over the rutted tracks, but a carriage had been promised them on the far side of the Forth. Mairi lifted her face to the sea breeze that reminded her poignantly of her first home and remembered with a pang, the desolate cry of the seagulls. The salty air would blow away the dreary thoughts of the journey and the sad partings and prepare her for the new life ahead.

For to her surprise, leaving Duntorin had been harder than Mairi had ever imagined. She had stemmed back the tears as her mother held her tightly, wondering when they would next be allowed to meet. But she was growing up and could not hang on to Florence's skirts for ever. Poor Isabel had lost her mother far sooner and more tragically in childbirth. On that last morning Mairi had taken her leave of the township, walking its rigged fields and saying farewell to the tranquil lochside.

Mary Bain, the blacksmith's daughter, had come with a posy of wild flowers to wish her good luck. Mairi had blushed at the show of friendship and inwardly chided herself for unkind thoughts towards the blue-eyed girl.

She had avoided Douglas until the last moment and her heart twisted as she recalled his formal farewell.

'I hope you will be happy at Court,' he had said, his dark eyes holding hers as if he meant something by the look. Was it accusing or dismissive? Then he had added more gently, 'I'm sorry if I have caused you any unhappiness, Mairi.'

She had found her throat aching with a lump that prevented her from speaking and she blinked hard to stem the unwanted tears. If he had not mentioned her name she would have been all right. But it reminded her of other happier moments when Douglas had seemed to care for her.

He must have seen her chin trembling because he leaned down and brushed her cheek with a kiss, murmuring, 'Be brave, my wildcat.' Mairi had quickly turned from him for fear of showing her feelings. The rest was a blur and soon they were caught up in the bustle of the convoy. With a sad pleasure, Mairi learned Sam was to accompany them as far as the Forth.

She remembered looking back at the gateway and seeing Douglas standing with a comforting arm about her mother and Duntorin's arms raised in a dramatic gesture of farewell that he could not put into words. At that moment Mairi had realised she would miss them all dearly. But, as the procession snaked its way south into new territory, it was the memory of Douglas's black unblinking gaze that haunted her and left a dull ache deep inside.

'The boat is ready, madam,' it was Sam's words that broke her reverie. Mairi smiled at his formal address; she was soon to be a lady of the Court. 'I must take my leave of you now.'

Her heart lurched. He was her last palpable contact with Douglas and she had found comfort in his presence on the hard journey.

'Thank you, Sam,' Mairi laid a hand shyly on his sleeve; 'you have been a good friend.' He smiled bashfully and kissed her hand.

'Perhaps it will not be too long before my master finds a pressing reason to bring him to Edinburgh.'

Mairi coloured, a flame of hope lighting quickly inside. But then Sam may not know of her quarrel with Douglas or have noticed the coolness between them since the night of the banquet. It was a slim hope indeed.

Sam said goodbye to Isabel and Mairi noticed the spark of interest light the blank eyes like a ripple in a stagnant pool as Isabel responded. She remembered the night of the Beltane dance when Isabel had gone quite happily with Sam. Perhaps there was a chance her stepsister might get over her infatuation with Zechariah Black in time.

The crossing was calm and they were met by servants of Bailie Greeves who shared a town house with Duntorin. The carriage ride was far worse than horseback riding and they jolted along painfully on the rough road into Edinburgh.

Yet the view that greeted them made them forget all discomfort. Mairi gasped to see the imposing Castle looming ahead on its black crag and the high walls of the town reflected in the glassy Nor' Loch. The procession rumbled round to the south and entered at the guarded Netherbow Port into the Canongate. Even Isabel looked awestruck at the towering stone houses packed cheek by jowl on the steep High Street and the burst of life about them.

Hawkers and sellers crowded about the Mercat Cross and merchants in dignified robes and scarlet stockings walked the cobbled causeway seemingly unaware of the waste splashed at them by the heaving carriage. Mairi covered her nose and mouth with a scented handkerchief to counter the blast of human stench in the street. The High Street was an open sewer in which fat pigs snuffled happily. But this did not prevent her fascination for this bustling giant town with its stone and timber mansions out of which inhabitants called to their neighbours in a robust Lowland accent.

Unselfconsciously, she gripped Isabel's cold hand in excitement. 'It's a different world,' she said, her voice muffled behind her mask. Her dark-eyed companion was silent but did not withdraw her hand immediately. Bailie Greeves greeted the travellers openly as they climbed out of the carriage into his enclosed court off the Mairi thoroughfare.

'Welcome, dear ladies!' he clasped his hands in front of his stout figure. 'Your rooms have been prepared.' His eyes twinkled out of creased pockets of skin in the round fleshy face.

Judging by his satin gown, girdled at the waist and the gold chain about his neck, he was a canny businessman, Mairi mused. She smiled back warmly at his kind fussing.

'Thank you for your generous welcome,' she curtsied before him. Isabel gave a small bob and nodded in agreement. At least she seemed to be aware of what was going on about her, Mairi noted with relief, she had behaved like someone drugged for the past few days.

'I'd be pleased if you would dine with me when you are rested and settled into your quarters,' the pink-faced merchant beamed shyly. 'Tomorrow you will be summoned to Holyroodhouse and afterwards will be too busy for a simple man such as me.'

'Thank you,' Isabel managed a wintry smile.

'It would be a great pleasure,' Mairi grinned at him reassuringly, touched by his concern and modesty. They were guided up the outer Mairi stair to their first floor apartments, above which Bailie Greeves lived and below which he kept his store house of bales of cloth and household goods. Mairi was eager to see Duntorin's town rooms where he came and stayed on business and used to come many years ago with his first wife, in the days of the gay Queen Mary, mother of the present King James. She knew her mother regretted that Duntorin never brought her to Edinburgh and hardly ever used the mansion.

The rooms were tastefully furnished with warm wood panelling and painted ceilings in bright colours. In spite of it being summer, a cheerful fire was lit in the Mairi chamber and a jug of sweet ale stood waiting to refresh them. Both their bedrooms were prepared with linen sheets and bowls of pot-pourri to mask the smell from the close below.

'The Bailie has been very thoughtful in his preparation for us,' Mairi said aloud. Isabel nodded.

'He has always been a good friend to Father.' She hesitated, picking up a silver casket from the table. 'Father says he was fond of Mother too. But she chose the older more persistent suitor.'

Mairi shot her a quick look, surprised by the softness in her voice.

'He never married?' she asked tentatively. Isabel shook her head and put back the silver box.

'Let us unpack,' she added briskly and went into her room.

Much later, Mairi lay back in the comfort of the big soft bed, the crisp linen pillowcase cool on her cheek. She smiled remembering the friendly intimate dinner party the merchant had laid on for them and his cheerful courteous banter. It seemed strange that she could feel so at home in unfamiliar surroundings, so soon after her uprooting from Duntorin and her mother. Isabel too had opened up like a late flower to the attention of their host, who knew nothing of the past unhappy events on his friend's estates north of Stirling. But perhaps her interest had been sparked by the late appearance of Robert Boswell, the younger son of the Earl of Brae.

65

He had swept in on the dinner party with a friend Ruthven, fresh from some drinking haunt on the High Street. Boswell was indeed striking, Mairi admitted uneasily, with piercing blue eyes and a rakish lock of hair that grew over his shoulder framing a ruby drop earring.

He was dressed in turquoise blue doublet and hose and paced about the Bailie's room like a predatory cat. The young courtier exuded charm with every sentence he spoke and smiled easily, though amusement never embraced the sapphire blue eyes. His companion Ruthven was overshadowed and shifted restlessly in his seat as Boswell held court in the dining-room.

'You're a sly old merchantman, Greeves, to be keeping two such beautiful women under lock and key,' Robert Boswell flashed a brilliant smile, his keen eyes sweeping between Isabel and Mairi like beacons.

The Bailie flushed with embarrassment and stuttered, 'Tut, young Boswell, they are guests only for the night, I regret.' Boswell swung a shapely leg over his chair arm.

'I trust these priceless treasures are to dazzle us with their brightness for longer than a night?' He shot Mairi a bold look that made her drop her gaze to her lap.

'We go tomorrow to the Palace to wait on the Queen,' Isabel answered with quiet authority and met his stare with her own answering dark one. Boswell smiled.

'Then I will not be desolate tonight fair lady, for I shall hope to glimpse you at Court.' Mairi noticed a faint pink flush tinge Isabel's cheeks and jaw. She could understand her stepsister's attraction to this handsome, almost beautiful, clean-shaven man, more than she would ever comprehend her fixation for the repulsive Black.

'These gentlewomen have had a long journey,' Bailie Greeves intercepted quickly. He was disconcerted by his uninvited guests and wished to take control of the situation again. 'They must be allowed to retire and rest.'

Boswell threw him a look and then the smile leapt to his lips once more. 'Of course, I am being totally selfish in wanting to share their company with you. Sir, you shall have them all to yourself - just for tonight.' He appeared delighted at the frown of impatience on the burgher's brow and jumped up. 'Your brother is well I hope?' the Earl of Brae's son asked Isabel.

Mairi felt her heart miss a beat at the reference to Douglas even though his name had not been spoken. It was ridiculous she should still feel this way. She must try to put him from her mind.

'He is well,' Isabel gave a becoming smile, 'and recently returned from Denmark. I did not know you knew him, sir.'

'But of course,' Boswell laughed, 'we used to fight constantly under the eagle eye of tutor Simpson at St Andrew's.' Noticing Isabel's frown of dismay he added disarmingly. 'We were the best of friends and Douglas let me beat him occasionally.'

They smiled at each other as Mairi bowed her head to hide the blushes that came so easily to her face. She glanced up to see Robert Boswell eyeing her with a vivid blue stare and her pulse fluttered in confusion. Surely she could not be so susceptible to two men?

This feeling had not left her after the two young noblemen had departed with much doffing of hats and gallant farewells. As they said goodnight to Bailie Greeves and wended their way down the stone steps to Duntorin's rooms, Mairi noticed Isabel smiling to herself.

'You are happy to be here now, sister?' Mairi could not help asking after the frosty silence of the journey. Isabel whipped round suspiciously but saw only a look of enquiry on the younger woman's face.

'We must make the most of what has befallen us,' Isabel said tartly, 'and that is what I intend to do.'

Mairi felt little respect for the step-relation who must now be her companion at Court, but she was glad Isabel had shaken off her queer detachment and that the unstable glint in her eyes had vanished.

'Quite so,' Mairi smiled, wondering wryly if Robert Boswell had a part in Isabel's plans.

As she lay now, drifting off to sleep, Mairi could not help musing if Douglas had ever used this room on his way to or from Denmark. He may have lain in the very same bed so recently. . . .

Mairi buried her burning cheeks in the pillow. She must forget Douglas for her own peace of mind. It was a foolish infatuation that he did not share. He was probably at this moment dallying with Mary Bain. Even if they had both wanted it, marriage between them would be forbidden by both parents on religious and social grounds. They had been quick to show disapproval and stamp out the flame of attachment that had first leapt between her and Douglas at the Beltane fires. Douglas knew as well as she did that Duntorin would have a greater match in mind for his only son and heir. She could be no more than a passing diversion for him and she ground her teeth to think of her naive stupidity. She lay and fought the picture of Douglas's dark bearded face that came when she tried to sleep. To banish the black commanding eyes, she conjured up the hypnotic blue of Robert Boswell's.

The next morning brought a flurry of expectation as Margaret and Bailie Greeves's maids helped the noble daughters of Duntorin prepare for their first audience with Queen Anne.

Dresses had been made of finest silk with pleated bodices and full skirts in the courtly fashion. Isabel looked a grown woman in the scarlet red that enhanced her dark looks, while Mairi's emerald eyes were matched in the vivid green of her shimmering gown. Margaret fussed and cooed as she dressed their hair and the girls donned hats of velvet.

'What precious jewels of Duntorin!' Bailie Greeves cried ebulliently at the sight of them descending to the courtyard. 'The Queen is lucky indeed.' Mairi giggled with excitement and Isabel smiled at the pleased face of the burgher. To save their pretty stockings and shoes he insisted they be transported to Holyroodhouse in his carriage.

As they swung down the High Street, through the Canongate, the Palace stood ahead imposingly, its massive turreted north wing shadowing the entrance of strangely carved figures. Behind it the sweep of a stranded mountain lay like a lion asleep. In the sunshine of a clear summer's day, the fawn-coloured stone glistened welcomingly like some fairy residence and rays of light sparkled on the large casement windows.

'It's beautiful,' Mairi gaped, infecting Isabel with the thrill of the new experience.

'Yes it is,' Isabel squeezed her hand in return and then let it drop self-consciously.

Servants in blue livery ran about the forecourt as they emerged from the carriage. The two country girls were quite overwhelmed by the grand scale of the royal house, with a chain of apartments linked to each other, overlooking an internal courtyard. As they waited to be escorted into the Queen's morning withdrawing-room, Mairi gazed in awe at the blue and gold painted plaster ceilings, the elaborate panelling depicting musicians and the richly coloured tapestries lining the walls. She had thought Duntorin rich in embellishments but this took her breath away.

'You must be Duntorin's daughters?' a silvery voice brought Mairi's gaze down to the level again. She pursed her mouth at the pretty fair haired woman before her, dressed in pale blue satin, her hair combed back fashionably to reveal high cheek bones.

'Yes we are,' Isabel cut in quickly to avoid a scene at this delicate stage. 'I am Isabel Roskill and this is my younger sister, Mairi.'

Mairi realised with a stab it was the first time in years Isabel had not used the formal 'step' term to address her. She recovered herself and smiled at the stranger.

'I am Lucy Seton of Hoddington,' she smiled back disarmingly, unaware of Mairi's initial frostiness. 'I've been here six months. Queen Anne is such fun to be with, you'll like it here, I'm sure. Did you have a good journey?' Her dark blue eyes widened with interest. 'You travelled further than me I believe?'

'It's nice to be out of the saddle,' Mairi could not help liking the chattering friendly Lucy. 'And we had a restful night at Bailie Greeves's house, thank you.'

'Ah yes, I've heard of him,' Lucy's face showed the struggle to recollect. 'Nice man, so I'm told, though I can't remember who told me, or when,' Lucy Seton laughed. 'I've got a head like a cook's sieve!'

They heard a bell ring from the courtyard below and Lucy jumped round. 'Oh, it's time we were going; we mustn't keep the Queen waiting. I'm to show you to her audience chamber.'

Mairi could not stop her heart pounding at the thought of meeting the Queen of Scotland. She had grown up in the Highlands thinking of the monarch as a distant make-believe figure who governed a far distant country dislocated from her own.

Now she was about to meet a royal personage, one she would have to work for closely. The doors were thrown open and Lucy glided in before them. Mairi and Isabel followed as in a dream. The redheaded Lismore curtsied low as they had practised in their stiff dresses and looked up through fair doe-like lashes. Her eyes met the smiling amused look of the Danish-born Queen. Mairi was surprised how young she looked, about Douglas's age, her hair the colour of corn, her cheeks made more pallid by powder. She wore a low-cut dress that spread out like a great ship in sail about her hips over the tip-tilted farthingale frame. Queen Anne was bedecked in strings of pearls about her neck and wrists.

'Welcome,' she spoke in a strange guttural accent, 'I am pleased to see such young girls at my bidding. They will be company for you Lucy, no?'

'Yes ma'am,' Lucy blushed with enthusiasm and grinned.

'Good,' Queen Anne ran her fan of feathers across her hand. 'Now we can sit and get knowing each other, I think,' she smiled and her attractive face lit with something of mischief. 'Perhaps you tell me why your father sent you here so suddenly?'

The Queen eyed them both, twisting a thin pigtail that coiled down from her crimped headdress of hair on to her shoulder.

Mairi and Isabel stood motionless like shy maids. Their mistress laughed. 'No I think not. You must be Isabel I'm sure?' the round amused eyes settled on the taller girl.

Isabel nodded. 'Yes ma'am.'

'Yes, you are looking like your brother, Douglas,' she tapped her fan against her chin. Both girls jolted up in surprise and the young royal laughed. 'You forget I met your brother on a visit to Denmark to see my brother Christian. Oh what fun we are having,' a healthy laugh bubbled out of her throat, 'my brother is liking your brother very much I think. And I too, he is brave, yes, and handsome.'

Mairi pulled her hands down her skirts to rid her palms of their clamminess. She could feel the pulse beating rapidly in her neck. It seemed she could not get away from the man who haunted her even at the Court. Must she be constantly reminded of her foolishness? She looked at the floor hoping the Queen would soon dismiss them, her throat as dry as dead leaves.

'And Mairi,' Queen Anne turned her attention to the red-haired girl, 'you are from the Highlands, yes?'

69

Mairi dragged her eyes up to the woman before her and nodded, gulping, 'Yes ma'am.' Would the Queen hold the same views as the King that the Highlands bred nothing but wolves and wild boars?

'We are having the same - what you say? - ancestors, yes? The Vikings?' Queen Anne smiled broadly and Mairi answered with a pleased flush.

'I'm honoured to think that we do, ma'am,' Mairi managed in a hoarse voice. After that the ice of formality was broken between them and the women chattered happily together, Mairi warming to the Queen's direct vivacious manner. As she dismissed her new ladies in waiting the Queen bade Lucy show them to their quarters.

'Now you be showing Isabel and Mairi what is doing, Lucy. Later we will be having fun, I think.' The girls curtsied and left.

They gabbled with relief and excitement, moving off noisily through the State Apartments. Turning eventually into the Long Gallery hung with royal portraits, they were stopped short by the appearance of a group of courtiers at the far end. The sun streamed into the long hall, setting off the blue-green and gold painted woodwork so that the room was spun with a web of colour.

Lucy gasped and sank in a deep obeisance, pulling Mairi's hand as she did so. As she followed, Mairi was aware of a brightly dressed figure leaning on the arm of someone teasingly familiar. She heard Isabel catch her breath and recognised the slim courtier as Robert Boswell.

'Your Majesty,' Lucy breathed in her high-pitched tone and Mairi's heart raced to think she was in the presence of King James VI of Scotland. Peering up as discreetly as possible she saw the almost comical bow-legged figure of the monarch, dressed in quilted doublet and padded hose that made him appear stout. It seemed incongruous that this ungainly man should have won the heart of the attractive blonde Danish princess they had just left.

'Rise, my ladies,' King James spoke in a deep assured voice and Mairi looked again at the man who ruled Scotland and it was rumoured would succeed to the English throne on the death of their old Queen Elizabeth. The large eyes were alert and his smile brought his face to life above the square-chinned beard.

The hand that rested on Boswell's arm was slim and bejewelled; the slender fingers were those of a scholar rather than a soldier and belied the dumpiness his clothes gave to his body. No doubt in this place of intrigue he preferred the protection of padding from the treacherous blade, his life had been threatened on more than one occasion.

'And are these my dear Queen's new maids?' King James asked pleasantly. Isabel and Mairi sank again to their knees and introduced themselves. As Mairi looked up she was aware of Boswell's sharp-eyed gaze boring into her. A slow thudding started in her chest and she found it hard to breathe. He was enjoying her discomfort she was sure and it did not reassure her to realise that this off-hand reveller of the previous night had the arm and doubtless, the ear of the King. She would have to watch her responses.

'Your Majesty,' Boswell seemed quite at ease in the King's presence, 'these fair ladies have left the quiet of Duntorin to grace your Court with their beauty. Thankfully they leave behind my old rival Douglas Roskill, who cannot prevent us from enjoying their delightful company.'

'Well spoken, Rabbie,' King James patted the young man's arm. 'I hope you will enjoy life here,' he added with a smile for the bashful women.

Mairi could not help looking into the hard piercing blue eyes of Boswell to gauge his words. They held hers challengingly, his lovelock curving around his handsome chin. Had he guessed from her blushing last night that she felt more than sisterly affection for Douglas and was now goading her? Or was it just the flowery empty words of the courtier? There was certainly nothing courtly about the brazen look he gave her and Mairi forced her eyes away from their hold. They were a cruel blue in spite of the smiles and flattering silken words.

Glancing across at Isabel she saw her mouth tighten in reproach. She had misread the looks passing between her and Boswell; Mairi wanted nothing to do with this man who attracted and repelled her at the same time. The King continued his progress, laughing and conversing with Boswell and the other accompanying young nobles. Mairi let out a soft sigh of relief.

'This is quite a morning for you both,' Lucy spoke in a hushed tone. Isabel threw Mairi a silent vicious look, reminding her of the glare with which she had stabbed her when Zechariah Black had come to Duntorin Castle. She blanched at the suspicious eyes. Lucy chattered on missing the wordless threat. 'Did you see the King's breeches?' she spluttered, a hand stifling a disloyal giggle. 'He could take off in the wind!'

Mairi was riveted by the sudden image and could not help grinning. 'And what about his latest "favourite"?' Lucy persisted, her eyes lighting to the smell of scandal. 'He seems quite taken with Master Boswell. And I can see why!'

'Lucy,' Mairi burst into laughter, 'you are quite incorrigible! Anyway, we met Robert Boswell last night at Bailie Greeves's,' Mairi added slyly, hoping to stem Isabel's petulance, he seemed very taken with my sister, said he hoped to meet her again.' She watched the warmth flooding into the tall dark woman's face.

'How delicious,' Lucy clapped her hands,' and he is unattached,' she smiled enjoying the gossip. 'Though I believe he and his drinking companion, the Master of Ruthven, are quite the ladies' men.'

'You shouldn't talk of such things,' Isabel snapped reprovingly. Lucy threw her a look of surprise, but changed the subject.

Later, as they settled into their new rooms Isabel was on the attack again.

'I think your manner is too bold for Court life, Mairi,' she admonished like a nurse, 'you must be careful here, this is not the wilds of the Highlands now.' Mairi felt a quick stab of irritation at the barbed comment about her background.

'From what Lucy says, this place is far wilder than any Highland dwelling,' Mairi shot back. 'Did you know the King once had to hide in an upstairs room from a mad Border nobleman after his blood?'

'Lucy is full of tales and gossip; you should not listen so much to her wagging tongue.'

Mairi looked sadly at her stepsister. 'I like her and I want to be friends. She could be a good friend to you too, Isabel.'

'She is too frivolous and shallow for my liking,' Isabel answered in her most infuriatingly sanctimonious tone.

Mairi looked astounded at the prim face. She condemned Lucy, yet it was more than likely that she would throw herself unthinkingly into another dangerous affair. But why argue, Mairi thought glumly? Isabel was a grown woman with little care for anyone but herself. The melting of Isabel's hardness that Mairi had sensed since arriving in Edinburgh was unlikely to develop into the friendship for which she had hoped. Still there must be a truce and the best way for that, Mairi realised was to keep out of Boswell's way, not giving him the chance to flirt with them both and exploit their rivalry.

The next days and weeks merged into a blur of activity and new duties and Mairi had little time to dwell on what was happening back at Duntorin or what the future might bring. Life at Court was hectic; the Palace halls and courtyards clattered to the sound of well-heeled noble shoes as well as rushing servants and guards. It would take months to put names to the faces who came and went; lairds and their ladies from the Lowland farmlands and the Border strongholds, merchants and councillors, ministers and foreign envoys, learned scholars and visiting entertainers.

Lucy was becoming a firm friend and delighted Mairi with her wicked gossip and her latest infatuations borne across the dance floors and dinner tables. Isabel kept her distance and as Mairi had expected, encouraged what contact she could with the King's favourite, Boswell. For herself, Mairi had kept deliberately out of his way.

'That English ambassador tonight was such a bore,' Lucy stifled a yawn with her fan, as they strolled in the King's park, enjoying the cool night air. 'I don't know why they didn't send the last one; he had the best pair of legs I've ever seen.'

Mairi chuckled, 'You, of course, are an expert on legs.'

'Naturally,' Lucy's light voice carried upwards to the bank of brilliant stars above them, 'I have studied them religiously and am quite a scholar on the subject.'

Their laughter tinkled like burn water. Mairi had never had such amusement with another friend as with this Border baron's daughter, just a year older than herself. Tonight Mairi had celebrated her sixteenth birthday and had led the courtly dancing to the accompaniment of the lutes. Her head was still full of the music and the attention and now she breathed deep, satisfying gulps of air. It was unusually mild with no raw east wind tearing up from the Port of Leith and she was contented walking in the grounds with her new friend. Queen Anne had dismissed them for the evening as a birthday gift.

'And which are your favourite pair of legs?' Lucy squeezed Mairi's arm conspiratorially.

Mairi felt a quick flush hot her cheeks at the impertinent question. But Lucy had long since prised out of her that she had feelings for Douglas Roskill. 'Are they the strong limbs of a Scottish mercenary perhaps?'

'Lucy!' Mairi let slip an embarrassed laugh, but she was enjoying the evening too much to care.

'I knew it,' Lucy said triumphantly, 'you have eyes only for your man of action. It's too bad when there are so many nice pairs of legs at the King's Court.'

'Hush!' Mairi stopped suddenly, 'there's someone ahead by the pavilion.'

'Oh,' Lucy whispered, 'have we come across some lovers?' Mairi flinched, her mind dragged back to the nightmare scene in the bothy. She would turn now and flee rather than pry on anyone again. They had strayed too far.

'Let's go back -'

'Look at the smoke,' Lucy urged her forward with her arm, 'do you think the place is on fire?' Mairi caught the strange whiff of pungent smoke and saw a cloud billowing out of the usually deserted pavilion that the tragic Mary, Queen of Scots had delighted in using. Since there were no flames as yet, they could perhaps be of assistance. She began to run forward with Lucy following at her heels. Arriving breathless at the doorway, Mairi peered inside, mystified that the smoke had dispersed.

'Ah, what sweet company do we have here?' the leisured voice gave her a start and Mairi gasped at the eerie figure sitting close in front. There was a short laugh and then a red glow burned at the end of a long pipe and the man rose out of his chair.

'Boswell!' Lucy cried incredulously at the figure emerging into the moonlight. 'What are you doing here?'

CHAPTER SIX

Mairi, breathless from running, could not quieten the irregular beating in her chest as Boswell's eyes glinted straight at her and his lips curled invitingly, as he answered Lucy's question.

'We await more sporting company to brighten a dull evening, dear ladies. Isn't that so Ruthven?' He turned briefly as a second pipe-smoker rose out of the gloom.

'Quite so,' the young nobleman withdrew his pipe and smiled handsomely.

'You're not,' Lucy dismissed the explanation. 'You've sneaked out here to have a smoke of your evil-smelling tobacco, because the King would have apoplexy if you set fire to your pipes in his presence, favourite or not!' The two men laughed out loud and Boswell swung down to stand right before them.

'You are too perceptive, Miss Seton,' his silken tones wrapped around them like the smoke, 'but now that two such delightful companions have chosen to join us, our evening is complete.'

'We did not choose to join you,' Mairi's voice betrayed a note of husky nervousness, 'we thought the pavilion on fire and came to put it out.'

Boswell turned his eyes on her and his voice was mocking. 'With your 'kerchiefs, I suppose?' Mairi felt her face scorching under his attention.

'Of course not, we would have called for assistance,' she rallied back. 'And now that we have discovered nothing more than a smoking house, we shall leave you to kipper in it.' She swung round but Boswell caught her hand and she tensed in resistance.

'Come, come, I was jesting,' he drawled. 'Please put up with our dubious company awhile longer.'

'I suppose we must,' Lucy smiled and took Ruthven's proffered hand, cutting off Mairi's objection. Her unease did not decrease as Boswell sat her on a bench next to him, floodlit by a full moon.

Mairi dared not look at him, but sat with hands clenched in her lap, wondering how the peaceful joy of the evening had been shattered by the appearance of the two young lords. Lucy was already in conversation with the Master of Ruthven. What would the Queen think if she knew her two charges were consorting alone with these young men? Worse, what would Isabel say if she heard she had met Boswell by moonlight?

'You are shivering Mairi,' he purred like a leopard and closed his hand over hers. 'We cannot have the Birthday Queen cold. I would that I could warm you.' Mairi jolted under his touch and the forwardness of his words.

'I am quite well, sir,' she drew her hand away ignoring his familiar use of her first name.

'Oh yes you are very well,' he murmured and swept her with his appraising look.

'Did you enjoy dancing with my sister Isabel tonight?' Mairi met his gaze straight on, determined not to be defeated by it. 'She talks of you often. I know her father and yours are good friends, so it is very fitting that you like each other.' For a split second he seemed taken aback and then the familiar taunting smile came again and he regained composure.

'She is a pleasant young woman, indeed,' Boswell leaned closer still so that the others, even if they had been listening, would not hear. 'But there is no need to be jealous, her young stepsister is far more entrancing and I would rather be friends with her.'

'You think too much of yourself sir.' Mairi was piqued, 'I feel no jealousy.' But her head swam at the dangerously bright eyes scanning her face. Her immobility belied her protest, as if she were detached somewhere afloat above them, watching herself drowning. Mairi could see the scene being played out, but she was no longer the redheaded woman below and had no control over her movements. The slim hand glided back to squeeze hers and this time she did not withdraw.

Boswell felt himself gaining ground with this alluring yet allusive woman. He had wasted much time trying to manoeuvre himself into such a position.

At last he had guessed rightly that she would take her favourite stroll here. Now from the pulse he could see beating rapidly in her chest under the becoming lace ruff, he could almost taste the sweet draught of conquest.

'You have been avoiding me, Mairi, I think,' he persisted in a low measured tone. 'Do I frighten you?'

'No sir, you do not,' Mairi gulped, amazed how calm her voice sounded.

'Good,' he smiled drawing her hand up to his mouth, 'for there is nothing to fear.' He kissed her warm fingers with soft lips. It felt pleasantly like butterflies caressing her hand. Mairi could not stem the unsteadiness of her breathing at his seductiveness. 'You are the most gorgeous creature I have had the pleasure to behold,' Boswell continued, the stark blue eyes flickering over her silk-encased bosom and her slim face with the full lips. 'You have the eyes of a tigress and no doubt the passion of one.'

'You go too far,' Mairi heaved her hand out of his grip as if it were a dead weight, fighting the hypnotic eyes. The detached Mairi warned that these were the words he spoke to all women. Lucy had said he was a philanderer. But the other part of her whispered that he was handsome and attracted to her. Why should Isabel have him? Douglas was far from her world, unobtainable and she should take what love and attention Boswell offered. It would fulfil Agnes's prediction of a lover at Court; it must be Robert Boswell after all.

Mairi felt a strange excitement stirring within her that was frightening.

'I go only as far as you want me to go,' Boswell sang like a night bird. 'I think we feel the same about each other and that is why you have avoided me. But I shall not allow you to run from me for long, we are meant for each other, it is our fate.'

Mairi sprang from the seat, appalled that his thoughts were so close to her own. She knew the type of man Boswell was and she must not succumb to his insistent caressing words. If she felt for anyone it was Douglas and she would not throw everything away on a brief flare of passion for the younger son of Brae, however inviting.

'Lucy, I think we should go now,' she said as evenly as possible. Her friend looked up and saw the agitation on Mairi's face. With a smile at Ruthven she stood up and went to her side.

'Of course, it is quite late and we will be missed,' Lucy slipped her arm through the other girl's for support. With concern she noticed a scowl of annoyance mar Boswell's good looking countenance. She hoped Mairi had not incurred his anger, she had heard he could be a deadly enemy when crossed. Lucy chided herself for not taking more care of what he had said to Mairi. She was still a young and inexperienced country girl.

'Then we will accompany you back to the Palace,' Boswell leapt up like a cat, 'you should not be walking abroad alone.'

'We arc in the safety of the King's park,' Mairi retorted, her confidence returning with the lessening of his proximity.

'Still, I would guide you home,' he insisted softly but with metal in his tone. Against her better judgment Mairi allowed him to take her arm and the four revellers walked back to the lighted Palace, the sound of minstrels still playing from within. Boswell's conversation was light and held none of the lustful menace of before. Mairi wondered if it was the effect of the wine and the moonlit pavilion that had made her mistake the young noble's meaning. He was the height of civility now in front of the others. At the Mairi entrance the men stopped. Boswell kissed her hand lightly but held on to it.

'We go now to meet friends in the town - a long standing arrangement I regret.' His grip on her fingers was surprisingly firm, the sapphire eyes razor sharp. 'But I wait with impatience for our next meeting, sweet lady and for better acquaintance.'

Mairi hated herself for the excitement that flared of a sudden, inside. Lucy threw a quick sidelong look at their leave-taking and noticed the heightened flush on her friend's face.

'Come Mairi, let us go in,' the fair-haired young woman stepped between them and broke the spell. Again the dangerous flicker passed over Boswell's face as he reluctantly let go Mairi's hand.

The Queen's maids bid a hasty goodnight and hurried back into the warmth and security of Holyroodhouse, leaving their escorts to head out of the portal into the Canongate. The dim lights and calls of the High Street beckoned them.

Boswell needed another drink. He also wanted company to slake the thirst with which the Highland girl had left him. He had seen the passion awaking in her cat's eyes and the lips like plums ready for the picking. Willing to bide his time to win her, Boswell would buy his pleasure in the meantime among the dark wynds of Edinburgh.

'Where have you been?' Isabel's pinched accusing face glared at her stepsister.

'In the park,' Mairi tried to control the erratic beat of her heart, still a confusion of feelings. She had entered her chamber thankful to be away from the crowds and to think.

'You shouldn't wander about on your own,' Isabel paced the room, a disturbed expression pulling at her features.

'I wasn't,' Mairi struggled to keep calm; the last thing she wanted was a lecture from this woman of all people. Isabel swung round her eyes black as coals.

'I knew it,' she nearly choked on the words, 'you were with him!'

'I was with Lucy,' Mairi added hastily, unnerved by the violence in her stepsister's face.

'Oh, the wonderful new friend with the brains of a mouse,' Isabel sneered as bile rose in her throat. 'No doubt she was leading you into trouble?'

'She was not,' Mairi finally snapped, her head pounding painfully so she could hardly think, 'unless you call Boswell and Ruthven trouble.' Isabel's face went ashen, the lines tight about the eyes and mouth.

'Tell me!'

'Why should I have to account to you?' Mairi flared, a hand pressed to her temple. 'You're no longer in charge of me.' Isabel came forward and gripped her wrist, twisting her arm back with a cruel wrench.

'I saw Boswell and Ruthven leave just as you did. You made an assignation with him didn't you? *Didn't you?*'

'No!' Mairi clenched her teeth at the pain and tried to push her away.

'Tell me that there's nothing between you,' Isabel clung on like a vice. Mairi saw the gaunt manic flash in the other woman's eyes and felt a frisson of fear.

'There is nothing between me and Robert Boswell, believe me,' Mairi spoke as normally as possible as if humouring a child. 'We came across him tonight quite by chance - we talked of you.'

Hesitation showed in the haunted face and Isabel relaxed her hold.

'Did he mention my name?'

Mairi nodded, hoping fervently Boswell would leave her alone in future. 'He likes you.'

Isabel shuddered and withdrew her hold. Within moments she was calm again like a blown out storm.

'Well.' she cast down her eyes, 'I must let you rest. Have you enjoyed your birthday celebrations?'

'Yes,' Mairi breathed, watchful of the other.

'Good,' Isabel glided to the door, her tall slim form controlled and graceful. 'Good-night, sister,' she turned at the entrance. Mairi returned the sentiment.

As Isabel left, Mairi stared after her. These flashes of mood were more pronounced than ever. The unpredictability of them frightened Mairi more than Isabel's temper ever could. Perhaps the strain of Court life was too great and the memory of the abortive affair with Black too painful to erase? Yet her stepsister had never once spoken of him. It might have been better if she had, though Mairi had no wish to talk of the lecherous minister. Her head pounded too much for her to dwell on it more, let the future take care of itself, she thought with Highland fatalism.

Sleep came more easily than she had hoped after the emotional evening. As Mairi drifted into unconsciousness, she walked again to the pavilion, drawn by some magnetism that would not let her go. Trying to pull back, her steps would not let her. Only when she arrived and peered into the gloom Mairi was no longer afraid. The eyes that greeted her were black not blue and the face that drew her was darkly bearded.

Queen Anne was in good spirits the next day, chattering as Lucy and Mairi helped her to dress for a Court appearance.

'My dear husband has invited King Christian, my brother, for staying,' she beamed at them both. Mairi's heart fluttered with excitement at the thought of seeing the man who had kept Douglas away for three years and whom her stepbrother admired so much. Her musing gave her unexpected warmth.

'Oh, ma'am,' Lucy gave a cry, 'that's wonderful. Will he bring the most noble and handsome of his lords with him?'

The Queen laughed, delighting in her maid's precocious outburst. 'Of course, all Danish nobles they are handsome,' the Queen pouted proudly. 'You must be watching them, for they show their feelings on their sleeves, yes?'

'Yes, ma'am,' Lucy spluttered with mirth, 'I'll be watching them if you say so.' Queen Anne wrinkled her face in the looking glass.

'I think I say wrong thing, yes!'

They chattered and laughed though Mairi was only partly listening. Would it be possible Douglas would be summoned to the Court to see his former Danish master, from whom he learned his soldiering? What if he did come, would they be like strangers again, or worse merely brother and sister? It was two months since Mairi had come to Edinburgh and she tried in vain to conjure up the tenderness she had glimpsed at their parting. It was imagined, for all she could remember was the angry hatred on his face the night he had stormed from her bedroom and the cold aloof contempt of the following days. They gave her little comfort that Douglas would be pleased to see her even if he were to come to Court.

'But Mairi is quiet, no?' her mistress eyed the other helper. 'You do not want to meet your Viking cousins?' Mairi flushed at being caught day-dreaming and smiled.

'I would indeed be happy to meet them and the King of Denmark since I heard so much about him from Douglas - ' Mairi stopped suddenly aware of both women looking at her intently.

The burning spread up from her chest and neck into her cheeks and up to the roots of her gold-red hair. The Queen smiled.

'Ah, yes, the handsome Douglas, who lives now as a laird, yes?'

'Yes,' Mairi whispered hoarsely and dropped her eyes to the comb she held in her hands.

'Perhaps it would be nice for Douglas Roskill to come to Edinburgh to meet King Christian, ma'am?' Lucy piped up in her provocative silvery voice.

'Do you dictate to the Queen?' the royal woman made a mock severe face at her maid. The two girls fell silent. 'But it would be nice for my brother to see his old friend, I am thinking also,' Queen Anne's eyes twinkled with amusement.

She received broad smiles from both her helpers and Mairi, still glowing with embarrassment, nodded.

'I know my stepbrother would be honoured,' she sounded almost prim in her reply, 'and it would be pleasant for both me and Isabel.'

'And I've heard so much about him, I'm dying to meet him,' Lucy added mischievously. Mairi shot her an anxious look but saw the laughter in Lucy's cornflower blue eyes.

'Then I will see if Duntorin can spare his son for a few days to dance and drink with us Danes. I think it is boring being a farmer, yes?'

'When will that be?' Mairi could not hide her impatience.

'In two weeks when it is high summer and the sea will not be as rough as a bear, yes?' Queen Anne smiled and pinched Mairi's cheek.

'Yes,' her maids chorused.

Douglas had been up early hunting with Sam on the high ground beyond the freshwater loch. The summer was well advanced and the unusually fair weather meant the crops were already golden in the fields. They cantered back. The feeling of the strong power of Elsinore beneath him and the rush of the breeze in his hair was his best tonic for relieving the frustration of being kept at Duntorin. To live here was an anticlimax after the Danish Court and fighting on the Continent. Or was the tedium the more marked since Mairi and Isabel had left?

He saw the promontory of the Beltane fires loom up ahead like a sore reminder of the early summer and his return to his father's lands. It seemed an age away and Douglas found his mind wandering once again to the dance with Mairi and of the times he had held her briefly in his arms, feeling the eager response to his kisses. He wondered who she allowed to kiss her now? She had the pick of the King's Court, Douglas thought savagely, now she was in her seventeenth year. But he would send himself mad with such thoughts; it was just the boredom playing tricks with his mind. Why was it he could not rid himself of feelings for the redheaded woman? Had he really missed her that much? Douglas spurred on Elsinore, leaving a puzzled Sam to follow.

Entering the Castle gates, Douglas noticed two strange steeds by the mounting block. They wore the royal livery. A message from the Court perhaps? He suddenly feared something was wrong. Duntorin was to be found in the new parlour, his face looking grim.

'Father?' Douglas enquired.

They understood each other with little need for words.

'We have messengers from the Court in Edinburgh,' his father eyed Douglas, gauging his response.

'Is all well?' Douglas asked rather too sharply. Duntorin grunted, unable to keep the smile from his craggy face at his son's concern.

'Aye, very well. Your sisters are spoken of highly by Queen Anne.'

'But they didn't send messengers just to tell us that Father,' Douglas answered impatiently.

'No,' Duntorin smacked the scroll of paper he held in his hand, against his leather hose. 'The King of Denmark is visiting Edinburgh and you are bidden to help with the hospitality.' Duntorin added dryly, 'No doubt King Christian will need someone to keep up with him in his hunting and drinking exploits.'

Douglas laughed. 'Then I must do the best I can,' he grinned at his father. Duntorin came forward and embraced his son in a rare bear-hug.

'You're hot-headed I know,' the older man said gruffly, 'and I don't want you starting feuds with every overbearing courtier who happens to displease you.'

Douglas gave him a wry look. 'No feuds, Father, I'll just settle the score there and then.'

'Hah!' Duntorin thumped him on the back. His son was all of his height and nearly as broad. He was secretly proud at the thought Douglas could take care of himself and stand equal to any other. 'And take care of your sisters,' he added.

Douglas saw his dark eyes moisten, though his father could never admit to him that he missed them both and their chatter, even their arguments.

'I will keep Isabel away from lecherous men and protect Mairi from the King's wrath about her hot Highland head,' Douglas chuckled. Duntorin saw the spark in his son's eyes and felt a grip of unease. Was he still too fond of his young stepsister? He debated whether to tell Douglas now of the other missive he held in his hand which would prove to his son that Mairi had captured the interest of someone else at Court. But he decided to remain silent; Douglas knew his wishes on the matter and he did not want them to part on bad terms. It was high time he put into action the plans he and Florence had discussed for Douglas before his return from Denmark. He had been dilatory in not doing so before now.

'Well go and prepare,' Duntorin smiled, 'and take your leave of your stepmother, she'll be inconsolable when you're gone.'

'Mairi!' Lucy burst into the tiny bedchamber. 'Come quickly, there's someone to see you.' Mairi's heart lurched at the look of barely suppressed excitement on her friend's face. Lucy had been like a wound-up spinning top since the Danish nobles had arrived, ready to spring and knock people over at any moment. Her enthusiasm was infectious and Mairi had entered into the festivities on their arrival three days ago with mischievous relish.

They had earned the King's displeasure by dressing up as page-boys at the first fancy dress ball. The Danish King suspected them and made them sing for their supper; only the delight of King Christian and his sister, Queen Anne, had protected them from being disciplined.

'It's a man and he's asked for you! He would not give his name, isn't that romantic?' Lucy bubbled pink with ecstasy. Mairi felt her heart jolt against her ribs. Had Douglas answered the royal summons and come straight to see her? Had he not asked for Isabel too?

'Is my sister bidden to see this mystery man?' Mairi tried to sound light, her fingers straying to the wisps of hair at her temple. Lucy shook her head in glee.

'Just you, now hurry up Mairi,' her friend grabbed her hand. 'From what I saw of him he's extremely handsome and so shouldn't be kept waiting.'

Mairi coloured and smoothed down her satin dress. 'How do I look?' she asked nervously.

'Lovely, as usual,' Lucy pushed her towards the door. 'He waits in the Long Gallery, you can see him quickly before his audience with King James.'

Mairi took a deep breath as Lucy opened the doors to the portrait gallery and entered. Lucy Seton dropped a curtsy at the figure standing in the light of the nearby window. Mairi came forward and then stopped dead at the sight of the stranger.

Her first thought was disappointment at not seeing Douglas standing there. Then curiosity quickened as she took in the straw-blond hair and fair-red beard. He was tantalisingly familiar, but her memory was a fog. Then he spoke.

'Mairi, is it really you?' The long unheard Gaelic came like a strange half-submerged tune to her ears.

The man moved forward, the green eyes smiling. 'You are quite grown up and a credit to Lismore,' he said in a soft, gentle lilt.

'Sandy!' Mairi let slip the childhood name for her brother Alexander and rushed into his open arms.

Lucy watched in open-mouthed amazement at the greeting, not understanding the words but only too well aware of the feeling between them. This could not be Douglas speaking in the barbarous tongue. How many lovers did this surprising Highland girl have? They were gabbling away together like a torrent in flood.

Mairi saw Alexander looking over her shoulder, his dark green eyes alive with interest. She turned, remembering Lucy was with them.

'Sorry Lucy,' she quavered with joy, 'let me introduce you. My brother Alexander, Chief of Lismore. Sandy, this is my greatest friend Lucy Seton of Hoddington and maid-in-waiting to Queen Anne.'

Alexander swept a bow, his golden hair rippling like a mane from his crown over his ruff.

Lucy blushed pink and coyly curtsied. 'I can see now how alike you both are.' Mairi looked pleased at her brother, awkwardly hampered by his best garb. She knew it was not his usual choice of clothing.

'It is good to know my sister is blessed with such a friendship. I can see the long journey to Court was worth it indeed,' he replied gallantly.

'Well spoken,' Mairi clapped her hands, unable to take her eyes from the man before her, surprised by the ease with which he spoke to her friend.

He was older than Douglas by several years, but ruggedly good-looking. This was the eldest of Florence's children who had borne the brunt of looking after the family and seeing them settled while pacifying their wild cousin Cailean and keeping the Lismore lands intact. There was no shred of bitterness or malice in Alexander towards her or her mother for deserting him, even if done so by force. She thought with a sudden prick of emotion how like her own father Alexander must be.

'I hope you will be staying in Edinburgh for a while?' Lucy's question brought Mairi back to the present. She could see the flush of interest on the fair cheeks and the sparkle in the indigo blue eyes.

Alexander smiled slowly, 'I think it would please the King if I stayed to observe the Lowland ways,' he spoke Lowland Scots with a hesitant soft tongue. 'And it pleases me too, in such company.'

Lucy gave a delighted tinkle of laughter and looked at Mairi. 'Your brother has Highland charm, far nicer than empty courtly words, Mairi,' she smiled prettily.

Their enjoyment was rudely broken by a curtain thrown aside and a group of young gentry sauntering in.

'The King will see Lismore,' a voice drawled condescendingly and Mairi knew without looking round it was Boswell. He caught sight of her. 'Ah, how touching, a family reunion.'

'Yes,' she flared at him, spinning round, 'I am proud to have such a brother, he is worth ten Lowland lairds!'

Lucy gasped at her friend's outburst, but Boswell gave a mirthless laugh. Alexander moved forward to put a restraining hand on her arm. His sister had lost none of her fiery temper, he thought with amusement. Instinct told him that caution was needed towards this simpering nobleman with the dangling red jewel in his ear, whoever he was. The Highland Chief lost none of the naked interest in Boswell's face as he goaded Mairi on. Alexander cut off the reply on the young lord's lips.

'Sir, I am ready to meet with the King,' Lismore said in his singsong way, belying the alert strength in the stocky body and the broad shoulders and neck. "Till later sister,' he kissed her hand and gave her a steady warning look. His eyes briefly met with Lucy's and he nodded a farewell with a smile.

As he went, Mairi realised she did not know his reason for coming to Court. Alexander had alluded to his defence of certain land titles. She hoped nothing was amiss, knowing the low opinion King James held of his Highland subjects.

They were proud and independent and did not take kindly to following dictates from a distant Sassenach monarch. They preferred to mete out their own justice.

She watched her brother follow the lean supple frame of Boswell, dressed in rich doublet and hose of pale green, his ruff intricately laced. He reminded her more of a cat than ever, like one of the strange feline beasts that prowled the tapestries in the Great Hall.

Lucy moved close. 'It was not wise to cross Robert Boswell like that,' she spoke in a hush, 'he is a dangerous man to provoke for all his smiles and flattery, Mairi.' Her face was worried. 'He pays you too much attention and it frightens me.'

'I know,' Mairi bit her lip, 'and I think I fear Isabel's jealousy as much as his interest, Lucy.'

The young Seton girl nodded. 'Isabel has eyes for no one else, yet Boswell practically ignores her.'

'I wish that he would pay her the attention and not me,' Mairi sighed.

'Never mind,' Lucy's eyes lit with mischief, 'Douglas will soon be here to warn Boswell off,' she squeezed Mairi's arm. 'And for my sake, you will persuade your handsome brother to stay on for the festivities, won't you?' The two friends laughed and left arm in arm.

Douglas and Sam stood squinting over the bright water of the Forth on the spot Sam had left Mairi two months ago. Young Roskill was impatient to be across and ride into Edinburgh. Sam watched him pace with silent amusement. He threw Mary Bain a knowing look.

It was just like his master and comrade in arms to think of their happiness in the midst of the hasty preparations. Sam knew Douglas had appointed Mary as housekeeper on this visit, so that they would not be parted. Since the time Mary had done so much to help the Roskill family, Sam's admiration had quickened into love. Initial opposition from her blacksmith father had been overcome and from the look in Mary's dancing blue eyes, Sam knew his love was returned.

She had only teased him once about his jealousy over her dancing with his master at the May Day rituals. Mary had insisted proudly she had been Queen for the day and could dance with whom-so-ever she wished. Now they were both Douglas's loyal servants and that was an end to it.

'I could do with some of Bailie Greeves's best claret, Sam,' Douglas clapped a hand on his friend's shoulder, 'we've ridden hard.'

'I'm sure there will be a generous welcome for you, sir,' Sam grinned, 'and much quenching of thirsts over the next few days.' He noticed the relief on Douglas's face as the vessel that was to transport them to the southern shore, hove into sight.

The Queen strolled in the park with her ladies-in-waiting, a black mask to her face to ward off the sun's rays.

'Tomorrow we practise the steps for the masquerade, yes?' There was an excited buzz like the droning of bees about her as they discussed their costumes. The Queen was going as Bel-Anna, the Queen of the Ocean and Lucy would be one of her nymphs.

'Mairi should be Goddess Diana of the Moon and the Chase, with such luxuriant hair,' Lucy cried excitedly. As they chattered and fluttered around their mistress, Mairi noticed Isabel looking smugly pleased with herself.

'You're looking forward to the Ball too, Isabel?' Mairi smiled.

'The more so because my brother arrives today from Duntorin,' she looked triumphant at Mairi's shocked surprise, watching the hot burning spread to her fair cheeks under her scrutiny.

'How do you know?' Mairi stammered, unable to hide the effect the news had on her.

'Bailie Greeves told me this forenoon,' she preened, 'he likes to be kept informed of our progress.'

Mairi's eyes widened further still. She wondered where Isabel sometimes slipped off to; the Bailie must have a soft spot for the daughter of his old love.

'Will you go to visit him Isabel?' Mairi felt warm and flustered all of a sudden.

'No, he will be at the banquet tonight,' Isabel waited a moment and then added softly, 'and he will not need my administrations about the mansion. He has the help of Bailie Greeves's servants - and Mary Bain, of course.'

Mairi felt as if she had been kicked in the stomach by those last words. Why had she put Mary from her mind until now? Could it be that Douglas had been in association with her all summer and now could not bear to be parted even for a brief visit to Edinburgh?

She felt hot tears of annoyance spring unwanted to her eyes. She could not believe how hurt she was by the news. Douglas had probably not given her a second thought since she rode away. If he had, he would have got word to her of his coming and not left it to the malicious tale-telling of Isabel. What an idiot she was to harbour romantic notions about her dark stepbrother, he would only laugh and tease her if he suspected she felt anything for him.

It was just as well Isabel had told her now, preventing her from making a fool of herself when she saw Douglas. This way, she had time to gain composure and greet him with the offhand coolness he deserved. Why should she expect the assassin of her father to behave differently from the hard-hearted man he obviously was? Mairi vowed to banish her weak feelings for him; she had her elder brother to protect her and allow her to hold her head high in front of these Roskills. She would show him that Lismores could be just as strong and cool-headed when necessary.

Lucy came to Mairi's side, afraid her friend was about to strike out at Isabel. She caught only the gist of their conversation but heard Douglas's name mentioned and that of another woman. It angered her that Isabel could so easily upset her friend.

'Come Mairi,' she steered her away from her stepsister, 'let's talk of our costumes.' Isabel watched them go with a spiteful triumph.

Despite her earlier self-admonishing, Mairi could not help the nervousness she felt as they made their way down to the Banqueting Hall. Would Douglas already be there carousing with his Danish friends? She had warmed to the big King Christian with his rakish pigtail falling over one shoulder and his booming laughter. She wanted to meet Douglas but only to hear news of her mother and Duntorin and Agnes.

Lucy's chattering swept over her head as they hurried to attend the Queen. She too was in high spirits and the girls sensed a long evening lay ahead again.

'Have you seen your brother Alexander?' Lucy whispered to Mairi.

'Not since his audience with the King, but he sent me a message to say he had been invited to dine here tonight,' she assured the eager fair face.

The doors opened releasing a volley of noise and laughter from the throng of nobles already assembled. Mairi recognised most of them, with a liberal sprinkling of Danish guests joining in the merriment. They bowed and made way for Queen Anne, who talked her guttural tongue and set them laughing and at ease.

As they parted for her to progress to her royal brother, Mairi's heart knocked against her breast at the sight of a tall familiar figure standing legs astride beside King Christian. Douglas's violet-black eyes met hers before he bowed to the Queen and she felt the resolution of the past few hours dissolve.

She watched as he made pleasantries with his Queen, quite at home in the surroundings of the Court and not in the least overwhelmed by the host of important people about him. Douglas was dressed in rich brocade and a silk slashed doublet, his velvet hose slimly hugging the powerful legs. His dark beard was newly trimmed about the firm mouth, the dark hair curling to the stiff white ruff around his neck. Mairi felt as if she had left him only moments ago instead of months.

'By the look on your face, that must be Douglas Roskill,' Lucy whispered cheekily, 'and I can see why you're in such a state.'

Mairi gulped. Was she so transparent that her friend could read her like a book of verse? She strove to regain composure. When Douglas next looked over to her, she glanced quickly away and turned to talk to someone else. In the general melee before the meal, Mairi noticed Isabel rush up to Douglas and make a show of seeing him again. Mairi was sure his reaction to his sister was cooler than usual, but she may have imagined it.

As they took their seats, Mairi was aware of Douglas trying to make his way over to her. She did not trust herself to speak to him at this moment and slipped away to talk to a couple of young Danish lords, who had enjoyed her page-boy prank of the other evening. Even as she sat down, Mairi could feel herself being watched and raised her eyes to see Douglas considering her speculatively, before he turned to greet a Danish friend.

The dinner dragged on for hours, with dozens of courses being brought to the groaning tables. Mairi felt her head buzz with the noise and the effect of the wine. The court minstrels had begun to play and the music swam in her mind leaving her mellow. To her pleasure she noted Lucy and Alexander keeping each other quite enthralled in conversation. She wondered what Alexander and Douglas would have to say if they were to meet? Would they like each other or be instantly on guard with their family enemies?

She needed air, Mairi decided suddenly, the heat in the Hall was oppressive. Excusing herself she slipped from the table and went out through the heavy curtain, through the antechamber to the Gallery.

Throwing open a window she breathed in the still night air of a balmy late July evening. The coolness felt reviving on her closed lids and burning cheeks.

'Am I to be avoided all night?' Mairi swung round at the deep voice right behind her. Douglas stood towering over her in the soft light of the Gallery, so near she could have put her hand out to touch him.

'I - I did not mean to avoid you, brother,' Mairi squeezed the words painfully from her dry throat. It felt as if a lead ball was stuck in her windpipe. She saw his face tighten at her use of the sibling greeting, but he let it pass.

'Well here we are anyway,' he looked her over with his dark gaze and she felt her pulse banging in her throat and chest. 'I would that you were as pleased to see me as I am to see you,' his voice rippled round her like a warm cloak.

She would not be taken in by sweet words or that bold look of his! He played with her as if she were a kitten that would purr nicely at such fondling. Well Mary Bain might be taken in and used in such a way, but she, Mairi Lismore, would not.

'Yes, it would suit you, no doubt, to have a small diversion at the Court while you enjoy yourself with your Danish friends,' Mairi replied haughtily. To her fury he began to laugh.

'Oh, I've missed your redheaded temper, Mairi, it's been so dull at Duntorin without you,' he leaned forward and stroked the wisp of hair from her eyes.

Mairi coloured in confusion. She had not expected this tenderness after Isabel's news. Her heart responded with a painful beat to his touch, she could not bear it.

'How is Mother?' she forced out the question and turned her back to him, breathing in the cool air at the window.

'She is well,' Douglas's voice was so close she could feel his breath brush the top of her hair. 'I bring a letter from her.'

'Oh!' Mairi spun round forgetting her caution. 'Do you have it?' she smiled eagerly.

'Yes,' he chuckled and drew the parchment out of his jerkin. She lurched for it, but he held it out of reach.

'Douglas, hand it over,' Mairi insisted, the frown knitting her fair brow.

'What price is it worth?' he teased in his low voice, the sensuous mouth twisting with amusement.

'What do you mean?' she asked with annoyance.

'A kiss perhaps,' he murmured, sweeping her with his insolent gaze once more, 'to welcome your - stepbrother - and show him how pleased you are to see him?'

'How dare you withhold the letter,' Mairi croaked huskily, hating the treacherous pounding in her breast at his suggestion.

He leaned down towards her, the spicy scent of his beard filling her nostrils. 'Just one kiss, Mairi,' he whispered, like a distant rumble of thunder. She knew he was about to have his way and part of her cried out for the taste of his lips.

'Is this how you blackmail Mary Bain for her favours?' Mairi warded him off at the last moment, not knowing from where the question came.

Douglas stopped dead, the black eyes boring into hers. 'In God's name,' he cursed under his breath, 'would you throw that old jealousy at me even now?' She heard the quick anger in his tone and the spell was broken. Douglas lifted her chin roughly with his hand, pinching the soft layer of flesh underneath. 'Why do you dislike Mary so?'

'I don't,' Mairi flashed back at him, 'but I won't be another notch on your tally of conquests!'

He clutched her violently by the shoulders as if he would shake her into submission.

'Mairi,' his voice cracked with anger, 'you can be so infuriating at times! Why can't you understand I -'

'Is he bothering you, Mairi?' the silken voice of Boswell cut across Douglas's outburst. Mairi froze at the unexpected appearance. How long had he been listening in the half dark? She saw the fire of displeasure crackle in Douglas's eyes as he held hers for one brief moment and then turned to face the intruder.

'Boswell!' he thundered with a mixture of wrath and surprise. 'You have not rid yourself of the childish habit of eavesdropping, I see.'

The young son of Brae threw him a cool look. 'It did not seem like the way a brother should greet his delightful sister -and so I thought it best to intervene on the gentlelady's behalf.' He relished the choked angry look on Douglas's face and Mairi knew young Duntorin controlled himself with difficulty.

'So you are no strangers to each other?' Douglas flung a dark demanding look at Mairi. She stared mutely back at him unable to find the words to reassure him there was nothing between her and the preening sly-eyed nobleman.

'Oh, the sweet creature and I are well acquainted,' Boswell drawled, stepping closer, a finger stroking the soft fashionable tuft of hair below his lip. 'She looks most enchanting on a moonlit walk, Roskill, believe me.'

Douglas looked about to strike Boswell for his insolent manner. Mairi saw him grip the hilt of his sword with white strained knuckles, his nostrils flaring with furious contempt. Only with supreme control did he stay his itching fingers.

'Is this so?' he glared at Mairi, the eyes black as whirlpools.

'We - we have only, just the once we . . .' she could not speak coherently under the accusing stare.

'Calm yourself Roskill,' Boswell smiled cat-like, 'you are upsetting Mairi.'

'Call her by her first name again and I'll strike you down where you stand, you blackguard,' Douglas said with a voice of iron. 'To you she is Miss Roskill.'

As Boswell laughed in his face, Mairi was spurred into action, her frozen limbs and voice coming to life again. 'I'm Miss Roskill to no man,' she blazed at them both, 'you speak to the daughter of Lismore and I will not be the subject of your squabbling.'

Her green eyes flashed from one to the other.

'You can carry on your schoolyard fighting if you wish, but I'll be no part of it!' At this she side-stepped Douglas's imposing frame and rushed for the Banqueting Hall, forcing herself not to look back.

'Such passion,' Boswell cast Douglas a challenging look, 'but this time she has outmanoeuvred us both, I fear.'

'Keep away from her,' Douglas threatened through clenched teeth.

'You don't change do you, Roskill?' Robert Boswell smirked, 'always wanting to pick a fight.' He pulled the lovelock of hair between his fingers. 'Be assured that I do nothing the girl does not want me to do.' And with that he turned on his heels and sauntered back to the banquet, leaving Douglas alone.

The Devil take them both, he thought furiously. If Mairi chose to make a fool of herself over a rogue like Boswell, let her go ahead. He had seen it happen before, even as a youth the youngest Brae had charmed girls into his bed. Why should it matter so much to him that Mairi might be involved with Boswell? He would spend his time here hunting with his Danish friends and forget about her.

Nevertheless, he had to admit that the force that had pulled him to Court had been illusory, the belief that Mairi would have missed him as much as he had missed her. But then he had parted with her on bad terms at Duntorin and said some terrible things to the young woman. She had her pride and was as stubborn as a wild Highland colt at times.

Douglas gnawed a knuckle, trying to calm his temper before returning to the feasting. He was plagued by the image of Mairi in her shimmering court dress of gold with the low cut neckline and the delicate lace across her breast. She was more beautiful than he had recalled, with her hair of burnished copper piled on the crown of her head, exposing the vulnerable sensuous face. Whatever happened he would not allow Boswell to have her, of that he was sure.

With a start Douglas realised he still held Florence's letter to Mairi. It brought a grim smile to his mouth, she would have to come asking for it. If he handled the situation with more self-control the next time, perhaps she would not spark so easily with her ridiculous notions about Sam's Mary. Consoling himself with the thought, Douglas strode back towards the Hall.

CHAPTER SEVEN

Mairi joined Lucy and Alexander, her heart still thumping at the shock of her encounter with Douglas, and Boswell's startling appearance.

'You look flustered sister,' Alexander saw her flaming cheeks with concern. 'Are you unwell?'

Mairi braved a smile, 'No Sandy, it is just oppressively hot in here.'

Lucy was not taken in by the excuse. She had been watching her friend's moves and had seen both Roskill and Boswell follow in her direction. She hoped nothing untoward had happened.

'Perhaps we could take a stroll?' Lucy suggested. 'I'm sure your brother would like to see the grounds, Mairi.' Alexander's fair face blushed with pleasure and his youngest sister wondered fleetingly if there was anyone at home who kept his heart or whether Lucy Seton was special in his eyes? He had not married, being too busy seeing to the affairs of his family to look after his own interests.

'I would welcome the night air away from the formality of a Lowland supper,' he replied with a smile.

'Oh, you must tell us about your wild Highland feasts then,' Lucy put a hand on his arm and giggled. Mairi glanced anxiously at the entrance to the Hall and saw Boswell reappear. She accepted Lucy's plan hurriedly.

With increasing alarm she noticed the brazen courtier scanning the room. Mairi dropped her gaze so that he could not single her out. They made their way towards the door as he moved away and with relief, Mairi saw him go to Isabel's side. Long may it continue, she thought fervently. He had delighted in provoking Douglas and played shamelessly with her. What was it Douglas had been about to say to her in the Gallery? She might never know, for she had rebuffed him and then Boswell had destroyed their meeting.

As they reached the entrance, the curtain moved and Douglas stood before them. For a moment Mairi stopped breathing as he looked from her to Alexander with his jet-black eyes. He looked in no mood for light conversation.

'Miss Seton, Lismore,' Douglas nodded at them curtly, ignoring his stepsister. It galled him to see her so at ease in the company of her relation, as if emphasising the Roskills were of no importance to her now she had found her own again.

'Roskill,' Alexander bristled, 'enjoying yourself with your Danish drinking companions?' Mairi looked at him in surprise; she had never before heard this sarcastic side of Alexander.

'And what brings you out of the Highlands?' Douglas kept his voice level, but Mairi could see a muscle working in his cheek.

'I'm on no business of yours,' the fair Chief answered tight-lipped.

'Come to grovel to the King for your lands, no doubt,' Douglas could not resist the jibe, 'like all the other Gaelic chieftains scrabbling to find their so-called charters. Though why they worry over their entitlement to some barren bit of waste, I fail to understand.'

Livid spots of pink spread into Lismore's cheeks. 'There is no doubt about my claim to the lands of Lismore,' he raised his lilting voice angrily. 'My ancestors have lived there for ten generations and I even have bits of royal paper to keep you Sassenachs happy, though they would not stop me and my people living there even if I did not!'

Mairi stayed him with a soft hand on his arm. It upset her to see the two of them take such an instant dislike to each other. Douglas suddenly smiled.

'I see the Lismore temper runs in the family,' he threw a look at Mairi which made her hot.

'Yes,' Alexander challenged him with green eyes as rebellious as his sister's, 'I'm glad to see living among Roskills has not daunted my sister's spirit.'

Douglas gave a short harsh laugh. 'Far from it, Lismore, she can still spit like a wildcat.'

Mairi gasped at the impertinent words. 'How dare you!' she lifted her chin at him.

'Don't worry,' Alexander flashed back, 'I will take care of my own now, Mairi's welfare is no longer your concern, Roskill.' Mairi saw the angry glint in Douglas's eyes and the tightening of his jaw. He was about to erupt when Lucy piped up.

'Gentlemen, this is the King's Palace not a baiting ring,' she smiled at them both, 'You can carry on this fascinating conversation at another time, but now the Queen's maids desire a walk.' She moved between them and slipped an arm through her friend's. 'Come Mairi,' she swept a dazzling smile at Douglas and pushed Mairi forward. Alexander quickly followed without another word.

Douglas watched them go, cursing himself for losing his temper with Lismore. He had not meant to ridicule the man; he had wanted to be friends with Mairi's real brother and end any bad feeling between the families. But they were plagued with such prickly pride, each one as insufferable as the next. It wounded him to think Mairi accepted her long lost brother so easily, while treating himself with suspicion and contempt.

Turning, Douglas saw Boswell watching him with a derisive grin as he led Isabel in a formal dance. The man was deliberately baiting him with his sister. He decided it was best ignored, he had promised his father that he would take care of Isabel and resolved to speak to her later. In the meantime he would join the raucous crowd about King Christian of Denmark.

The air was cooling down rapidly outside and calm had returned to the

Lismore siblings.

'Young Roskill sounds just like his overbearing father,' Alexander commented dryly.

'It was not his fault that you quarrelled just now,' Mairi found herself defending Douglas, 'and he is not usually so abrasive.'

Alexander shot her a quick look. 'So you have some affection for the man?' he enquired.

'He was often kind to me as a child,' Mairi parried.

'Still, the Roskills killed our father and for that I cannot forgive them ever,' Alexander said shortly. Mairi realised he could not know of the rumours she had picked up as a child that Douglas had done the killing himself, his first blooding. She hastily changed the subject.

'Sandy, what does bring you to Court? It worries me to hear talk of charters and entitlements; surely the Lismore lands are safe?'

Alexander stopped and distractedly picked a leaf from trailing ivy. 'It is not our lands that are insecure,' he spoke low. 'I have complied with King James's wishes and produced my charters. They show clearly Lismore is mine.' He hesitated and glanced at Lucy. She smiled reassuringly.

'I will keep anything you say in confidence, sir.'

Alexander smiled back at the pretty young woman at his side and continued. 'It is our cousin Cailean,' his voice grated with irritation.

'He chooses to ignore the King's decree and will not produce charters to his land. Probably he has none. Like any Highland chief he feels the lands of his forefathers are his by right, no matter what a mere King of Scotland says.'

'Keep your voice down,' Mairi urged nervously, looking about her for spying courtiers. Alexander stuck his chin out proudly but lowered his speech.

'King James is just waiting for some fool like Cailean to defy him, so that he can make an example of him and his clan.' His bearded face creased in worry. 'And that means the Lismores of Glen Garroch will be put to the sword - wiped out, Mairi!'

His sister shuddered with horror. 'Surely the King would not resort to such a measure against his own subjects?' She thought of their ungainly but amiable monarch. 'He is our friend, Sandy.'

Alexander smiled down at her wistfully. 'You have been sheltered from much of the world's ways,' he answered, gently touching her cheek with a rough hand. 'The King will do whatever he feels he must to preserve his own throne,' he dropped his voice to a soft whisper, like an evening's breeze rustling through grasses. 'If that means subduing Highlanders who go their own sweet way, then he will do it, even if they were his own kin and however bloody the result.'

Lucy listened in silence. She knew Alexander spoke accurately for she had witnessed some of the unrest that blighted her Border home, which King James fought to keep in check. Mairi looked appalled.

'Have you come to plead for Cailean then?' she asked in hushed tones. Alexander nodded.

'The King is in good spirits at the moment with his Danish guests to hunt with. He listened to me civilly today and I hope he will give Cailean a reprieve.'

'Perhaps I can put in a good word for him to the Queen?' Mairi murmured.

'That would be a kind service to our kinsman's people,' Alexander took her hand and squeezed it, 'you are a thoughtful sister.'

But that night, Mairi could not sleep. She tossed and turned in the narrow bed, images of angry men conjured up before her sleepless eyes. Stupidly she had failed to secure her mother's letter from Douglas and she yearned for news from Duntorin. How was Agnes? Were things calm again after Black's despicable witch hunt? Did her mother miss her fondly too? Douglas had been quite wrong to withhold the missive, but had not her heart raced at the thought of being kissed by him again? She blushed in the dark to think Douglas must have been sure of her response, he knew the power he had to stir her. He had been angry at her mention of Mary Bain. Mairi could not tell if it was because she guessed the truth about them or whether the blacksmith's daughter was really of no consequence to him.

Had she misjudged Douglas? It pained her to think she might have scorned his attempts to be friends with her again, after their quarrelling at Duntorin over Isabel and Zechariah Black.

Her feelings were so juggled about, it would have been better if he had never come to Court. Though as she finally drifted off into fitful sleep, she prayed she would have the chance of speaking with Douglas once more.

The next day there was much gay laughter about Queen Anne as her gentlewomen practised the steps to the masquerade. It was to be the crowning entertainment for the Danish lords before they embarked for Denmark in a week's time. The Queen had declared the most elaborate costumes must be worn and no expense spared for the revelries. She cared not what the killjoy element of the Scottish Kirk thought of her ploy.

Mairi threw herself into the preparations trying to forget the clashes of the night before and teasing Lucy for her interest in an unsophisticated Highland Chief.

'Are you changing your Lowland mind about the merits of Celtic looks?' Mairi joked.

'There must be exceptions to every rule,' Lucy rallied back. Isabel broke in on their conversation. 'A word, Mairi,' she commanded. Mairi raised her eyebrows at Lucy but stepped aside. 'We are bidden to dine at Bailie Greeves's tonight. He and Douglas are laying on a supper for King

Christian and my brother wishes us to be there to entertain the Danes.'

Isabel watched for the reaction on Mairi's transparent face, her eyelids fluttering rapidly and crimson stains spreading across her cheeks at the words.

Just the mention of Douglas's name affected the girl, Isabel thought with irritation.

'Then we must be there,' Mairi nervously smoothed her hands over her dress as she answered. Isabel considered her in silence. 'But you do not look pleased, Isabel,' Mairi held the dark eyes. 'I thought anything your brother wanted agreed with you?'

The dark eyes narrowed. 'I just wondered what trickery you had been up to, that's all,' Isabel replied with a hiss.

'I have no idea what you mean,' Mairi was impatient to get back to the dancing.

'Oh no?' Isabel pinched her upper arm. 'Then why has Douglas seen fit to invite that uncivilised brother of yours and Lucy Seton, and not his old school friend Robert Boswell? You have said something against Robert to spite me.'

Mairi's eyes widened into amazed green pools of light. 'How kind of Douglas to include Alexander,' she cried with pleasure, 'it is a generous gesture. As for Boswell, maybe they were not the good friends he led you to believe.'

Isabel nipped her arm viciously. 'You stop at nothing to thwart my happiness, do you?' her voice was venomous. 'Well just remember that your dear mother packed you off to Court so you could turn my brother's head no more. I will be watching you with him.'

Indignation flashed in the green eyes. 'Your brother is old enough to know his own mind,' Mairi shot back, 'and I don't need the likes of you to tell me how to behave.'

She unfurled Isabel's grip with her free hand and walked over to Lucy. Ignoring her stepsister, she broke the good news of the banquet to her friend. Nothing was going to stop their enjoyment, least of all the spiteful jealousy of the thin-lipped Isabel. Judging by Lucy's ecstatic reaction, she would hear of nothing else for the rest of the day, Mairi thought wryly.

Mairi wore her favourite gown of green silk with shimmering silver gauze over the sleeves for Bailie Greeves's supper party. The excitement she felt mounted as Lucy rushed into her room in peacock blue, showering her with compliments and speculation. She may mean little to Douglas, Mairi thought, but she would hold her head high and look as dignified as a chief's daughter should.

Together with Alexander, Isabel and a couple of the Danish nobles they had come to know and like, they stepped up the High Street in good spirits. They joked in the flickering torchlight that the servants carried ahead of them. In the semi-dark the filth of the cobbled streets was obscured and

Edinburgh took on a magical quality of its own. Lights burned from the windows of the tall stone houses, twinkling invitingly.

'I'm pleased you have agreed to come, brother,' Mairi linked arms with Alexander and smiled up at the fair bearded face. He grunted.

'I do this for you and not for the satisfaction of Roskill,' he said with embarrassment, 'after all, his family have looked after you and mother well in spite of their faults.'

'Oh Sandy,' Mairi tugged his arm impetuously; 'I wish mother were here with us now to enjoy your company, she would love it so.' His expression softened.

'Perhaps one day we will all meet,' he speculated, 'but nothing in this world is sure.'

'Listen how the pipes greet us,' Mairi cried excitedly on hearing the blast of music in the close. She almost skipped into the courtyard. King Christian had already been received and noise of loud conversation wafted out of the upstairs windows of the mansion. Three pipers stood by the steps giving their musical salute. Mairi blinked and looked again.

'Rory!' her face was a picture of delighted surprise on recognising the old Gaelic-speaking piper in the middle of the trio. She had not seen him since the Beltane dance. Mairi rushed forward and gave him a friendly hug. His ugly weathered face broke up in a creased map of lines at the gesture. 'How do you come to be here?' Mairi grinned at him. 'Is this not too far south for you?'

'Young Duntorin requested it and the chance of seeing the fair Maid of Lismore would make me travel far.'

She flushed with delight. 'Rory, this is my brother, Chief Alexander,' Mairi introduced him proudly.

'Indeed Mairi, I know Rory well. He often cheers our hearth with news from afar and the music of the ancient bards,' Alexander smiled. 'It is good to hear God's language spoken among the heathens, Rory of the Pipes.'

The young Chief jested in Gaelic and they laughed until Lismore caught the perplexed look on Lucy's face. 'Forgive me, Miss Seton, it is rude indeed to speak our tongue in your presence. From now on I shall struggle with your Scots.'

Lucy took his proffered arm with a dazzling smile. It warmed Mairi to see it. They proceeded up the narrow outside steps, Mairi thinking what an age away was their first travel-stained arrival here, traipsing up this very same flight. Now she approached the Bailie's apartments with a nervous beat of the heart and a tense dryness in her mouth.

The kind merchant welcomed them in with outstretched arms, keeping close to Isabel as he led the way into his withdrawing-room. As usual the Danish King had an amused audience about him as he recounted great tales in halting guttural English and much gesticulation. Mairi's pulse began to race at the sight of Douglas drawing near. He was heart-stoppingly dressed in a deep brown velvet jerkin and hose, sumptuously decorated in silver and pearl. In the candlelight he looked taller and manlier than ever, striding with unselfconscious ease in spite of his height. A smile played on the strong mouth above the dark bearded jaw.

'Welcome,' he kissed Lucy's hand and then Isabel's cheek. 'Lismore; I'm glad to see you at our table,' Douglas greeted him formally but with no hint of irony. Mairi saw with relief her brother bow graciously and return his good wishes. They might never be friends but at least they could be civil to one another for an evening.

Douglas turned his lively eyes on Mairi. 'Dear sister, you look enchanting,' he swept her with a challenging look. 'Remind me to pass on a letter to you - I had meant you to have it yesterday, but you rushed off in such a hurry.' Mairi coloured at the teasing in his voice and reproached him with her emerald eyes.

'As long as there is no tax to pay on the document, sir,' Mairi replied with a provocative jut of her chin. Lucy and Alexander exchanged bemused glances, unable to follow their fencing.

'It will be freely given on my part and no tax at all,' Douglas fixed her with a wicked look. Mairi bit her lip and turned to her brother.

'Come Sandy, and meet some of our Danish friends,' she recovered hurriedly, 'Queen Anne calls them our cousins.'

Douglas let them go with an amused twitch of the mouth and his spirits rose. He felt a strange energy in the company of his stepsister that revitalised him. All was not lost.

The merriment continued as the guests proceeded to the Bailie's table. Mairi noticed with a start she was to sit up near King Christian next to Douglas, with a Danish lord to her other side. As Douglas sat beside her the pulse in her slim neck began a frantic hammering of its own. She kept up a string of conversation with her other partner and heard Douglas banter happily in Danish with the King.

The thin veil of decorum with which the evening began, evaporated and soon the noise in the room grew to a deafening level, some of the men smoking as the Scottish monarch was not present. For the first time, Mairi caught a glimpse of Mary Bain hovering in the doorway. She saw Mairi and smiled her broad, generous smile.

Mairi forced herself to respond, a sickness welling up inside. So Isabel had spoken the truth, Many had come with Douglas to Edinburgh. Hot furious tears pricked her eyes, but she would not show them how she felt. She sat, her hands gripped tightly in her lap, a fixed painful smile on her full lips.

Douglas saw the change in her and looked up to see Mary directing operations to the servants. The little fool, he thought with affectionate irritation, Mairi's jealously blinded her to the truth of his feelings. Some devilry in him decided he would teach her a lesson and play on her ridiculous notion a while longer. He leaned towards her and spoke under the din of the guests.

'Mary is so efficient a housekeeper, the Bailie is quite envious of her skills, Mairi, he would steal her from me.'

Mairi's face burned with indignation. He would rub her nose in the squalor of his affair while she could not escape. He was more despicable than she had imagined. How did she ever allow herself to think of him romantically? Douglas was as two-faced and spiteful as Isabel.

'How nice to be so easily pleased,' Mairi responded with a smile, while her eyes remained cold.

'Oh yes, I am well pleased,' Douglas mocked and leaned closer, so that his warm breath tickled her ear. She smelt the musk on his beard and gulped, her pulse beating erratically. 'You understand how I could not have left her behind.'

Mairi's green eyes smarted with fury. She would not stay to be insulted by his insinuations. All at once, she pushed back her chair and rushed from the table. No one appeared to notice as she escaped out of the door to the outer stairs and the cool night air.

He was hateful! She should never have come, she blamed herself. If only her brother knew how Douglas humiliated her, he would put an end to his overbearing mocking ways. Mairi took deep breaths to calm her emotional state, trying to concentrate on the normal sounds of the town.

Steps behind made her swing round. Douglas stood looming above, a smile still playing on his insufferable face.

'Go away,' she cried, 'I hate you!' She heard a soft laugh deep in his throat as he came down to her.

'Mairi, forgive me,' Douglas stretched out to reach her, 'it was wrong of me to goad you like that. I did not realise how much you believed in your own imaginings.'

'Don't give me that,' she shrunk from his touch, backing off down the steps. 'I know exactly what is going on.'

'No you don't,' Douglas was more serious, 'and now I must tell you once and for all.'

Mairi's green eyes were like hard glass as she glared into his dark ones. 'I don't want to hear,' she put her hands over her ears.

'Mary is betrothed,' Douglas continued, following her down the steps.

'No,' Mairi was on the verge of tears, 'let me be!'

'She and Sam will many in the spring, Mairi,' Douglas gripped her arm hard. 'Do you hear that?'

'You're just saying that,' Mairi gawped at him, her hands sliding from her ears.

'It's true - ask Sam, he's pleased as punch,' Douglas smiled.

Mairi, balancing on the second last step, faltered and began to fall.

Douglas lunged to catch her, pulling her back with a rough forceful tug. Mairi gasped as his arms went about her body, bringing her to him. 'It's true, my wildcat,' he kissed her forehead, 'there must be no more misunderstanding between us.'

Mairi felt the resistance seep out of her as she slumped willingly against his chest.

'Oh Douglas,' she whispered, 'why didn't you tell me before?'

'I was never given the chance,' he laughed low in her ear and nibbled the lobe. 'You went off like a firework when I tried to explain last night.'

Mairi buried her hot face in his doublet, unable to meet his eyes. Gently he lifted her chin and made her look at him. The black-violet eyes were deep with tenderness, his bearded mouth amused and sensuous.

'It's you that I want, Mairi,' he spoke so low she wondered if she had heard correctly. She wanted him to go on holding her, stroking her hair, telling her words that thrilled. She could not speak for the tightness in her throat. 'Ever since the Beltane dance I've thought of little else,' he admitted, his fingers caressing her cheek, running down her throat. He felt her gulp at his touch and carried on.

Mairi could not protest, thankful the lower stairs were in shadow. His very fingertips set her skin alight, so that she tingled the length of her being. 'Tell me you feel the same, my love,' he urged her, bending to plant delicious kisses on her eyebrows, her cheekbones, her chin.

'Douglas, I - ' Mairi was so full of emotion she could only respond by slipping her arms about his neck, her fingers entangling in his thick mane of hair. Briefly their eyes engaged, filled with a passion that neither could speak. Douglas's mouth sought hers and she answered with equal longing. It shook her to the core to taste his mouth and feel him press her against him as if he would crush her.

Douglas released Mairi, her head spinning from the embrace. His breathing came unsteadily. 'I must not kiss you like a kitchen wench on the Bailie's steps,' his voice sounded strangely cracked. He laughed quietly, his eyes full of merriment and warmth.

'No,' Mairi looked at him coyly from under her lashes. 'What would the Danish King think if he knew what his host was up to?'

'He would be jealous as the Devil, I warrant,' Douglas grinned and squeezed her waist. Mairi let a shy giggle escape.

They heard footsteps approaching at the entrance above. Mairi did not care who was about to discover them, but a flash of impatience crossed Douglas's face. He quickly kissed her hand with warm lips, his eyes lingering on her for a moment.

'We must find a way to be alone together, Mairi,' he whispered in a deep rumble, 'and it must be soon.'

Mairi did not have time to answer as a figure appeared above them in the Bailie's doorway. In the lamplight Mairi recognised the golden rugged head of Alexander. He peered out, unable to see his sister standing close to Douglas in the dark.

'Mairi, are you there?' he called in Gaelic.

She moved up the steps and into the light. 'Yes, Sandy,' she smiled back feeling warm with the excitement of the past minutes. 'I was taking some air.' She heard him sigh with relief.

'Good, I thought you had run off upset and I saw Roskill go after you,' he sounded disapproving.

Douglas heard his name mentioned, though not understanding Alexander's words. He gained the steps quickly behind Mairi. She started at the touch of his hand on her bare neck and saw the suspicion cloud her brother's green eyes.

'So I was right,' he reverted to Scots, 'what is the meaning of this?'

'She was safe in my company, Lismore,' Douglas was gently mocking, 'you have nothing to fear.'

Anger smouldered in the weather-beaten face as Alexander took a step nearer them. 'If you are your father's son, then I rightly fear for my sister. I told you before, it is now my duty to protect her, not yours,' his lilting voice took on an icy edge, 'and I can see from the look on her face, it is from you she needs the most protection.'

'Sandy,' Mairi felt stung into a retort. 'I am old enough now to choose my own friends!' She was acutely aware of Douglas's thumb rubbing the back of her neck. 'And Douglas is my friend,' she gulped.

Her stepbrother smiled amiably at the scowling Highland Chief above him. 'You see, Lismore, your worries are without foundation. Surely you would not selfishly keep Mairi to yourself for ever?'

The redheaded young woman between them tensed. Douglas was wickedly trying to provoke Alexander again. Somehow he seemed to be able to get under her brother's skin and irritate like a pest. He was foolishly jeopardising their chances of being together.

'It's time we went home, Mairi,' Alexander commanded, ignoring Douglas's provocation.

A second figure appeared at the doorway; it was the rosy-cheeked Lucy. She took in the scene at a glance, remembering how the two men had sparred before.

'Will you not come back to the feast gentlemen?' she reproved them in her gentle high-pitched way. 'It appears there are more people on the stairs than at the table.'

Mairi smiled thankfully at her friend; Lucy was much better at taking the heat out of the situation than she was. Mairi seemed only capable of fuelling an argument. Douglas laughed and Alexander flushed boyishly.

'It is time I escorted you back to the Palace,' he spoke in his normal quiet tone, 'and leave King Christian to his hosts.' The young women thought it best not to argue at this point and returned to take their leave of the

Bailie and collect Isabel. Douglas mounted the rest of the stairs, stopping Alexander with a hard grip.

'I can see you, too, are not unaffected by a woman's charms,' he spoke low but clear, 'do not try to stand in the way of my happiness Lismore, your sister means much to me.'

Alexander shook off his hold and answered proudly. 'Mairi will decide where her happiness lies and in the meantime I'll safeguard her interests Roskill.'

Douglas saw the challenging look on the Chief's face and his bristling dislike of the man was grudgingly mingled with respect. He should welcome the fact that Lismore felt a protective affection for Mairi and yet it niggled to see the way she acquiesced to his wishes and ignored his own.

Mairi hardly looked at him as they bade farewell. Even as he gave her Florence's letter at last, she did not seem pleased. Was she having second thoughts about her show of feeling towards him? He cursed her brother's untimely appearance; their meetings so far in Edinburgh had been thwarted with bad luck.

Mairi was silent on the walk home, clutching her mother's letter which Douglas had thrust into her hands as they left. He had seemed angry and eager to be rid of it. So he was not going to use it as an excuse to seek her out alone after all. Douglas was behaving like a typically ill-tempered Roskill because he could not get his own way for once. She had agreed to go with Alexander and the others and he obviously felt she should have stayed by his side. But it was not that simple and she still was unsure of his motives. Desire her, she knew Douglas did, but she would not just be his plaything until his father arranged a better match. He had yet to prove to her he was sincere in his feelings and not just sporting with her.

The evening, however, had gone flat and Mairi did not feel like joining in the chatter of Lucy and Alexander. Even Isabel was animated and talked without malice, several times mentioning their kind host Bailie Greeves. How strange she was in her likes and dislikes, Mairi mused, she would never understand her contrary stepsister.

Alone in her chamber, Mairi tore open the letter from her mother and devoured it word by word, her eyes misting up with tears at the naked affection in the beautiful script. Her mother had been born to a scholarly Lowland nobleman and had been tutored in reading and writing like a son. It was Florence who had instilled the same learning into her daughter during the first long dreary days at Duntorin.

Sarah and the servants asked for news of her, Duntorin was impossibly bad-tempered since the young people had all left and Zechariah Black had gone from the parish of Duntorin. What good tidings.

Her heart quickened at the next phrase.

'But something of importance may bring us to Edinburgh before long.

It concerns you too, my dear child, and your stepbrother Douglas. Perhaps you can guess?'

Mairi fell her stomach turn over at the words. She dared not hope they could mean marriage between them. Had Duntorin, on reflection, had a change of heart? She could not wait to see Douglas again and show him the letter. He might know more of their thinking. If her mother backed such a union, it would not take much to persuade Alexander that it was a good idea. Happiness bubbled up inside and Mairi felt like bursting into song. She wanted desperately to be with Douglas now, to share in the expectation, to see the tenderness in the dark eyes shining for her alone. Was it possible he had known of the plans ever since he had come to Edinburgh? It would be so like him to tease her and not let her guess until he was sure of her response. Well he had received her answer in the willingness of her kisses.

Mairi turned to the last page of the letter and continued to read.

'My dear one, I must now tell you the sad news and you must bear it bravely. Our Agnes passed on a fortnight ago and was buried in the family graveyard. She was a true friend to us all and to you especially, Mairi. You returned that love generously with your own, I know. To her last day she spoke of you and now she rests at peace.'

Mairi's eyes burned with tears of regret. Her first friend at Duntorin was gone and she would never again hear the infectious cackle or listen to the old woman's stories. Closing her eyes, Mairi felt the hot tears squeeze from under her lids and course down her cheeks.

From nowhere, Agnes's words of warning echoed in her head. 'Trust no one; promise me you will trust no one, Mairi.'

CHAPTER EIGHT

Douglas was restless after the departure of his guests. He wanted to carry on drinking, but the Bailie was tired and wished to retire. He decided instead to walk off his pent up energy in the High Street; the night air was sharp and would clear his head of conflicting thoughts.

Douglas strode out of the close, fretting about Mairi. He was sure she felt strongly for him and yet he was not satisfied. She was passionate by nature and responded naturally to his advances. But had she not equally flared at Boswell when he had disturbed them in the gallery? He could not be sure she did not feel the same for the aggravating vain rake, who had been Douglas's rival at school. He wished Boswell had stayed and had his sport in England instead of returning to ingratiate his way into King James's confidence. Their intelligent and wily monarch appeared to have lost his head over the young arrogant courtier who could do no wrong.

Candlelight still flickered low inside a nearby tavern. On the spur of the moment, Douglas decided to stop and find company with the late-night drinkers.

Bending under the low archway he squinted into the dim room. For a moment he paused as his eyes grew accustomed to the gloom. In the corner four men were huddled over a table in deep conversation, while nearer the door the tavern-keeper and two local women sat joking by a cask of claret.

The cackle of their laughter drowned out Douglas's arrival for several moments. He glanced again at the corner table seeing two behatted men rise and, taking their leave, slip out by the back storeroom. Something in the covert way they left, struck Douglas as suspicious, the men not wanting to be seen leaving by the High Street entrance. No doubt they were smugglers completing a bargain, but it was no concern of his. Still it puzzled Douglas that one of them had looked oddly familiar. By his clothes he was a gentleman and the flicker of candlelight across his features showed a man more mature than Douglas by some years. The other could have been foreign; he was dressed in the southern way.

Suddenly he found the place stiflingly distasteful and he had no wish to be caught up in anyone else's intrigue. But as Douglas turned to go, one of the women saw him and called loudly for him to join them. Young Duntorin hesitated not wanting to appear rude and in that moment one of the remaining intriguers kicked out a stool for him.

'Well, well, if it isn't the Danish man of action,' a familiar voice drawled. Douglas swirled to meet Boswell's mocking face, flickering distortedly in the candle's flame. 'Come to find some solace with Beatrice here no doubt?'

Douglas clenched his jaw, not wanting to give Boswell the satisfaction of seeing him provoked.

'A last drink in pleasant company is all I ask,' Douglas looked across in contempt. 'But seeing you here shows me that cannot be.'

Boswell laughed.

'But I insist you join Ruthven and myself, Roskill, or are you pining too much for your sweet stepsister, to hold your drink with men?' A bawdy shriek of laughter from the women goaded Douglas across to the vacant stool, all the time the mysterious figures of the departed noblemen nagging at the back of his mind. What devilry was Boswell concocting now? Douglas allowed an empty goblet before him to be filled, intrigued to discover his game. He knocked back the bitter draught that sent fire into his limbs. Boswell was slurring his words but Douglas instinctively felt it was an act, covering up a quick-thinking maliciousness.

'And how are your sisters,' Boswell leaned over the table, 'as tempting as ever?' Douglas felt the muscles taut in his face. He yearned to answer Boswell's insinuations with a swift blow to the smug pretty face. 'If I have to choose though, I'd prefer the charms of that delectable redhead.'

Douglas jumped to his feet, knocking the stool from under him and was across the table and taking Boswell by the throat before anyone realised it.

'Don't speak of her you worm,' he spat the words in the scared face. 'I'll have you skewered if you so much as touch her!'

Ruthven grabbed him from behind and tried to pull Boswell's aggressor off, but he clung like a vice.

'Too late,' the youngest brother of Brae gave a strangled cry, squirming in his grasp, 'I already have.'

Douglas felt his head fill with blood as he smote Boswell with a ringing blow to his jaw. The young rival went down with a thud and a curse, staying on the floor for safety's sake. He felt his chin and winced with pain. Douglas stood trembling above him, Ruthven braving his fury to drag back his arms.

'I will not hit a man who cowers on the floor,' Douglas shook him off roughly and stood glaring with hatred at the frightened man rolling in agony. 'You lie Boswell,' Douglas's voice was strained with anger, 'and you will take back those words that besmirch Mairi's name.'

Boswell threw him a petulant loathing look, 'I cannot take back what I say - and cannot give back what has already been taken,' he hissed spitefully. 'Ask your innocent stepsister about the Queen's Pavilion in the Park and see if she blushes.'

Douglas resisted the supreme temptation to kick Boswell out into the street and make him fight like a gentleman for his boasts. But a wicked doubt inside mocked him; it was possible Mairi had been foolish enough to succumb to her wild emotions and given in to this philanderer. She would not be the first by any means and she had been away from Duntorin for several months. Why should she have waited for him? He had given her no

103

indication before she left that she was still special to him, parting with cool words and reproachful looks.

Yet he found it intolerable to think Mairi enjoyed Boswell's company; she was an independent spirit who could not be taken in by his empty words and gestures. He hated himself for even considering Boswell's story, it was said merely to provoke.

The felled courtier saw Douglas's hesitation and took advantage.

'I don't want to fight over a woman, Roskill,' he tried to make light of the situation, 'but I have heard that Mairi was first sent to Court by your father to keep her apart from you.' He watched warily at the muscle flinching in his rival's cheek. 'I only press my case knowing that she is out of your reach Douglas - and because the lady has a certain attraction for me, I must confess.'

'Get up,' Douglas hissed savagely, 'get up, you whimpering dog!' He inwardly cursed Isabel for her meddling; the information could only have come from her, unless Mairi . . .? He could not bear to think of her discussing their relationship with this wretch.

The landlord stirred himself to come between them and Douglas realised he had no more stomach for their company. Even the pleasant Ruthven seemed totally in Boswell's power.

'Just keep out of my way,' Douglas spoke with deadly calm, 'if you want to die of old age.'

He went, the words of the viper ringing in his ears, nagging his tired mind with doubts. Douglas decided once and for all he must discover Mairi's true feelings for him or whether Boswell was already her lover. He did not trust himself to see her just now; he must think things over calmly.

As he took the steps to Duntorin's apartment, it came to him; one of the secret visitors at Boswell's table was Ruthven's older brother, the Earl of Gowrie. What was such a powerful baron doing skulking in a High Street bothy with a stranger? And what, in heaven's name, were they all up to, he wondered uneasily?

Mairi's fitful sleep was filled with tantalising dreams of Douglas reaching out for her and then disappearing like mist on autumn hills. She woke, strangely uneasy, her mother's letter crumpled beneath her pillow. The next two days were hectic with preparations for the masked ball and Holyroodhouse echoed to the shouts and movements of servants and guests. Mairi revelled in the practice dancing, life had never been so full of joy and excitement and Lucy delighted in her friend's happiness, the only one to share her secret hopes brought by the letter.

'I have spoken to the Queen of Alexander's plea for my cousin Cailean,' Mairi told Lucy as they laid out the fancy dress costumes.

'Oh, Mairi, does that mean Alexander will be leaving?' Lucy's face crinkled with worry.

'I know he will not want to leave,' she answered gently, 'but his mission is a matter of life or death for many people. If the King relents and gives Cailean more time to produce his charters, my brother will have to return soon and bring Cailean to Court with him.'

Lucy's face brightened a fraction, 'Then let him return swiftly,' she answered, unusually shy, 'for I shall miss him greatly.'

Mairi reached out and hugged Lucy close. She would like nothing better than to have her friend become her sister by marriage, but this was a hard, dangerous world and tomorrow's happiness could not be assured. They must take their pleasure while they could.

'Come Lucy,' Mairi chivvied her companion, 'Alexander is here for the masquerade and we will have fun tonight.' Her friend laughed, unable to hide her high spirits for long.

As Mairi dressed in the privacy of her own room, she felt a pang of anxiety; there had been no word from Douglas since the night of the banquet and she was impatient to see him again and talk of their parents' proposed visit. There must be some simple explanation, she blushed at her own wish for haste; he had been hunting with the two Kings or doing business for his father. Alexander's threats could not have put him off; Douglas would see them rather as a challenge.

She put on a white loose gown scattered with a design of birds, fruit and flowers. On top of this Mairi wore a silvery gauze overgown which Lucy had helped decorate with spangles and edge with lace. She called in Margaret to help her comb out her long hair and set the crescent moon of pearls as her headdress. Her chattering servant had picked fresh scented flowers which she entwined in her unbound red-gold tresses.

'Did you pick these with your Tam?' Mairi asked, squeezing her maid's hand. Margaret blushed and giggled in reply.

'They make you look like the real Goddess Diana, Mistress,' the girl answered proudly, looking approvingly from the blue and white pearled slippers up to the white slim neck and cascading gleaming hair.

'Thank you Margaret,' Mairi flushed pink with nervous pleasure. 'Tonight I feel ready for music and hunting by moonlight! Look, I even persuaded Prince Henry to lend me his toy bow and arrow.'

Soon joined by Lucy in sparkling sea-green and blue as the Queen's ocean nymph, Mairi rushed to attend Queen Anne at the grand entrance. Mairi pulled her spangled gauze veil over her face as the others attached their red masks to their faces. Queen Anne looked magnificent in her elaborate costume and crown of gold and jewels and feathers. The King would certainly be impressed by her queenly grace and bearing. Their royal mistress declared that they would dance first before the assembled guests and then dine. Lucy squeezed Mairi's hand in encouragement and she smiled back nervously, her heart racing as the doors opened to the Banqueting Hall and the minstrels began to play.

The room was ablaze with light and the hubbub of noise rose into gasps of appreciation as the procession appeared. Mairi thought the hammering in her breast would drown out the lively music of the flutes and strings. She concentrated hard on the dance, not daring to look around for Douglas until she felt more composed. She was the goddess of the moon and the chase and threw herself into the imaginary part with a light step and a glint in her eyes.

The women followed the torch bearers, carrying garlands of flowers for their Queen. Finally the music stopped and the King came forward to congratulate his wife and bring her to his side. Mairi knew he did not care for dancing himself, although he loved the spectacle of the masque. It was now the turn of the masqueraders to invite the guests to dance. Mairi looked around in trepidation for Douglas, wanting only to dance with him.

Their eyes met across the room and Mairi smiled shyly at his dark handsome face. He looked stern, but it must be a trick of the light catching his strongly cut features. He could not still be smarting at Alexander's words. With relief she saw him move towards her in long quick strides. Douglas took her hand and kissed it roughly, his dark eyes smouldering as they took in the loose flowing hair and the small figure outlined in the fairy-tale gown. To Mairi's growing dismay he pulled her into the dance without a word.

'Is there something wrong?' she whispered under cover of the music. His dark velvet eyes flashed down at her questioningly.

'You are enchanting, sweet Mairi,' he seemed to mock her with the compliment, 'and I wonder for whom you dress so divinely?'

'I do not understand you,' Mairi flushed and answered haughtily. He must know it was he she sought to please, though she would not be made to say it. His jealousy over her brother was ridiculous; if he had eyes in his head, he would see Alexander was so besotted about Lucy Seton he did not even notice with whom his sister danced.

'I thought I understood you,' Douglas said harshly, a sardonic smile on his lips that did not warm the accusing eyes, 'until I met with Robert Boswell.' Mairi jumped at the name and Douglas gave a short cruel laugh, watching the scarlet confusion flood up into her cheeks. 'So it is true, my little wildcat,' Douglas gripped her hand painfully in the dance, 'you and Boswell are lovers and I am a fool.'

Mairi could not believe what she was hearing. What lies had that evil son of Brae been speaking about her? She could not bear to see the hurt harrowed look on Douglas's face.

'Whatever he has been telling you, is not true if it concerns me,' she answered defiantly. 'I dislike Boswell and am shocked you believe his lies,' her green eyes were reproachful. 'Anyway it is Isabel you should worry about,' Mairi turned in the dance to face him directly, 'she is as obsessed with him as by the foul Zechariah Black.'

Douglas gripped her arm tighter, wordlessly searching her face for the truth. He had disbelieved Mairi once before about Isabel and the minister and had been proved wrong. She had been sent from Duntorin as a result of his mistake, could he trust her now? He too had noticed Isabel's interest in Boswell and had not cautioned his sister.

Mairi gave back his look, a defiant goddess dazzling in the spangle-sparkling gown that floated around her like waves in the candlelight. The crescent moon of pearls twinkled as a crown on the molten red hair. At that moment, Douglas cared not what poisonous words Boswell had said. The beautiful woman who looked at him now had not a trace of secrecy or guilt in the glassy green eyes.

Douglas swept her hand impulsively to his lips.

'Forgive me,' he whispered hoarsely, 'I was consumed with jealousy at the thought.'

A smile of relief trembled at Mairi's red lips. She must not allow Boswell or anyone to come between them. She would take care to avoid the feline courtier, who at least for now, was content to flatter and dance with Isabel. He must know that it was Douglas who held her heart and not him. It was just wicked sport that had led Boswell to needle Douglas about her. As the dance finished, Mairi looked eagerly up at her dark partner.

'I have news I must discuss with you,' she gave him a coy look; 'perhaps you know it already?'

'What is it that brings such a becoming flush to your face, wildcat?' he asked amusedly. 'Has the Queen ordered some new page's outfits for you?'

'No,' she slipped a hand through his arm, 'guess again. It concerns my mother's letter.' Douglas's eyes widened.

'I'm not in the habit of unsealing private correspondence,' he joked, 'so unless you enlighten me, I will be guessing all night.'

She hesitated suddenly embarrassed to mention the words that set her heart racing.

'Well, it concerns the two of us . . .' her gaze dropped to the floor at her tongue-tied state.

'Douglas Roskill,' it was the Queen's voice that called across the top table, 'come and be sitting near to me.'

Their heads shot round at the royal command and Douglas bowed in acceptance. He quickly turned to Mairi.

'Let us meet somewhere after the masque.'

Mairi gulped excitedly. 'The Queen's Pavilion in the grounds,' she answered swiftly, 'it is quiet and away from the Palace, no one goes there.' She noticed Douglas's brow draw into a frown at the suggestion and wondered if he thought her too forward. 'Or where you wish,' she added more subdued.

'Then let it be there,' Douglas answered curtly. 'I will wait to see you leave and then follow.'

He moved away from her, a smile and gracious comment for the Queen. Mairi looked after him, puzzled by his sudden change of mood. She consoled herself with the thought they would be alone soon and once she had shown him her mother's letter there would be no more doubting, only celebration. Her pulse quickened in anticipation.

She watched the rest of the merry masque as if from a distance, the Danish lords enjoying their last evening to the full. She rejoiced at Alexander's attentiveness to the wide-eyed and vivacious Lucy and with thankfulness noted the only attention she received from Boswell was the occasional insolent sweep of the hard blue eyes.

Mairi took Lucy aside and told her of her plan to meet Douglas. The fair haired young woman gave her an encouraging squeeze of the hand and said she would keep her brother out of the way this time. With her duties done, Mairi picked her moment to slip from the dining-hall, catching Douglas's eye before she disappeared.

Through the empty lobby she ran and out into the antechamber that led to the spiral staircase down to the ground floor. Out into the night past the guards, she felt the cool air gusting about her white shift and delicate gown, quickening her pace to reach the darkness of the ghostly Pavilion, away from the prying eyes of the Palace.

The trysting place was empty. With a childish laugh she threw herself onto the bench and waited. Within moments she heard his steps, soft and conspiratorial. Mairi felt the ache of longing and excitement squeeze her insides. She jumped up to meet Douglas with a welcome kiss. The dark shadow of her sweetheart showed in the doorway. Something checked Mairi's eager step; the atmosphere was not right, the statue of the man was too slight.

'Waiting for me, my lovely creature?' the syrupy tones of a familiar voice oozed in the dark towards her. 'I knew you would be here in our special meeting place.'

'Boswell!' Mairi exclaimed, her heart freezing. 'What are you doing here?' He laughed softly and she began to make out the slim outline of his face and smooth chin in the dark.

'Don't be so coy,' he swung himself from the doorway towards her, 'you expected me to follow, wanted me to, didn't you?'

'No,' her reply was a strangled whisper, 'you must go away. Please Boswell, go away!' Mairi felt panic rising tide-like up through her chest and throat. Douglas would be here at any moment and could not be blamed for believing the worst. How could Boswell do this to her? He must hate her or Douglas to do such a thing.

Had he been watching them all evening, ready to make his move and cause a scene between them? It came to her in a rush that this was why

Douglas had turned cold at the mention of the Pavilion; Boswell must have spoken of their meeting here before. She was in no doubt that he would have coloured the chance encounter differently and the idea of his scheming made her suddenly mad with anger.

'Stand away from me!' Mairi snapped. 'You know it is not you I wish to meet here.'

She saw Boswell check his stealthy advance. His next words were said lightly but with an undercurrent of menace.

'You do not mean that you wait for that hot-head Roskill, my sweetest? If so, you are foolish to encourage him.'

'I do not need a man of your reputation to advise me!' Mairi threw the words in his face.

He sprang forward like a beast striking its prey and grabbed her upper arms. Mairi froze in shock.

'You will soon understand that no one denies Robert Boswell, sweet wench,' his soft tone belied the cruel set of his mouth and glint in the jewel-hard eyes. 'You will soon be mine.'

'Why me?' Mairi whispered in fear. 'It is Isabel who loves you.' His lace came close to hers so that she was overpowered by the sickly perfume on his chin and clothes.

'Love is for children,' he spoke contemptuously, 'and it is you I desire.'

Boswell pulled her on to his wiry body and descended on the mutinous lips. Mairi was appalled. The kiss revolted her and she wondered how she had ever found him attractive.

Douglas heard no movement as he strode quickly towards the shadowed building, wondering if he had mistaken the place of rendezvous. He was about to turn and look for another such summer retreat when he caught the sound of rustling and a person's breath. Gaining the entrance, his eyes began to distinguish between the shadows and he saw the two figures locked together. It took only seconds to recognise that the man entwined with Mairi was Boswell. A red rage blinded Douglas as he sprang to wrest them apart.

'You blackguard,' he bellowed, seizing the impostor by the shoulders, 'release her at once!'

Boswell neatly side-stepped Douglas's heavier frame and eluded the hands that tore at his peacock blue velvet doublet. He panted, the taste of Mairi's lips arousing his appetite.

'Turning up like a faithful dog again, Roskill,' he sneered, 'can you not leave the maid alone?'

Douglas pulled back his right arm and sent a clenched fist swinging against Boswell's nose. Mairi heard a cracking sound and a yelp of pain from the victim. In the near dark she saw the black stream of blood spurt from his nostrils. Douglas spun round on the mute and shaking Mairi. He could not see her expression under the gleam of the crescent moon in

109

her hair. He had acted so swiftly he had not stopped to think if he was in fact breaking up a lovers' embrace.

Surely Mairi could not have lured him here to flaunt her affair with this hell-raiser? Was it revenge for the way he had cruelly treated her at Duntorin, all an elaborate plot to inveigle him here and ridicule his passion for her? She did not rush into his arms with tearful thanks, he thought savagely.

Douglas could not see the silent dry sobs convulsing her body. Mairi watched him, painfully aware of the fury he directed towards her. He would never now believe that she cared nothing for the hateful son of Brae, having caught her in his arms in a seemingly intimate embrace. How Douglas must loathe her at this moment; Mairi had never seen such disgust register on his dark bearded face.

'You see, Roskill,' Boswell's voice sounded muffled with his handkerchief pressed to his broken nose, 'she does not thank you for your interference. You make a fool of yourself.'

Douglas let out an angry oath, restraining himself from further damaging the pretty face of Boswell.

'Douglas - ' Mairi forced herself to speak to defend her reputation and salvage some of his hurt pride.

'I don't want to hear,' he shouted at her, 'I can see with my own eyes what has happened.'

'No you don't see,' Mairi responded with pent-up frustration, 'I did not know he would be here. It's another of his vicious tricks to make you despise me.'

'I don't know what to believe,' Douglas replied angrily, 'but you will not stay with this toad a moment longer. It is an insult to both the houses of Lismore and Duntorin!' He seized her by the arm and pulled her after him.

'You will regret this indignity towards me!' Boswell screamed after them. 'This is not the end of the matter by far.'

Douglas did not stop to argue more. Mairi wriggled to release his grip, mortified to be dragged about like a naughty child.

'Let go!' she railed against him. 'You hurt me.'

Douglas, for the first time conscious of what he was doing, let her loose. His head throbbed with the uncontrolled outburst he had allowed to happen. Never had he made such a spectacle of himself over anyone. Why, he wondered, did the woman he cared for most, always inspire such pain and anger? His attraction to Mairi was beyond comprehension. She walked beside him in silence now. He had won his battle with Boswell and yet he felt Mairi more distant to him than she had ever been. Perhaps they could never be close as he had so wished since his return from Denmark.

'I will see you safely to the Palace,' he spoke with rigid courtesy, 'then you will no longer be troubled by my presence.'

Mairi bit her lip in anguish, hot tears stinging her eyes.

'Yes Douglas,' was all she could manage. It was a hopeless task to make him trust her. He did not want her explanation. Now that he was icily polite, she yearned to hear the teasing in his voice again and see the warm laughter in his eyes.

How could she tell him of her mother's hints at their marriage? It was all too late, their brief happiness destroyed by the serpent Boswell for his own perverse reasons. Even if a marriage was planned for them, Douglas would never go along with it now, his pride and faith in her too blighted.

As he turned and bowed curtly at the entrance to Holyroodhouse, he seemed a thousand leagues away from her. Mairi was too full to answer his abrupt goodnight. She pivoted round in her flowing gown and fled. Gone was the goddess of the moon and the hunt with expectations so high. The dress was a cruel reminder of the joy of the masque and she could not wait to be rid of it.

Douglas watched her go with a heaviness of heart he had never felt the weight of before. Isabel found him in the courtyard about to leave. She had seen with satisfaction, Mairi fleeing in distress to the upper apartments, ignoring her questions. She had looked away with hurt green eyes and hurried on in a shimmer of gauze and spangles. It was clear to Isabel she had argued with Douglas who turned restlessly on his heels. It was a relief to see that the feeling between them was fading. Mairi was no good for Douglas; he must make a better match than a wild-tempered, Gaelic-speaking Highlander. For that was what Mairi still remained in spite of the civilising influence of her upbringing at Duntorin. Her brother would marry a high born woman of grace and bearing to be mistress of Duntorin, someone who would respect the special relationship Douglas had with his sister and always take second place.

'Brother,' she caught up with him, 'there is no need to hurry away so soon. Stay and dance a while longer.' Douglas looked down into the dark eyes fixed on him lovingly and could not help wishing they were the sea green of Mairi's. Isabel saw the grim set of his mouth and the puckered brow forbidding light conversation. Then his expression softened into its customary smile, though more wistful.

'I do not feel like dancing at this moment, sister,' he laid a hand on her shoulder. 'It has been a long evening and tomorrow I ride with the King to Leith to bid our Danish friends a safe voyage home.'

Isabel smiled. 'Does that mean you will shortly be leaving for Duntorin again Douglas? I shall miss you so.'

Douglas squeezed her shoulder lightly, his eyes looking beyond.

'Perhaps I shall stay a while longer. King James will need someone to hunt with when the excitement of the royal visit is over.'

Isabel's face tightened. It would be better if he left soon and forgot his feelings for Mairi; she did not trust that, with the redheaded girl around,

Douglas would not be quick to make up his quarrel.

'Are you not needed at home?' she asked primly. 'Father has been patient in letting you come to Court at such a busy time of year for our lands.'

'I'll not be lectured by my younger sister too,' Douglas replied sharply. 'I may return to soldiering in Denmark if my relations continue to nag like old nurses.' Isabel flushed at the rebuke.

'That is not what I want,' she assured him, laying a diffident hand on his arm. 'It's just you will have responsibilities to take on soon Douglas. You should be thinking of a wife, for instance, and heirs for Duntorin.'

Douglas started at the bold look in his sister's eyes and her forward speech. The thought had crossed his mind of late, but after recent events he was not so sure. The woman he wanted did not return his advances and he would not be rushed into a marriage of convenience just to please his father.

'And what about my sister?' he gave her a sardonic look. 'I should see her married off before I take a wife.' He watched with glee as the pale face changed colour in the dim light. 'Perhaps you have an opinion on the matter Isabel?'

The dark gaze dropped from his and Douglas saw her lost in childish confusion for the first time in years. He had guessed the truth; there was someone special in Isabel's heart. At once a cold foreboding gripped him inside and Mairi's words came back like chimes to remind him. 'It is Isabel you should worry about, she is obsessed by him . . .' she could not seriously want to marry Boswell?

But why not? His family were one of the most powerful in Scotland, only Robert was a younger son and would need to make a good marriage of his own. Duntorin would probably approve as a past comrade of Brae's, unaware of Boswell's increasing notoriety with women. He would dismiss Douglas's fears with the retort that it was youthful sport and the man would settle down in marriage.

And if Boswell were out of the way, he could not take advantage of Mairi, Douglas thought selfishly. The picture of her embracing Boswell in the dark Pavilion rushed unwanted into his mind. What a damn fool he was to think that would make any difference. Boswell was determined to have Mairi and she seemed reluctant to parry his advances. He should admit it now, she cared more for young Brae than she did for him and he would not make a laughing-stock of himself by chasing after Mairi.

Isabel looked at him cautiously. 'Why are you so silent brother? Can you not guess who I love?' She saw Douglas's face cloud angrily and he jutted out his black-bearded chin.

'If it's Boswell, then you should forget him,' he answered tersely. Isabel's eyes narrowed with annoyance.

'You do not wish me to be happy with anyone I care for Douglas,' she was petulant, 'bur this is different. We have both declared our love for each other.'

Douglas could not bear to see the expectation shining in her face. She was cruelly deceived by both Boswell and her stepsister, as he was too.

'Don't say that!' Douglas cried with exasperation. 'It worried me that you might feel something for this man with the habits of a cur.'

'How dare you call him that,' Isabel flared back at him, her body trembling with indignation, 'and he a friend of yours.'

'He is no friend of mine, be sure of that,' Douglas answered bitterly, 'and of yours neither.'

'Stop it Douglas,' Isabel was furious, her dark eyes gleaming with uncontrolled rage. 'I will have him!' she screamed in the tranquil courtyard. Douglas was suddenly unnerved by her outburst. He had seen this madness in her eyes once before. He came forward and put his arms about her to stop her shaking.

'Do not trust him,' Douglas said with quiet authority, 'his interests lie elsewhere Isabel, I'm sorry but it's best you know.'

Douglas felt her struggling to throw him off. 'You are hateful,' she spat at him, 'and you lie about my Robert.'

Douglas was full of a quick anger. 'I found him trying to seduce your stepsister,' he said harshly, forcing her to look at him. 'And from what I saw, I was wrong to interrupt,' his voice was a cold dead rasp.

He heard her moan as her head dropped back and she began hitting him with her captive fists. The look in the tortured black eyes was hate-filled. She still would not believe him. At that moment there was a scrape of feet behind them and a lithe shadow appeared, faltering at their unexpected presence. Isabel looked over Douglas's shoulder at Boswell. She saw the bloodied enlarged nose and froze. No words passed between any of them as he sauntered with studied indifference into the Palace.

The fight went out of Isabel. The broken nose and the hostility between the men told her Douglas's story was true. So Mairi had run in tears from the scene because her brother had torn her away from Boswell, not from a lovers' tiff between themselves.

A deep loathing stirred like a waking snake in the pit of Isabel's stomach at the thought of her pretty stepsister. Mairi would always stand in the way of her happiness as long as she lived. How she hated her at this moment; the thief of her beautiful Boswell.

She allowed Douglas to steer her back to Holyroodhouse without protest. She was numb with shock, but there would be revenge. There must be some way of slaking the jealousy that festered like a sore in her breast, else she would go quite mad.

Her silence worried Douglas more than the screams and blows. He wondered bleakly if he had been wrong to tell her the truth. Everything he did seemed to make matters worse for everyone. Perhaps Isabel was right and he should leave soon for Duntorin, putting all these troublesome relationships behind him.

CHAPTER NINE

Florence watched as her husband rode in at the head of his entourage and wondered nervously if his mission had been a success. The set craggy face under the tall feathered hat told her nothing; it could mean the satisfaction of negotiations accomplished or the grim mask of rejection. She thought with a smile, it rarely denoted the latter. John Duntorin was not easily refused.

It had been days since she had last heard his gruff bark and felt his robust presence about the Castle. Blissful peace had descended at first, but now Florence was eager to have his company once more and hear the dry wit of his observations.

The door to the parlour burst open and John Duntorin strode in still booted and wrapped in his cloak. His arms flew out to receive his wife.

'Florence!' his face creased into a broad grin. She smiled with welcome, the pale green eyes glistening warmly. 'I hate going away,' he enfolded her in a hug, kissing the silver stand in her hair, 'but it is worth it for the returning.'

Florence laughed into his deep-throated chuckle.

'It's nice to be missed,' she kissed him back. 'And were you well received at Hoddington?' she slipped her hand in his and led him to the window-seats.

'My old friend Seton was well pleased, my love,' he answered with a grin. 'It seems his daughter has already talked of our son since his arrival at Court. So the young couple should be content with our arrangements.'

'Good,' Florence sighed with relief. She felt better with the thought that Douglas must have got over Mairi and made his mark elsewhere. She did not want to see her stepson hurt unnecessarily.

'And the dowry is most generous,' Duntorin clapped his hands.

'The Setons show how they value their daughter's marriage with the heir to my lands.'

'And such a presentable young man too,' Florence smiled encouragingly. It would be nice to have a young woman in the household again to lessen the aching void she still felt at Mairi's departure.

'And so my dear wife,' Duntorin said brightly, 'I must prepare for the journey to Edinburgh. I wish to see things underway. I'll send word to Bailie Greeves that I'll be there by the end of the week.'

Florence's face clouded. Surely he was prepared to lay the old ghost of his first wife to rest and take her to stay at the Edinburgh mansion? She longed to see her daughter and partake in the celebrations of Douglas's betrothal.

'John, you cannot leave me here while you go to see our children?' she asked in disbelief.

He pulled at his grey beard, the bushy brows knitting together in thought. 'There is rumour of a shortage of water in the town,' he avoided her look, 'and I fear an outbreak of sickness during such a hot spell.'

Florence pulled him gently round to meet her eyes. 'There cannot be danger if you are willing to go,' she chided. 'I will risk the inconvenience of scant water to see my child and to be with you.'

Duntorin smiled quizzically at his wife. 'I am lucky indeed to have you,' he growled low. 'But if there is the slightest hint of fever, we will leave immediately.'

Florence's face lit with joy at his acceptance. 'And what of the other matter, John?' she asked tentatively.

Duntorin knew at once what was on his wife's mind; he had wrestled with the dilemma while riding back from the south.

'That shall be arranged too,' he promised gruffly. Florence smiled and leant up to kiss his ermine flecked beard. He had acquiesced on this point too and they were now in agreement. Strange then, that she could not help the feeling of unease clutching her at the thought of Mairi.

Lucy found Mairi in the nursery playing listlessly with the Princess Elizabeth. Prince Henry had gone off to find someone with whom he could play bows and arrows, as his favourite Queen's maid was no fun this morning. Lucy went to the window and gazed out.

'Have you made no attempt to see him yet?' her fair friend turned to ask gently. Mairi pressed her lips together stubbornly and shook her head. 'Mairi, he may return home without ever realising how you feel,' Lucy sounded more abrupt. 'At least he is still within reach while he spends days hunting with King James.'

Mairi shot a quick look and saw the uncharacteristic sad light in the cornflower blue eyes. She was selfish not to notice the pain Lucy was in too. Alexander had left for the Highlands the day the Danes had departed, over two weeks ago. The customary sparkle and mischief had deserted her with him. Even Queen Anne had noticed the difference in her maids and scolded them for being poor company indeed.

'What's the point of trying?' Mairi asked obstinately, tickling the kitten which scratched playfully at her hand. 'Even Isabel believes Boswell and I are lovers. She has become as tight-lipped and withdrawn as she did after the Black affair. They have both closed their ears to me.'

Lucy came over and knelt beside Mairi.

'You're both as stupidly proud as each other,' she answered with more force. 'It's obvious to me he feels as deeply as you do. What does it matter what Isabel thinks anyway? It's Douglas who's important.'

Mairi smiled wanly at her confidante. Lucy was pining for Alexander her brother, but would not let melancholy overtake her, as she did. Her friend looked forward to the day the Chief of Lismore would return, bringing the recalcitrant Cailean back to Court with him, to pay respect to King James. Mairi's pleas via the Queen had at least not gone unheard.

The Seton daughter persisted against the defiant silence of Mairi.

'If you don't make up your quarrel with Douglas then everyone will assume Boswell is your man. Go now and see Roskill,' Lucy urged. 'Boswell is at least away on some jaunt of his own at the moment, so now is your chance. I know Douglas will listen.

'Why else do you think he remains in Edinburgh so long after the Danes have gone?'

Mairi felt a flicker of hope. It was true; Boswell and his friend Ruthven seemed to have disappeared since the masque, no doubt to allow his nose to mend out of the eye of the King and the Court. Was it possible Douglas might accept her word without rebuttal? She would not go begging for his forgiveness, after all, it was he who had assumed the worst of her. Apologies should come from him.

She fought with her feelings, pride battling against the love she felt for the dark, tempestuous noble. What if Lucy was right about Douglas's feelings for her? She could be throwing away the last chance of happiness between them. If Duntorin found out the rumours she was Boswell's woman, there would be no thought of her being allowed to marry his son anyway. If she did not act now, she might never see Douglas again to find out what he really felt.

'Perhaps you are right,' Mairi agreed slowly, looking sidelong at Lucy, who smiled generously.

'Then you will go?' she asked. Mairi nodded stiffly, releasing the kitten. 'Good,' Lucy got up, 'I've arranged for Margaret to accompany you into town,' she said briskly. 'I happen to know Douglas does not hunt with the King today. There seem to be preparations going on for a visit to the Bailie's house.'

Mairi's eyes opened wide with amazement. 'You little schemer!' she cried at Lucy's pink amused face. 'You expected me to agree all along didn't you?'

'Of course,' Lucy pouted, 'I know you well enough by now, Mairi.' They both laughed for the first time in days. 'And on the subject of visits, I expect my father at any moment; he is in Edinburgh on business.'

'Oh, I'd like to meet him Lucy,' Mairi smiled. The small Princess gurgled with laughter too, roughly rocking the baby Prince Charles in his cradle. 'Careful with your wee brother, Elizabeth,' Mairi caught the podgy hand, 'we want him to grow up into a big strong Prince.'

Mary Bain came in and curtsied swiftly. 'There's a visitor for you, sir,' she smiled openly at Douglas, catching Sam's eye on the way out. Sam nodded and followed Many, saying he had much to do before their guests arrived on the morrow. When Mairi heard Mary close the door behind,

Douglas was bent over a table full of papers and accounts.

It seemed an age before he looked up and she thought him deliberately ignoring her and making her wait like a servant. But when he glanced up at the visitor he seemed quite taken aback.

'Mairi?' he stood regarding her with dark pools for eyes. Douglas looked tired, his dark hair tousled, his silk shirt open beneath the leather jerkin like the soldier she had first encountered at the Beltane dance. The pulse under her chin began to hammer at his unguarded use of her name. She had determined to take control of her emotions while she explained everything to him. Biting her lip, Mairi took a step forwards.

'I - I thought you might be leaving soon,' her voice was dry and strangely high-pitched. 'I didn't want you to go still thinking the worst of me.' She held her head with dignity, clutching at the sides of her blue cloak, seeing the tense muscle pull in his cheek. He said nothing. Mairi ploughed on wishing she had never come; he was still angry and she had misjudged the situation.

'I am not involved in any way with Robert Boswell, nor wish to be,' she controlled her voice better than the thumping of her heart. 'It hurts me deeply to think you ever doubted me, but I can see the evidence pointed against me. So for that I forgive you,' Mairi's green eyes were moistly defiant. Involuntarily, she put her hand up to the silver Viking ship that swung from her neck and caressed it as if drawing confidence from its shape. She saw Douglas start at the sight of his gift and something flashed in his enigmatic black eyes.

'I had always hoped - ,'Mairi tried to find the words but the numb detachment in which she had cocooned herself for the visit, crumbled away. A lump formed in her throat and she turned from his stare. She had said enough and just wanted to run from Douglas's stony, disbelieving face. Her retreat was stopped by strong hands on her shoulders. In two long strides Douglas was with her and spinning her round to face him.

'Hoped for what?' his grip was hard as he searched her face with coal-black eyes. Mairi found herself trembling under his touch; she had never expected to feel his warmth again. Now it flooded from his hands into her shoulder blades and rippled down her spine. She answered him with a toss of the head and her fierce eyes took on the challenge of his gaze.

'That we might both be together,' she breathed unevenly, burning at the boldness of her words.

Douglas pulled her roughly to him and bound her in an embrace that squeezed the breath out of her as if he would never let her go. The suddenness of the gesture made Mairi faint, patterns of light breaking up before her eyes. Her hearing sounded muffled but she caught Douglas's rasp.

'I love you,' he growled and covered her lips in a scorching kiss. Light-headed, she threw her arms about his neck, the pain of the past weeks vanishing in the sureness of his words. They embraced with equal ferocity aware only of their need for each other. It sent shivers of delight down Mairi's body, not wanting the kissing to end.

Douglas loved her and she never wanted him to let her go again. He tasted her lips, her cheek, her chin, her throat, his beard tickling her chest as he brushed the pulse in her neck.

'We shall be together,' he promised, 'no one shall stand in our way this time, my love.'

Mairi thrilled to his intimate endearment, her heart banging rapidly at the feel of his mouth on her face and neck. In a moment she would forget where she was, forget there was a household of people beyond the closed door. With an effort she pulled herself away, fumbling in her cloak for Florence's letter.

'I bring good news too,' she smiled lovingly into his animated face. 'I wanted to show you this before.' Mairi blushed to think of how that plan had gone so horribly wrong. Douglas linked his arms loosely around her waist and smiled.

'Nothing is better news than what you have just told me.'

Mairi unfolded the letter and read the words concerning them both. 'What do you think it means Douglas?' she looked up shyly. 'Do you imagine they might have changed their minds about us?' Mairi burned with sudden embarrassment, unable to bring herself to use the word marriage. Douglas had mentioned love but never promised more.

The look on his face did nothing to reassure her. He was growing distant again, the lines of his brow puckering into a frown. She had spoiled their moment of reunion by showing him the letter and reading more into it than there was.

'You - you don't agree?' Mairi felt her eyes stinging as his dark one's hardened. 'I see you don't hope for the same good tidings as I do,' she pushed his arms away from her. That registered at once and Douglas clasped her face in his hands.

'I wish for as much as you do - even more,' he answered sternly. 'But I do not trust my father could have had such a swift change of heart. We Roskills are as stubborn as any Lismore,' he grunted.

'What does it mean then?' Mairi's face clouded with worry. 'Why should my mother mention us both in their plans?'

Douglas looked grim. 'I don't know, but we'll soon find out, our parents arrive tomorrow.'

Mairi gasped, momentarily overjoyed to think of seeing her mother again. She was optimistic; her mother would never agree to something that would hurt either Douglas or herself. Douglas was just being overcautious.

'They cannot separate us now, they will see how we love each other,'

Mairi whispered shyly, crimson flooding into her cheeks at Douglas's amused smile. He hugged her close.

'Tonight, Mairi,' he brushed her ear with a kiss, 'we shall dine alone in my apartments.' The words sent her insides somersaulting.

'And tomorrow we will face them together?' Mairi asked quietly. He studied her for a moment.

'Tomorrow I hunt with King James near Falkland Palace. When I return we will confront my father.' Douglas smiled tenderly down at her worried expression. 'This evening I shall send Sam to accompany you from the Palace and we will forget everyone else for a few hours.'

Mairi almost ran back to Holyroodhouse, her heart as free and light as a skylark. Douglas loved her and wanted to be with her. Together they would stand against any opposition. The dark lover of dear Agnes's prediction could be no other than Douglas and so she had nothing to fear. She banished the old nurse's words of warning to trust nobody, knowing now she could rely on Douglas.

She went in search of Lucy to tell her the good news and to thank her for her part in reuniting her with the proud heir of Duntorin. Instead Mairi found Isabel sewing in the upper withdrawing-room. The older girl noticed at once the flush of happiness on her stepsister's fair cheeks. Her insides knitted with jealousy.

'Who allowed you to go off on your own?' Isabel asked with cold disapproval.

'No one,' Mairi smiled and hugged herself. She was unable to keep her joy to herself; even Isabel was a better confidant than nobody. 'I have been to see Douglas,' her green eyes shone as she spoke his name. Isabel looked up in surprise, her needle poised to stab the cloth. 'I am dining with him tonight, just the two of us.'

Isabel jolted and pricked her thumb. A spot of red blood oozed into the sampler. At that point the door was flung open and Lucy rushed in. She saw the room occupied and froze, pale as a winding-sheet. Mairi had never seen her fair friend look so shocked, the deep blue eyes like huge dull mirrors staring at her. She had been crying.

'Lucy, whatever is the matter?' Mairi came forward full of concern. She remembered Lucy had been looking forward to seeing her father; she must have received some bad news. Her friend was breathing in great gulps.

'No Mairi, keep away,' she backed to the doorframe. 'I can't tell you.' She looked on the verge of tears again. Mairi ignored the plea and went to comfort her.

'Is it bad news from home Lucy?' she asked softly. 'You can tell me.'

Lucy Seton put her hands to her face, covering her mouth. The eyes were distraught. 'It's terrible,' she was almost incoherent, 'for both of us.' Mairi gaped at her nonplussed. Lucy dropped her hands. 'I'm to marry Douglas.' Then she was running from the room, running from the disbelief in Mairi's eyes.

For a long moment Mairi stood staring at the spot where Lucy had stood, as if the empty space would somehow conjure her back. She was trying to comprehend what her friend had gabbled before fleeing from the room. Lucy was going to marry Douglas, her Douglas; the man whose warm arms she had just left, whose kisses still tingled her skin. It was a horrible prank, a sick joke. But she had never seen Lucy act so convincingly before.

'At last my brother is to take a wife,' the metallic voice cut through Mairi's numbness. 'Lucy should show more gratitude than that. She is highly honoured to be chosen as the future mistress of Duntorin Castle.'

The words stabbed Mairi in the chest like needles; she felt her breathing coming painfully. Slowly she turned to face the pale Isabel and saw the glee in the night-black eyes taunting her.

'It's not true,' Mairi said, drained of all colour. 'Douglas would never accede to such a match.'

Isabel gave a hard shrill laugh. 'Don't be such a fool; Douglas will do whatever is best for Duntorin. He will always put that first, as well he should.'

'You're wrong!' Mairi shouted at the smug aloof face. 'We love each other. Douglas knows nothing of this arrangement and he will not agree to it.'

Isabel strained forward, her embroidery pulled taut in her hands, the dark eyes flashing with cruelty. 'You arc more stupid than I gave you credit for,' she sneered. 'Of course Douglas knew of the marriage. Do you think it was not discussed before he left my father? Only you are so vain and conceited that you imagine my brother's passing fancy for you should override practical considerations. Father would never agree to a marriage between you and Douglas and you know it. He has his duty to Duntorin. It is hardly fitting, in the circumstances, that you dine alone with Douglas now you know of his engagement, Mairi. It would only cause scandal.'

Mairi could not bear the disdainful smile on Isabel's face. She turned and made her escape, only wanting to be alone, to nurse her shocked and bruised feelings, to try and understand what was happening.

Even the thought of having Lucy near her made Mairi shrink from human contact. She was not to blame, but she could not trust herself to be civil to the pretty older girl. Had Alexander had any inkling before he left of what was going to occur? Mairi suddenly longed for her gentle brother to be near to comfort her and reassure her among these two-faced Lowlanders, who were still strangers to her after all this time of living among them.

Isabel was right when she said it would be scandalous to accept Douglas's invitation, knowing he was betrothed to someone else. She would save herself the humiliation. As much as Mairi tried to tell herself Douglas could not know of his father's plans, she could not forget the veiled look on his face when she had shown him her mother's letter. He had not been pleased. It came to her clearly that he could have known and the letter was merely a sharp reminder of his duties to come. Douglas had wanted his sport with Mairi first and she thought bleakly that he had never actually mentioned marriage between them at all.

Was his promise that they would stand together in the face of opposition, to be a token gesture of resistance soon to be followed by willing capitulation into a liaison with Lucy? It would not be an onerous task, for Lucy Seton was a lovely and vivacious young woman.

As Isabel had stressed, she was eminently suitable and for her part, Lucy had never made a secret of how handsome she thought Douglas. Mairi knew her friend was in love with Alexander, but with him far away, would she not give in eventually to the idea of Douglas becoming her husband? Trust no one, Agnes had warned; it seemed she could not.

Torturing herself with such thoughts until she was unable to stand the confines of the Palace any longer, Mairi set herself free, climbing the mountain behind Holyroodhouse. She walked up by the still loch, set like a jewel in its heart, its banks unusually parched. Here nature could be a balm to her emotions and she drank in its soothing freshness and desolate quiet.

It was dark and Douglas paced impatiently across the boards of his parlour. Everything was set for their intimate dinner, the heavily carved wooden furniture flickering in the mellow candlelight and the smell of roast woodcock wafting in from the kitchen. Still Sam did not return with Mairi. Douglas was on edge, what could be keeping them? Dark thoughts of Boswell's intervention sprang unwillingly to mind, or had Mairi had a change of heart? He must have frightened her with the quickness of passion he could not restrain when she was near him.

Soft steps approached on the outer stair. With a flood of relief, Douglas rushed to welcome his guest. Sam entered alone and shut the door behind him.

'Where is she?' Douglas barked, clenching his fists behind his back. Sam hesitated, hating the role of bearer of bad news.

'I'm sorry Douglas, Mistress Mairi will not be coming to dine tonight.' There was wariness in the soft hazel eyes that Douglas could not read. Or was it pity? He would not be pitied.

'Damn it Scott, what do you mean?'

'She is unwell,' he began evasively, 'and wishes to rest.'

Quick concern flashed across Douglas's stormy face. 'Then I must go to her, Sam,' Douglas answered impatiently.

'No,' his servant stopped him with quiet firmness, 'she does not wish to see you.'

Only Sam would have dared say such a thing to Douglas and as his close comrade, Sam knew reluctantly that he must give the full message. 'She says that, for reasons you will understand only too well, she cannot meet you again unaccompanied.'

'What in Heaven's name is that supposed to mean?' Douglas fumed and paced to the glowing fire. It hurt Sam to see the pain and incomprehension on his master's face. He had no more idea what was going on than Douglas did. For two people who seemed so drawn to each other as Douglas and Mairi plainly were, he could not understand why they were so frequently at loggerheads.

'I don't know,' Sam shrugged with embarrassment, 'but she seemed very distressed.'

Douglas gave a short exasperated cry. 'I will never understand her, Sam,' he leaned against the mantelpiece and ran a hand through his hair. 'Why can't Mairi be as straightforward and uncomplicated as Mary?'

Sam gave a short amused snort. 'Then she would not be Mairi,' he commented.

Douglas knew he was right. Mairi was unpredictable and quixotic, passionate and yet unapproachable, and he loved her for it. 'I'm going out,' he cried impatiently, 'you can devour the supper if you wish.' Douglas threw Sam a bleak look, 'I have no appetite left.'

Douglas rode out before sunrise the next morning with Sam, keen to join the King's hunting party at Falkland and rid himself of pent up frustration. He had pondered Mairi's strange message until he was plagued with doubts about her true feelings for him. He would not be kept waiting like a lovesick schoolboy again. She could play her coy games with someone else, but not with him.

Only briefly did he think of Florence's letter and its allusion to plans for himself and Mairi. He could not believe his father would have arranged anything behind his back and yet it niggled that he was still treated like the undisciplined youth he was before he went to Denmark. Why did he have the uneasy feeling that his father had been keeping something from him those last days at Duntorin, something that Florence had seemed on the point of telling him more than once?

Spurring on his horse, Elsinore, Douglas responded to the distant hunting horn of King James's party. Arriving at the group already gathered in the twin-turreted gatehouse of Falkland Palace, Douglas noticed with annoyance the presence of young Ruthven.

He exchanged a brief look with Sam who knew his distrust of the nobleman. Did his appearance mean the unwelcome Boswell was near at hand too? A quick inspection of the assembled hunters suggested not. Douglas did not want a day's hunting marred by Boswell's simpering spiteful tongue. A glimmer of sun broke out from behind a colourless blanket of cloud and lit the conically shaped turrets. There was hope of a good day yet.

Mairi and Isabel went in silence to the Edinburgh mansion of Duntorin. Mairi was pale, her green eyes huge and sunk in tired rings of sleeplessness. No smile played on the full lips at the thought of the meeting ahead. She dreaded the confirmation of Lucy's bolt from the heavens that had turned her insides to stone. Isabel was quietly gloating at the thought, Mairi knew. Lucy had avoided her since yesterday, taking duties that did not coincide with her own. It was hurtful, but Mairi was relieved she did not have to think of pleasantries or worse congratulations.

Thankfully, Douglas would be away on his royal hunting trip and she would not have to face him. He seemed to have accepted her excuses without protest which reinforced her suspicions that he knew all along about the proposed marriage.

Still, as they entered the close and saw the bustle of pack-horses and servants, her heart leapt at the thought that her mother was nearby. It was so long since they had last clung to each other for comfort and she needed to grieve with someone about Agnes.

Mairi fell like a different person from the one who had left Duntorin in May and wondered if her gentle mother had changed also? Duntorin appeared at the doorway with the Bailie. He threw out his arms in a welcoming gesture at the sight of his daughter and foster-child.

'The fair Queen's Maids!' he called to them above the general clatter. 'Come and greet your father.'

Isabel rushed swiftly up the stairs to his waiting hug and Mairi followed, her throat feeling dry and cracked. She kissed him on the cheek and murmured a welcome. Catching sight of the silver streaked and becapped head of her mother, she rushed to the door and flung her arms rapturously about the familiar figure.

'Mother!' Mairi buried her face in the scented warmth of her bosom. 'I've missed you.'

She experienced an answering hug, then her mother pushed her to arms length. 'Let me see you,' she smiled. 'My daughter is quite grown up,' Florence took in the adult cut of her dress and the styled copper hair.

Mairi smiled too, though the shadows showed in the sad green eyes. Her mother noticed with unease that the youthful sparkle was gone. Her daughter was subdued.

'I will send in some ale and cakes,' Bailie Greeves announced brightly, 'and leave you to be reacquainted with your family, John.' He threw a questioning look at Mairi but her eyes slid away. He had heard the servants gossiping and it saddened him to see her unhappiness, still it was no business of his.

The two men clasped hands and the thoughtful burgher disappeared to look after their needs.

'Well daughters,' Duntorin put an arm about Isabel's shoulders in the privacy of the apartment, 'we have much to talk about, your life at Court for instance.' Isabel beamed up at him.

'It's wonderful to see you father, but do tell us what brings you to Edinburgh.'

'Family business,' he replied rather shortly as he settled down in a chair. Mairi shot her mother a look and saw a nervous smile creep across her face. The redheaded girl's heart sank even lower.

'I hear a troupe of English players are to visit the royal burgh soon,' Florence tried to divert the conversation for the moment, sensing it was not the right time for their news. Mairi attempted to join in.

'There is some doubt as to whether they will be allowed to come, mother,' Mairi sighed. 'Rumour has it there is fever in the town of Newcastle where they entertain now and there is fear of it spreading with the players.'

'And a good thing too,' Isabel was dismissive. 'The Kirk is trying to prevent the good people of Edinburgh from attending the performances if they do arrive and I tend to agree with them. They inspire immodest behaviour and bawdiness.'

'Well your mother will see them if she wishes,' Duntorin cut in with a warning look, uncomfortable with the conversation.

'Yes stepmother,' Isabel bowed at Florence insolently.

'I had hoped your brother Douglas would have been civil enough to attend our arrival,' Duntorin continued gruffly, 'but it seems the King cannot hunt without him.'

Mairi's stomach churned at the mention of his name and she gripped her hands in a tight clasp in the folds of the satin dress.

'We will see him at dinner, John,' Florence tried to soothe him. She looked worriedly at her daughter who had fallen unnaturally quiet. Something had happened; she would question Mairi later when they were alone.

'Oh yes, and it will be our first chance to congratulate him on his betrothal to Lucy Seton, won't it Mairi?' Isabel goaded her unmercifully. Mairi blinked back hot angry tears, but held her peace.

'So you know already?' the Laird thundered in surprise. 'I can see nothing remains a secret at Court.'

'Lucy told us herself,' Isabel smiled sweetly. 'She seemed rather overcome with emotion at the time.'

'Not with pleasure that's for sure,' Mairi broke her silence with a fiery denial. Both parents looked at her with shock. 'Lucy loves my brother Alexander,' she turned her blurred gaze on her mother, 'she does not thank you for your interference.'

'Don't you speak so impertinently!' Duntorin blazed, quite taken aback by her criticism.

'Alexander?' Florence whispered. 'You have seen him, Mairi?' Her pale eyes sparkled with hope.

'He has been to Court, mother,' Mairi smiled genuinely for the first time. 'He is a fine man, a credit to Lismore,' she raised her chin proudly.

Her mother was quite overcome by the news. 'I would that I had been there too,' she answered, her voice quavering with emotion. This then was the reason for Mairi's sadness, that her dear brother and friend were in love but not destined to be together.

'Lucy showed only a young maid's nerves at the betrothal,' Isabel intercepted swiftly to please her father. John Duntorin glowered at his wife and stepdaughter.

'It is settled with Seton anyway, Florence, so let us have no second thoughts.' He turned and patted Isabel's hand. 'Please go and see if you can help the Bailie,' he winked. 'I have something I wish to discuss with your sister.'

Isabel smiled demurely, flinging a mocking last look at Mairi and did as she was bidden. Duntorin stood up and paced to the fireplace, his back turned to the women.

'I have at least something to put the smile back on your sullen face, Mairi,' he scrutinised the decoration on the panelling above the fire.

'John,' Florence interrupted, 'do you think this is quite the right moment?'

Her husband wheeled round. 'This is what you wanted, remember?' he warned, his temper dangerously close to the boil. 'You put Mairi's interests before her elder sister's, didn't you?'

'Yes,' Florence agreed, but had a sudden pang of doubt. She wished for more time with Mairi first, to discover what troubled her.

Mairi glanced at her mother questioningly and got a weak smile of encouragement. Her stepfather turned to face her.

'Your mother and I have your best interests at heart always and would like to see you happily married too.' Mairi stared at him, her mouth uncomfortably dry. 'I have had a proposal of marriage for you from the son of an old friend of mine,' Duntorin smiled.

Mairi felt her head begin to throb, drum beats of noise in her ears.

'We hear you are fond of the young man too,' her mother reached and squeezed her hand.

'He has recently been to see us to press his suit further and we found him sincere in his wish to take care of you,' Duntorin persisted uneasily, watching the aghast look on his stepdaughter's face. 'Of course we will provide you with a handsome dowry.'

Mairi did not dare to speak, she dreaded to hear the name she feared the most. Florence looked at her strangely. Duntorin's voice rang out in the hushed room, 'You must know the man we speak of is Robert Boswell?'

126

Mairi's heart hammered. It was a nightmare coming so quickly upon the shocking news of Douglas and Lucy's engagement. Never in a hundred years had she expected Boswell to make a bid for her hand. She had thought his intention was merely a dishonourable affair.

Mairi could not think what he gained from such a move. Was it the supreme provocation he thought it would bring Douglas or was it the dowry? Surely he would have a greater portion if he had asked for Isabel's hand? The thought of being finally caught in his paralysing web made her shiver with horror and fear.

'Mairi,' her mother urged, full of disquiet, 'you must thank your father for arranging such a match. Boswell is the son of one of Scotland's most powerful families; it is a great honour he seeks to do you.'

The young woman was stung into defence by the collusion of her mother. 'Never!' she sprang out of her seat. 'I will not marry the lecherous son of Brae. How could you ever agree to such a thing?' The accusation whipped like a smack across her mother's face. Duntorin lunged forward and shook her by the shoulders.

'You will do as you're told girl,' he roared. 'I can see being a Queen's maid-in-waiting has not improved your manners a jot. You will not disobey your parents or insult the Braes by such slanderous insults!'

Mairi gritted her teeth at the bruising pressure on her upper arms.

'It is true,' she gasped, 'the whole Court knows of his loose behaviour. I will not marry a rake, I do not love him. It is Isabel who wants to marry Boswell, not me.'

Duntorin flung her away from him at this last comment. He strode to the fire, slamming his fist down on the mantelpiece. Florence moved to steady Mairi and steer her to a chair.

'Your father has made a special exception for you Mairi,' she spoke soothingly. 'By rights, Isabel should be married before you. But Boswell was adamant in his choice and led us to believe you felt as strongly for him. He was quite charming. Now you treat your father ungraciously and without the respect he deserves.'

'I tell my stepfather the truth,' Mairi shook with emotion. 'I will not be made to marry a man I do not care for; my brother Alexander would not allow such a thing to take place.'

Duntorin pointed an angry finger at her. 'Lismore is not here to allow or disallow anything. It is your mother and I who protect and care for you.'

'Sandy will be back soon,' Mairi answered spiritedly, 'and I will go with him when he does, you cannot stop me!'

'By God I can,' the Laird of Duntorin thundered. 'If necessary we will take you back to Duntorin where we can keep an eye on you until the wedding is arranged. By All Hallows E'en you will be married, Mairi!'

Without another word, she ran from them and the claustrophobic parlour. Throwing herself down on the bed of her old chamber, Mairi wept into the soft bedspread. Her fragile world of happiness was crumbling about her like leaves in autumn.

CHAPTER TEN

Florence looked up helplessly at her furious husband. She knew Mairi's words hurt him deeply. He had hoped to make her happy with this match to the eligible Boswell and secure her future. John Duntorin had even placed Mairi's welfare before that of his own daughter and from the harrowed look on his face she knew he was now regretting it. There was only one real explanation for Mairi's uncontrolled outburst and moody behaviour; she was upset about Douglas's betrothal as much as her own.

Florence Roskill and her husband looked at each other in silence, both thinking the same thing. Mairi was still emotionally involved with Douglas. It only remained to be seen what Douglas's reaction to the whole situation would be. Florence thought with dread, she could already guess the answer.

'What about Isabel?' she whispered the question.

Before Duntorin could respond, the door opened and the tall dark young woman came in bearing a tray of titbits for them to eat and a jug of ale.

She registered surprise at the silent apprehensive faces of her elders, noticing Mairi was not there. She took it to mean there had been a scene about Douglas's betrothal. Well, she would just have to get used to the idea, Isabel thought dismissively.

'Has my younger sister been difficult again father?' Isabel could not keep the satisfaction out of her voice.

'Yes,' Duntorin replied through clenched teeth, 'she is finding it hard to accept the plans we have for her.'

'Oh,' Isabel looked puzzled, 'what plans?'

The Laird briefly caught Florence's eye and took a deep breath.

'She is shortly to wed Robert Boswell, younger son of Brae,' he spoke dully.

The tray clattered on to the table, ale splashing over the polished surface. '*Boswell,*' Isabel choked, 'not Boswell surely?'

Duntorin began to bluster, stemming off another tantrum from their offspring.

'Yes Boswell. He has asked for her hand in marriage and I have accepted. They will be wed at Duntorin before the winter, after Douglas's marriage to the Seton girl.'

'And what about me?' Isabel was hoarse with indignation. She narrowed her eyes at her father, the thin lips pulled into a tight line of protest.

'We will arrange a match for you soon, daughter,' he answered shortly, striding up and down the wool rug.

'So Mairi is to get first choice as usual?' she spat the words at him. 'It should be me who marries Boswell, me! Mairi only plays with his affections; she bewitches him and takes him from me.' Isabel began to sob tearlessly, shaking off Florence's attempts to calm her.

'You will not cause a scene,' Duntorin shouted, wondering what he had let loose. 'Go to your room until you can behave yourself. I will not have the Bailie hear you screaming like a fishwife!'

Isabel walked away, her drawn face pale and tight with hatred. Without a word to his wife, Duntorin picked up his cloak and marched for the outer stairs, leaving Florence to ponder the spilt ale and untouched food.

Douglas was disturbed by Ruthven's presence and kept watch on the young man's movements. He had again taken King James aside and was talking most urgently, though Douglas could not catch what he said.

'I don't like it Sam,' he murmured to his companion as they waited with the hooded hawks. Not one of the hunters could explain why Ruthven had ridden over from the family house in Perth so unexpectedly.

'His Majesty's servant Ramsay, says the young lord is trying to get him to ride to Perth to see his older brother Gowrie,' Sam answered quietly.

'Why?' Douglas felt growing unease. The Ruthvens were not close to the King and had caused him trouble in earlier years. The whole situation was contrived and made him suspicious.

Sam shrugged, his eyes intent on the private scene. 'Ramsay said Ruthven made mention of a man with foreign gold - perhaps a spy - Ruthven has apprehended him and has the gold in safe-keeping. He wants the King to look into the matter.'

Douglas remembered with a jolt, the undercover meeting of Ruthven and Boswell in the High Street tavern and the disappearing shadowy figures of the Earl of Gowrie and a man of southern fashion. The Ruthvens were ambitious, and Boswell was greedy. He, no doubt, had dubious contacts from his months in England. Douglas felt instinctively there was a plot afoot, but he had nothing but his unease to prove it.

'It sounds so unlikely, Sam,' young Roskill fretted, 'I warrant Boswell is behind all this.'

'The thing of most concern, Douglas,' Sam said even lower, 'is that Ruthven insists King James rides to Perth without his party.'

Douglas shot a grim look at his servant.

'That we do not allow,' he was firm. 'Whatever happens we ride by the King's side.'

To their relief, the King seemed to dismiss Ruthven's persuasions and insisted they continue the hunt. The sullen look on the young noble's face was noticeable, but he did not depart. He would wait for the hunt to climax at the kill and then try again.

The day turned out bright after all and a deer was finally caught. This time King James in a good mood, acquiesced to Ruthven's request to visit Perth.

They rode ahead but Douglas and Sam kept close behind, not stopping for fresh horses, while the other noblemen followed in the rear. The Earl came out to greet them, though Douglas was sure he blanched to see a whole party had proceeded with the monarch. The royal guest was invited in immediately by his hosts; the others being told they must wait while extra provisions were sent for from the town. They were invited to stroll in the gardens before they dined.

Douglas paced restlessly while the other gentry sucked cherries and spat out the pips in the sunshine. Eventually they were called inside to eat a modestly prepared meal. There was no sign of Boswell, but Douglas could almost smell his presence. He posted Sam by the stables to guard their horses and see who came and went.

The youthful Gowrie appeared in the doorway, a goblet raised in his hand.

'Let us drink the King's health!'

Douglas rose with the others, relieved that King James was now to join them. But he did not come.

'Where is His Majesty?' Douglas spoke up sharply. The young earl gave him a quick smile.

'He has gone upstairs to question a suspicious character we detain under our roof, Roskill.' Douglas saw him lick dry lips.

'Then I will go with him,' Douglas moved towards the hall. Gowrie crossed like lightning to block his way and the guards at the door put hands to their swords.

'No need,' Gowrie's face was tense, 'my brother accompanies the King and the prisoner is unarmed. No reason to fear, Roskill, Ruthven can easily call for assistance.'

Douglas saw they were outnumbered by Gowrie's attendants and cursed himself for allowing such a disadvantage to arise. However, the other nobles seemed prepared to believe their host's story, although Douglas was restless with disquiet.

'Come Gentlemen,' Gowrie pressed his advantage, 'it is a beautiful afternoon. Let us go into the garden once more.'

He led them through the inner room where the King had recently dined and out into the sunshine again. Long moments dragged on while some of the party smoked a pipe with the earl. Douglas sat watching the upper windows of the house and rubbed the hilt of his sword. Surely the King had questioned the spy by now? Perhaps Ruthven and he were counting out the gold? It would be welcome to the high-spending monarch and Douglas was sure it was the lure of the currency that had brought King James to Gowrie's lair.

His eye suddenly caught a retainer hurrying towards Gowrie. 'His Majesty has left, sir,' he shouted breathlessly. 'He has ridden off for Edinburgh.'

Douglas jumped up at the words. Surely the King would not leave so hastily, unless he took the casket of gold with him?

'Then my lords,' Gowrie smiled with regret, 'you must make your way back and join the King. It has been a pleasure to entertain you all.'

Douglas did not wait to see what the others made of this. He ran round to the gateway and found Sam leaning up against the wall.

'Has the King ridden out yet, Sam?' he shouted urgently. Sam was on the alert at once.

'No sir, I would have told you.'

'Follow me!' Douglas barked and strode back towards the garden. Before they could tell the other hunters of Gowrie's lies, a window was thrown open high above them and a muffled voice screamed out, 'Treason, help me - !'

Stunned seconds passed before the assembled group realised it was their monarch crying for assistance, impeded by someone's hand. But Douglas was already flying to the entrance, sword drawn and lunging past the unsuspecting guards.

The door at the main stair was locked.

'Help them here, Sam,' Douglas ordered, leaving his servant to heave at the heavy oak barrier. Douglas in his watchfulness, had guessed there was a smaller winding stair up to the turret, betrayed by the roundness in the outer masonry. If he did not find it quickly, King James could be murdered before he could get to him. He swore at himself for being out-manoeuvred by the sly young earl.

A commotion had broken out on the main stair. The loyal nobles must be facing resistance from the Gowrie household. There were cries and sounds of clashing metal. He trusted Sam to do his best to beat them off.

The panelled door in the wall gave way on to a small unguarded stairwell. Douglas leapt up it. Arriving at the top he kicked in the rusty latch and heaved a powerful shoulder against the door frame. It gave way.

On the floor, Ruthven wrestled with the King. Like an attacking wolf, Douglas sprang on to the treacherous noble and ripped him from the half-throttled monarch. He had him in his grip when a crashing blow came down on Douglas's bare head. A flash of light blinded him and he reeled forward on to Ruthven, his sword clanking to the wooden boards.

Seconds passed as Douglas's vision cleared. Ruthven was up again, sword at the ready to swipe at the dazed opponent. For a brief moment Douglas glimpsed another man, dressed in armour, heading for the open stairway. He was masked and unrecognisable, but it was he who had struck from behind.

Ruthven thrust his sword at Douglas who, at the last second, rolled away and the sword stuck in the floor. Douglas, on his knees, went to tackle the escaping knight, catching his ankle. The armoured stranger tripped but gained his balance on the door frame, jarring his helmet as he did so. A piece of chainmail tinkled to the ground and then he was out of the chamber.

Douglas, through ringing ears, heard the King cry a warning to him. Turning, he saw Ruthven coming at him again. He twisted and felt the sword blade rip at his doublet, piercing his side. Gasping with red-hot pain, Douglas struck Ruthven across the face with his right arm.

It just gave him the chance to pull out his dagger and strike with the left hand into Ruthven's belly. The man fell from him and hit the floor. Waves of dizziness swamped Douglas's pounding head and his side burned in agony as he staggered to King James's side to see if he was all right. Through coughs and splutters the monarch tremblingly assured his rescuer he was unharmed.

With a supreme effort, Douglas turned and forced his steps over to the open door. The sounds of fierce fighting came from beyond the chamber on the main stair. The young Roskill heaved his body against the door and swung it shut and with his last conscious effort, pulled the buckled iron bolt into its bracket. Sinking to his knees, he fell like a guarding hound across the entrance, blessed unconsciousness delivering him from the searing pain.

The Laird of Duntorin grew more angry at his son's absence. They had dined like mourners at a whisky-free wake, silent and pale-faced. The jolly reunion of expectant young hearts he had imagined had been turned into a dirge of sniffles and crying. He would have no more of it. Tomorrow, Mairi and Isabel would be sent back to the Palace to ponder their rebellious behaviour. Following that, there would be an exchanging of rings with Boswell and with Lucy Seton. That was if Douglas ever returned from his hunting jaunt.

Noise broke out in the close below to interrupt Duntorin's thoughts.

'What drunken brawling is this?' he got up sharply.

Mairi sat mute and distant, disinterested in what might be taking place outside. Duntorin threw the door open and peering out, saw the white worried face of the Bailie on the stair.

'It's Douglas,' he called up in a fearful voice, 'Sam says he is wounded.' The Laird clattered down the steps.

'Let me help him,' Duntorin growled at the men who carried Douglas from Elsinore. He could see the deathly pale face of his son beneath a makeshift head bandage. Douglas groaned as Duntorin supported his bloodied aching side. 'You're home now, Douglas,' Duntorin said more gently, taking the weight of the powerful young body on his broad frame. Sam took his other arm round his shoulders and they hauled him carefully up the steps.

'He was defending our King,' Sam explained breathlessly, his voice husky with pride. 'Douglas saved him from the treacherous Ruthven dogs.'

Briefly he told the story of the Perth visit. 'The whole of that town is now a riot of protest - their lords, Gowrie and Ruthven, have been killed. But Douglas slew Ruthven to save the King's life.'

Duntorin was silenced by the news and looked in awe at the battered soldier in his arms. A fierce pride swept through his veins. They brought Douglas through the door and cries of shock filled the room. Mairi's eyes were riveted on the ghostly face, so drawn behind the black beard. There was dried blood on his clothes and matted hair.

Forgetting the reasons for her own grief, she ran instinctively towards him. The dark pools of eyes seemed to look through her as she cried his name.

'Keep back!' Duntorin ordered gruffly. 'We must lie him down.'

Mairi put her hands to her mouth to stifle a cry as they took Douglas to his bedchamber. Soon Mary Bain and Bailie Greeves's housekeeper were there to tend his wounds, while Florence sent for a doctor.

Mairi fretted in the parlour with her mother and a tearful Isabel. The garbled story from Sam sounded like an attempted kidnap of the King that had gone wrong. Both Ruthven and Gowrie were dead. Mairi wondered if her fiancé Boswell, Ruthven's close companion was involved too? She wished in desperation that it was the insolent son of Brae who had been killed at Douglas's hand.

Eventually the helpers retreated from Douglas's room.

'The doctor assures us that he will live,' Duntorin said in a dull voice. 'He has lost a lot of blood, but the lad is strong and fit - ' His voice suddenly broke and he could say no more. Mairi had never seen him so overcome with emotion.

'Please may I go in and see him?' Mairi gave him a pleading look. Isabel quickly sprang up.

'I must be allowed to see Douglas first,' she cried petulantly, 'he is my blood brother.'

'Go then Isabel,' Florence assented quickly, seeing her husband could bear no more argument, 'for a brief look and then Mairi shall be allowed to see him too.'

Isabel's eyes glinted with triumph and she hurried to the chamber. 'Do not tire him,' Florence added, 'he must be left to rest.'

The dark sister found Douglas looking feverish, his brow damp along the line of his bandage. The eyes flickered open as he felt her approach.

'Isabel,' he smiled wanly. She squeezed his hand and kissed his brow.

'I have heard how brave you were, Douglas,' she found her eyes brimming with unexpected tears. She had insisted on seeing him to spite Mairi, but now it came home to her how much she loved her brother. The thought of his brush with death sent a shiver through her. Isabel felt even Boswell would be shocked to hear of Ruthven's attempted treason and she was inwardly thankful her beloved courtier had had nothing to do with it. She knew now that the reason Boswell had left Court was to ask Duntorin's permission to marry Mairi and he would be preparing his household at this very moment, she thought bitterly.

Douglas's eyes glazed over as he struggled to focus on his sister. 'Where is Mairi?' he whispered. 'I thought I saw her - ?'

Isabel mouth tightened; even in such a weak state he could think only of her loathsome stepsister.

'No, you must have been mistaken,' Isabel could not resist saying it, even though she saw the pain ripple across his tired white face. 'She is at the Palace keeping your betrothed Lucy company.' She wanted him to think only of the fair Queen's maid.

'Lucy?' his face took on a perplexed look. 'No you are wrong...' His eyes fluttered closed.

Isabel wondered for a moment if Douglas indeed did not know of the match. Surely he was party to their father's plans? Or had he too been a pawn in the dealings between the powerful noble houses?

Mairi looked up eagerly as Isabel re-entered the parlour.

'He sleeps,' she replied shortly. Mairi's face fell.

'Did - did he ask for me?' Mairi queried timidly, her look a supplication. Her face was at once vulnerable and open, transparently a picture of hope, the full lips parted, waiting. Isabel paused. What was the use of encouraging Mairi when she was to marry elsewhere? Isabel shook her head.

'He spoke Lucy's name before he slept.'

Mairi's head dropped, tears stinging her green eyes. At that moment Isabel wished she had not said it, pricked with guilt despite her jealousy.

Florence went to her daughter and put her arms about her shoulders. She needed no more confirmation that Mairi was in love with Douglas. She knew with a stab that the young redhead must have harboured feelings for her stepbrother ever since his return from Denmark. She had been foolish to think Mairi's passion would have evaporated.

Now it seemed Douglas did not share her feelings, no wonder Mairi was so unhappy. There was nothing she could do to alleviate that pain, except pray that her daughter would come to love Boswell in the same way.

'You must get some rest,' Florence cooed softly, 'and in the morning you and Isabel will return to Holyrood. Douglas will be cared for well, here.'

Mairi slipped into a deep sleep, drugged with tiredness. A noise woke her in the pitch black. Or was it just a feeling? Wide awake, she pulled on an overgown and left the room she now shared with Isabel, intending to sit in the parlour for a while. To do so she had to pass through the room where Douglas lay. Halfway across the chamber, Mairi heard a soft moaning; he

135

was speaking in his sleep. With heart hammering, she crept nearer, pulled irresistibly towards the man in the bed. He may not love her, but she just wanted to look at him without him knowing how much she cared.

Mairi could hardly make out his mumblings as the glistening head moved restlessly on the white pillow. In the guttering candlelight his face looked boyishly trusting, though the sheet half thrown off his dark haired chest, revealed the virile body of a man. Mairi gently touched the bandage wrapped around his middle. He felt nothing, a soft sigh escaping the dry lips.

Without realising what she was doing, Mairi bent forward and kissed his mouth, her long unbound hair falling to brush his chest. She experienced a deep sorrow that Douglas could not respond, would never again kiss her lips with the mingled passion and tenderness that had made Mairi feel a woman. Silent tears streamed down her cheeks at her sense of loss. Tomorrow they would be parted and distant to each other when they met in future. There would be no intimate suppers and no secret trysts to anticipate. Douglas would never be the lover for whom she had hoped.

Mairi looked again at the shadowed face. His eyes were open; She caught her breath and stepped back. Their blackness consumed her and she could not look away, but as Douglas said nothing, she doubted he recognised her. With relief she realised he would think her a ministering nurse, a blur in his fevered brain.

His fingers stretched out weakly towards her and then dropped. Mairi gulped and slipped his arm under the sheet, her cheeks burning at the thought of her proximity to him. Douglas's eyes began to flicker shut again. Turning to go, to get away quickly from his room and his nakedness, she jerked back at the faint whisper, 'Mairi.' She was sure he had uttered her name. Now there was only the rasp of his uneven breathing and the sight of still closed eyes. Tip-toeing from the room, her spirits rose within. Douglas had recognised her and whispered her name - not Lucy's - in his dreaming.

The Palace was noisy and tense with lawyers and courtiers recounting the events of the August day in Perth. The King had ordered the questioning of Gowrie's retainers and issued a pardon for the mystery man in armour to come forward and give evidence against the dead Ruthven. For there were enemies of the Crown who whispered that it had been a royal plot to rid the realm of the awkward Ruthven clan and that Gowrie and his brother had been innocents. King James wanted swift justice and called on the Kirk to denounce his attackers and clear him of blame for the deaths.

This the Kirk refused to do, saying the facts were too muddled and reports contradictory. One young zealous minister left the King's audience chamber swiftly, having aggravated the monarch beyond endurance with his pious admonishing. He made his way down to the courtyard, pleased that he had the power to unnerve the King. However, he must not push the timid man too far. He would preach to his new congregation on the misuse of earthly power as well as subservience to the greater spiritual leadership of the Reformed Kirk.

Crossing to the entrance, Zechariah Black ran straight into two young women that he knew well. It shook him for a moment to see the Roskill girls standing in his way, but he soon gained composure. At one time they could have been of use to his career, but strict self-control must be practised now. It did not stop him noticing how attractive they were in court apparel, especially Mairi's growing voluptuousness like a ripening plum.

With annoyance he saw her recoil at the sight of him, as if she had seen an adder. The dark girl's eyes were not so cold and distant though.

'Minister,' Isabel said with shock, 'what are you doing in Edinburgh?'

'Miss Roskill,' he bowed in the new black gown that he felt made him distinguished, 'I am the leader of a parish within the town walls.'

'I see,' she faltered, unaware that Mairi was drawing away, 'and what brings you to Court?'

'I have been setting out the Kirk's position on the Gowrie affair,' he smiled haughtily at his own importance. 'I know something of local opinion on the matter,' he preened, 'my duties taking me to Perth on occasion. And now if you'll excuse me, I have pastoral work to carry out.' Black swept past them, pleased with the obvious impression he had made, the woman must still have a soft spot for him.

Mairi looked warily at Isabel. The man had not shown a shred of warmth or recognition that their past affair deserved. He was as cold as a fish.

Isabel did not like her stepsister's pitying look. 'That is all quite over,' she snapped, 'it was a stupid infatuation, that's all.' Mairi kept silent not wanting to provoke her temper, though by the way Isabel was shaking it was plain the encounter had affected her. The shock of seeing the man who had tried to have her branded a witch and hastened Agnes' death, filled Mairi with apprehension.

Their lives seemed plagued with inauspicious events, as if someone had put a curse on them all. And there was more unpleasantness to come.

Duntorin had told her to prepare for a formal meeting with Boswell on the morrow to announce their betrothal, now that he had returned from his estates in Brae. Her stepfather seemed the more impatient to settle everything and leave Edinburgh as soon as Douglas regained his strength. Mairi wished with all her heart it was Isabel who prepared for the occasion. The thought of seeing him made her skin crawl. She would rather die than accede to becoming his wife, she thought fiercely.

After two nights and days of rest, Douglas was quickly recovering. He had sweated out the fever and colour was returning to his face. He was still too weak to leave his bed, his head spinning sickeningly when he attempted it.

'Am I not to be treated with carrageen jelly, mother?' he teased Florence with a boyish smile. 'Or is that only for when your favourite daughter is ill?'

She laughed indulgently, though the mention of Mairi made her uneasy. Douglas sensed something troubled her and took her hand, traced with delicate blue veins.

'You do not like me to mention Mairi, do you?' he probed gently. 'Why is that?' Florence blushed at his perceptiveness and dropped her eyes.

'It will not be seemly for you to tease her as you do, Douglas,' she began hesitantly, 'now that Mairi is engaged.'

Douglas jerked up, the blood rushing to his temples. 'What do you mean?' he asked sharply, wincing from the pain in his side. Florence was taken aback by the quick change in mood.

'Why, her betrothal to Robert Boswell, of course,' she stammered. 'I — I assumed your father had told you about it?'

Anger flared in the deep sunken black eyes. 'No, he has not,' Douglas snapped. 'He cannot seriously expect Mairi to marry such a dishonourable man as Boswell. He has bedded half of Edinburgh!'

He saw his stepmother flush crimson at his basic speech and bit back further abuse. 'I'm sorry, but the man has no principles. He may give her a title, but he will not remain a dutiful husband.'

Florence watched him carefully. He had shown too much concern for Mairi's well-being. They were the outraged feelings of a lover not an older brother. If he loved Mairi as much as she appeared to love him, perhaps she and Duntorin had made a terrible mistake in forcing them apart? She only wanted happiness for her daughter and yet she was denying her the very thing for which she yearned. Florence sighed and asked, 'Has John spoken to you of your own marriage proposal then?'

'Damn it, am I not trusted to choose my own wife?' Douglas cried in exasperation. He was furious.

Florence was frightened the shock might be harmful to his recovery. 'I'm sorry; I should not have said anything.'

He gripped her wrist with surprising strength. 'Oh, but you will tell me,' his eyes burned into hers.

'Lucy Seton,' Florence whispered, 'we hoped you cared for each other, we had heard - ' She was stunned into silence by Douglas's laugh, loud but mirthless.

'Oh dear lady,' he looked at her unhappily, 'she will not come willingly. Miss Seton's heart lies with your own son Alexander, I believe.'

Douglas lay alone, tormented by thoughts of Mairi and Boswell. Was she pleased with the arrangement? Had she secretly wished for this all along and let her mother know her wishes? If she had cared only for him, she would have been to visit him before now. He had dreamed of her coming to him in the night, dressed in her white shift, her hair loose about her shoulders. She had kissed him and the memory had comforted him for long hours. The thought of seeing her again had spurred on his recovery, of that he had no doubt and he longed for the tonic of her generous smile and quick-fire conversation. Even her red-cheeked arguments would be preferable to neglect, he thought morosely.

It came to Douglas with a sickening realisation that Mairi must have somehow learnt of his betrothal to Lucy, the night they had arranged to dine alone together. It was not girlish nerves that had kept her away, but the belief that he had agreed to marry her best friend. No wonder she did not come to visit him, she probably loathed his very name.

Bailie Greeves had offered his rooms for the formal meeting of Boswell and Mairi and Duntorin. Mairi sat, sick at heart, her mouth as dry as sand. She wore a demure silk dress of apricot with a modest neckline and plain trim. She would not dress her best for a man she despised. Her rich hair was scraped back into a cap and crowned with a heart-shaped French hood. It gave her an older more severe look.

Duntorin paced the room making Florence and Mairi nervous.

'Please sit, John,' his wife remonstrated. A noise on the outer stair saved them all and the Bailie appeared with Mairi's future husband.

Boswell swept a deep bow at them all, his face set with a charming smile. His love-lock curled becomingly around a pearl-drop in his ear, framing the smooth shaven chin. Mairi could smell the overpowering scent about his person, permeating the lilac and green of his clothing. It made her queasy. Mairi noticed with satisfaction his nose was no longer beautifully straight.

His voice droned like a bee as he spoke with her stepfather. She hardly listened, thinking with a beating heart, how close Douglas lay in the apartments below. A rebellious voice within, urged her to run and join him, to escape the web that closed in about her, to defy them all. She had felt a growing reluctance in her mother to this meeting, but Mairi knew she would do nothing to defy Duntorin and his temper.

'Mairi,' her stepfather called commandingly, 'do not be shy, do as Robert asks.'

She looked up in panic; she had not been listening. Now Mairi saw Boswell eyeing her intently with an ice blue gaze, the red lips smiling. The pleasure on his face was a mask over his irritation at her reluctance. He stood waiting to present her with the ring that would forge the promise between them. Mairi was frozen to her seat.

'Come,' Boswell coaxed, fidgeting with the piece of hair below his lip. 'I would mark our betrothal with this ring, my dearest.'

Duntorin, fearing refusal, took Mairi by the elbow and propelled her out of her seat. He would not allow her to insult the young noble. With concern, he felt his stepdaughter shaking and looked to see her usually proud chin, trembling. He had never seen her so cowed, but it must just be girlish nerves on such an occasion of honour. One of the most powerful young men in the land wished for the hand of this small redheaded Highlander of sixteen years. She was a pride to her mother and himself. Why then did he feel a twinge of doubt at seeing Boswell clasp Mairi's hand so eagerly?

Mairi went through the motions as if in a dream. She was aware of the ring being slipped onto her finger and Boswell's cold hand taking hers and raising it to his lips. He left a moist mark on her fingers like a seal of their fate together. Soon she would be his for ever, at the mercy of his hateful lust. The men discussed a date for the wedding ceremony and Duntorin clapped a hand on Boswell's shoulder.

'You are keen indeed, young fellow,' he was falsely hearty, 'but we cannot arrange things at Duntorin Castle so quickly. It must be done properly, say by All Hallows?'

'That is nearly three months away,' Boswell tried to sound light, but did not quite mask his annoyance.

'There will be much to prepare,' Florence piped up, 'although your impatience is charming.'

Boswell flushed slightly and gave her a quick smile. 'You can understand why, I am sure,' he gave Mairi a flashing look. Her stomach turned at his insinuations and she dropped her eyes. 'Perhaps you would allow me a moment alone with my betrothed?' he challenged them.

Florence glanced concernedly at her husband but he nodded curtly.

'For a moment then.' They left the room, closing Mairi in with Boswell.

He walked forward swiftly and chucked her chin painfully in his hand, forcing her to look into the bold cold eyes.

'It's not like you to be so coy, my dear,' he mocked, 'I would that you showed me the willing affection of a bride-to-be.'

'You expect too much then, Boswell,' she answered disdainfully, 'for I'll do nothing for you willingly.'

He forced his lips on hers, maddened by her haughty indifference, but felt no response.

'I do not need your agreement,' he sneered viciously, 'there are plenty who will come without protest, nay eagerly, to my bed - your sister Isabel for one, I'll warrant.'

'You disgust me!' Mairi threw the words in his face, her green eyes flashing with hatred. 'If it is Isabel you want, then why not marry her? You may receive a better dowry, isn't that what you're really after?'

He gave a cruel laugh. 'You underestimate your attractions,' his voice

140

was icily calm. 'Apart from wanting you Mairi, I stand to inherit your Lismore lands, once these heathen Highland boars have forfeited their titles.'

Mairi gasped in sheer disbelief in what he was implying. He continued, 'The King grows impatient with the likes of your uncouth cousin and if your brother cannot bring him to heel, we will share in some of the spoils there too. King James draws little distinction between degrees of barbarian.' He found her horror amusing. 'So you see, my beauty, it is you I must have - *will* have,' he gripped her face and stole another kiss before Duntorin returned.

CHAPTER 11

Sam found Douglas looking grimly out of the window. He had struggled into a pair of breeches and a loose shirt.

'You should not be up yet, Douglas,' his friend chided, knowing how Mary would scold if she found their patient had escaped.

'I cannot rest knowing that poxy knave is flaunting his engagement upstairs,' Douglas ground out the words with distaste. 'He makes a fool of us all!'

Sam could not help a wry smile at Douglas's impatience. He knew what drove his master to recovery and it saddened him greatly to think that Mairi and Douglas were to be divided by loveless marriages while he looked forward so eagerly to his own with Mary. But they were of a different rank and must be sacrificed to the forging of ties between important families. Sam doubted whether either would go easily.

Mairi's engagement to Boswell had also complicated another issue. Sam had hesitated to approach Douglas with his suspicions; it might make matters a lot worse. Nevertheless, Douglas's loyal man felt in his heart of hearts that he must speak up.

'You have something on your mind I can tell,' Douglas eyed his childhood companion. Sam took a deep breath.

'When the King let us into the inner chamber at Gowrie's house, you were unconscious.' Douglas nodded. 'But when we moved you Douglas, you became agitated, kept trying to tell me something important,' Sam looked keenly at the young Duntorin willing him to remember, 'about Ruthven perhaps, or another conspirator?'

Douglas's head jerked up as a memory surfaced.

'A man in armour,' he whispered, not sure if the blow to his head played tricks with him.

'Go on,' Sam urged, 'did you notice anything about him?'

'He was dressed in chain-mail and plated sleeves,' Douglas struggled through the mist in his head. 'His face was masked.' Puzzled lines creased his bearded face. 'Yet there was something about him . . . I was half blinded by the blow and then he escaped down the staircase.' Douglas gave up with a shrug.

Sam said nothing. He reached into his woollen jerkin and pulled out a small rag. Unfolding it, something bright caught in the light of the window as Douglas leaned forward, holding his side, to have a closer look. It was a ruby-drop ear-ring; the kind the King's 'favourite' wore.

'Where did you find this?' Douglas hissed savagely, ignoring the pain in his ribs that the sudden movement caused.

'On the floor where you lay,' Sam answered quietly, 'by the entrance to the back stair.'

'It must have fallen as he fled,' Douglas tried to picture the scene again. 'The man caught his footing in the door frame as he recovered from my tripping him.'

The two men stared at each other as the full implication of what they suspected sunk in. 'Boswell,' Douglas murmured, half in disbelief, half in a dawning realisation, 'I knew I could smell the presence of that rat about the place.'

'But why would he be involved in a plot to kidnap the King?' Sam voiced his doubts. It was this bewildering fact that had held him from speaking earlier. The piece did not fit the jigsaw, Boswell was already favoured by the monarch, so why jeopardise his position?

'Because he cannot contain his own greed,' Douglas's face set with cold anger. 'Whatever their plot, be it for ransom or political gain, Boswell would have planned to remain anonymous in case things went wrong,' Douglas guessed. 'He was their contact man for something. Boswell will never be happy as he is, he will always grasp at more,' the future laird rasped angrily, thinking of his rival's bid for Mairi's hand.

'They say an English ship was lying off anchor the day of the incident,' Sam added, 'but rumours in the burgh are rife at the moment.'

Douglas grunted, once more reminded of Boswell consorting secretly with the Ruthven boys and a foreigner in the tavern. He would not put it past Boswell to have hatched a plot with ultra Protestant sympathisers south of the Border. The results of such unspeakable treachery, had it come off, were too terrible to contemplate, plunging Scotland back into a dark age of uncertainty. Douglas kept his thoughts to himself. He took the ear-ring and chucked it in his hand.

'Unfortunately this is not enough proof to condemn him, Sam,' Douglas looked at him evenly. 'It would be our word against his that he was ever there and Boswell could easily accuse me of stealing this to make a case against him. I can hear him now, saying that I acted out of jealousy over his marriage to Mairi.'

'But surely the King would believe you,' Sam remonstrated, 'you saved his life? King James is well aware of Boswell's connections with the Ruthvens, you said yourself he tried to discourage their friendship.'

'He will not get away with it,' Douglas clenched his teeth as he picked up his sword with one arm. 'But I wish to settle the score myself.'

'What are you saying?' Sam tried to steer Douglas to a chair. 'You are not well enough to move.'

'I intend to denounce Boswell as a traitor and challenge him to a duel if he protests his innocence. Either way, justice will be done.'

Sam stared incredulously at his foolhardy master.

'That is courageous talk Douglas, but you are not fit to fight the stable boy, let alone a swordsman like Boswell!'

'You will carry the message to him, Sam,' Douglas ignored his protest. 'He can chose the day and time.'

'I will not let you get yourself killed,' Sam's face set in stubborn disobedience.

'You will do as I say, Sam Scott,' Douglas answered angrily.

The sudden likening to his father Duntorin was marked, Sam thought distractedly. He had no choice; he must carry out the order. But he would play for time and think of a way for the duel to be avoided. Boswell should be condemned by the courts.

'Send for Mary to re-dress my wounds Sam,' Douglas asked more calmly. There was silence between them as he stretched and tested his legs and arms. Sam thought himself dismissed, but as he reached the door, Douglas called him back.

'One more Thing,' his master looked away as he spoke, 'I wish you to arrange a visit for me. I would call on my betrothed, Lucy Seton.'

Sam's jaw dropped open at this surprise change of heart, though he had not heard any protests from Douglas over the Laird's plans. Perhaps he was reconciled to the idea that he could not marry Mairi and was therefore making the best of the situation. After all, Miss Seton was one of the most attractive and lively women at Court.

Still, it bothered Sam unnecessarily that Douglas should give up his quest for the fiery Highland girl so easily. He felt a tenderness for the once carefree sparkling young woman who had outshone all at the Beltane dance and whom he had saved from the witch hunt just in time.

'What are you waiting for?' Douglas shot him an impatient look, the dark eyes showing no emotion. Sam turned on his heels and left to carry out his unwelcome errands.

He found a subdued pair of Queen's maids in the upper withdrawing-room to which he was admitted. In spite of their parents' unwanted meddling in their lives, the two were still friends. Mairi could not hate Lucy for her betrothal to Douglas, knowing the Seton daughter's reluctance. Mairi's heart went out to her brother Alexander who knew nothing of these plans and for Lucy who pined after the strong-gentle chief. Somehow she must think of a way to warn Lismore of Boswell's dangerous greed.

As Sam was shown in, Mairi's heart rose. Douglas had sent a message to her; he was planning a way to release her from Boswell's grasp. Her sad pale face broke into a sunshine smile of greeting, a spark lighting the moist green eyes.

Sam felt a stab of guilt at her transparent hope and slid his eyes to the unusually quiet Lucy Seton.

'Sam,' Mairi jumped out of her chair, letting her favourite volume of ballads drop unheeded to the rug at her feet, 'what news do you bring for me?'

He bowed shortly and Mairi could see the pity in his hazel eyes. The smile gave way rapidly to dismay on her young face.

'I come with a message for Miss Seton,' Sam croaked with embarrassment and cleared his throat. A pale flush crept under Mairi's cheeks and her mouth clamped shut to silence her disappointment.

Lucy looked up warily, seeing the hurt in her friend and the reluctance on the servant's part.

'My master, Douglas Roskill, wishes to meet you officially as his betrothed,' Sam delivered the message in emotionless terms. 'He will call on you tomorrow if it so suits.'

Lucy nodded, her reply a whisper, 'It does.' Then she hurried from the room, unable to meet Mairi's pained expression. Mairi longed to ask if Douglas had mentioned her, but pride prevented it. She raised her head proudly and gave a smile that wounded her inside.

'I have not had the opportunity of congratulating you on your engagement to Mary,' her eyes were unnaturally bright as she spoke. 'I'm very happy for you both Sam,' she said with feeling. They at least deserved their joy.

Only after Sam had retreated did Mairi give way to the tears of hopelessness and bitter betrayal that she felt. The world seemed suddenly a bleak place with few friends and with nothing to which to look forward. How right Agnes had been. It was a future filled with dread.

Much later that night, the hot sultry oppressiveness of the last days broke. As east winds picked up and brought squalls in from the North Sea, a Queen's maid did not sleep. The window was left open so that rain poured down the panelled wall and the casements banged angrily in their freedom. The candle on the floor blew and spluttered but did not quite go out.

A slim hand braved the flames by holding a piece of wax upside down in its heat. The fire spat greedily as the lump of putrid tallow melted and fizzled blue and white in protest. It was crudely moulded into the shape of a woman's form and bound around its neck was a strand of long red-gold hair. A second waxy shape, distinctly male, lay waiting for the fire, pins mutilating its head and belly.

A passer-by would have thought the strange mutterings from the room were the whispering of the winds. There was a gasp, as of the night sighing, as she dropped the figure, her fingers too scorched by the wayward flame to hold it.

The dark muffled woman leaned forward to blow out the candle, the ritual spoilt by a freak gust. For a moment it lit the tortured gleam in Isabel's dark eyes as she thought of the revenge she took on the two she hated most in the world. Then the room was veiled in the black of a moonless night.

Douglas bandaged and stiff in movement, bowed before King James VI whom he had last seen gasping by the window in Ruthven's inner chamber. He had been summoned and the stern look on his monarch's face did not augur well.

'Young Duntorin,' King James gestured for him to rise, 'I wish to thank you for saving my life.' A smile played briefly across his wary face, lighting the round eyes, 'you shall be rewarded.'

'I would do it again, Your Majesty, for nought,' Douglas replied gallantly and the King was pleased.

'However,' King James sniffed and cleared his throat as his eyes withdrew behind hooded lids, 'I am displeased to hear of the brave Rosklll making certain accusations to our friend Rabbie Boswell and throwing down a challenge to duel.' Douglas was silent, but a muscle worked like a hammer in his cheek. 'I will not have my subjects taking the law into their own hands, do you hear? Now what do you have to say for yourself?'

Douglas, biting on his indignation, produced the evidence of the ear-ring and noticed with satisfaction the King's eyes widen in recognition.

'Perhaps this was stolen to bring a false charge against Boswell?' The royal gaze considering Douglas was as sharp as a hawk's. 'I know you are rivals and he has got the better of you in affairs of the heart, Roskill.'

Douglas, tugging his beard to control his temper, protested; 'Your Majesty, my man Sam Scott found the ear-ring in the chamber where you were captive - bravely fighting for your life,' he added quickly. Douglas watched as a flicker of doubt entered the unblinking eyes. Something about the mystery figure must remind him of Boswell after all. It faded. To Douglas's disappointment the King continued in a deliberate calm manner.

'You need more than an ear-ring to point an accusing finger at a son of the powerful Brae.' He paused before delivering the blow. 'You were not to know Roskill, that while you lay at your father's house recovering, we put out a pardon for the man in armour to come forward and speak. You realise, of course, that an eye-witness was needed to support my word against Ruthven's cronies in order to round up all traitors?'

Douglas looked thunderstruck. 'Then Boswell is to go free?'

The King was stung by his incredulity. 'It was not Boswell who came forward,' King James snapped back, 'it was Gowrie's own chamberlain.'

Douglas gripped the gloves in his hand, his jaw clamped to suppress the anger he felt. Boswell must have coerced or bribed the unfortunate man into answering the plea.

'We will forgive this attempt to blacken Boswell's reputation because you are loved by your liege,' the wily monarch ignored his subject's defiant stance. 'You will stay at the Court, I have need of you. Let Duntorin and his wife return home and prepare for your future bride. You will dine with us tonight, of course?'

Douglas bowed as much to hide his frustrated fury as in respect, wishing to be gone. But King James seemed to want to talk now that the confrontation was over.

'I need men like you and Boswell to bring stability to the realm. We have had too much fighting,' he sighed. 'Together you can bring order to those wild lands to the north.'

Douglas was suddenly alert.

'Together, Your Majesty?'

'Yes.' the King smiled thinly, 'Boswell and yourself may well benefit from the forfeiture of - certain lands, if my Catholic subjects continue to defy their King's decree to produce their charters.'

Douglas tried to hide his creeping concern at the words, spoken so matter of factly.

'Alexander Lismore is surprisingly civilised for a Highland wolf, but he will not be able to deliver his cousin, of that I am sure. There will be treasures to award those who please me and new estates would be a fitting reward to Boswell once he is married to Mairi Lismore, of course.'

Douglas felt cold fingers spread from his wounded side across his back at the thought of Boswell and Mairi together. How she would despise Boswell's intention to grab her kinsman's estates with brutal force if necessary. He hardly listened to any more of the King's chatter, his mind working furiously to decide on what action to take.

He would send Sam to Alexander without delay to warn him of the impending danger from Boswell and that his monarch's patience was fast running out. And Mairi? He must hasten the meeting he had secretly planned to hold with her, if Lucy would agree to be go-between.

Mairi could not prevent herself from stealing to the casement window to watch Douglas's arrival. Her heart squeezed to see the dark crown of his head bound in a bandage and the energetic stride of his tall strong body. It reminded her of an earlier time when he had come impatiently to see her, his temple bearing the cuts from Cailean's men. Douglas was dressed in his best black velvet to see his new love. Tears of hurt filled the sad green eyes that gazed down on him. To think that he could so easily dismiss his feelings for her, while her heart broke.

For the rest of the morning, Mairi forced herself to be busy about the Queen's duties. There was a strange restlessness about the place which was not just hers. Mairi attributed it to the general nervousness following the attack on the King and the trial of Gowrie sympathisers that would soon take place. Or was it the rumour of Roskill's challenge to Boswell that set the place on edge?

Strangely no pedlars appeared from outside the town that morning and she could not recall hearing the bagpiper playing for the daily opening of the town portals. The thought perplexed and then was forgotten as Lucy burst into the room where Mairi sewed. Looking up startled by the suppressed excitement on her friend's face, Mairi felt her insides lurch at the effect Douglas had had on her.

'Mairi!' Lucy cried and ran across to kneel at her chair. 'Douglas wants to see you.'

Mairi stared at the pink animated face in amazement. Was Douglas even now prepared to play ruthlessly with her emotions? She could not bear his teasing ways any more and sat silently, questioning Lucy's dark blue eyes.

'It's true you dunce,' her friend put a reassuring hand on hers, 'he just used me as a way to get a message to you.' Lucy smiled eagerly. Mairi gulped, a rush of warm blood lighting her face.

'Where am I to meet him?' she whispered, clutching Lucy's hand in return.

'At the Pavilion — tonight after we have supped,' the dark blue eyes sparkled wickedly. 'I'm to make sure no one follows you.'

Without another word, Mairi threw her arms tightly about her friend and held on.

'There's one other thing you ought to know,' Lucy held herself away. 'Douglas's challenge to Boswell has been forbidden by the King. Boswell has been cleared of Douglas's accusations of treason — this morning Gowrie's chamberlain came forward as the masked man,' she sighed.

So the rumours that had been rife since yesterday were true, Mairi thought, relieved the duel was not to take place. Douglas would not be harmed, but it made her unwanted fate the more inevitable.

'Then nothing can stop my marriage to Boswell,' her voice sounded hollow.

'Douglas will,' Lucy urged, 'I think he has a plan to release us all from our parents' promises.'

Mairi looked hard into Lucy's face. 'You once cared for Ruthven, I think. Does his death make you angry with Douglas at all?'

'No!' her friend's answer was quick. 'I care only for Alexander; he's the first man I've ever truly loved.'

Mairi could not tell Lucy of Boswell's threats towards her brother; there was little point in upsetting her now. She resolved to get a message to her brother at once to hasten his return.

Neither was aware, as they chattered excitedly about the events to come, of the listening shadow at the open door. Isabel stood hidden in the antechamber on her way to answer the Queen's call. She had meant to ask Lucy of news of her brother's health, but on seeing her fly so quickly to seek out Mairi, Isabel had stopped intrigued to hear what she had to say.

Her first reaction was viciously to expose Mairi's rendezvous with Douglas to her father and stop any foolish fancy her headstrong brother might have for their coquettish stepsister.

But if she allowed Douglas to foil her father's plans, there would be hope yet that Boswell would take her as his bride. If Mairi disobeyed and insulted the young noble by breaking their betrothal, it would only be honourable that her own hand in marriage would save wounded pride. Mairi would be disgraced and she would get Boswell. Isabel slipped away unnoticed.

Mairi was alive with anticipation at seeing Douglas that evening. She called Margaret in to help her dress in the green and gold damask gown that Douglas had admired so much at Duntorin. Even in her excitement she noticed the feverish look in her servant's eyes. They were glassy and distant and beads of sweat hung like a string of pearls across her forehead. Perhaps she was overworked with her duties at the Palace or had she been jilted by Tam her apprentice brewer in the town? She would suggest a holiday for the young maid; Margaret could go back to Duntorin with her mother in a few days time after the English players had been.

'Will you fix the silver ship around my neck, Margaret, please?' Mairi looked at herself in the mirror while her maid fumbled with the catch to Douglas's gift. To Mairi's horror she saw the girl slip out of view in the dull reflection and fall with a thud to the ground.

Calling for help, Lucy came quickly to the rescue. Margaret lay moaning on the bed where they rested her, her limbs and face burning to the touch. With a start, Mairi saw a rash of rose-red spots on the girl's chest. They bathed her body with cold damp cloths, neither daring to speak their fear.

'I will stay with her,' Mairi said firmly, 'it's a touch of summer fever, that's all. I'll remain here until her breathing comes more easily. Will you ask the physician to come Lucy?'

'Of course,' her friend looked deeply troubled, 'but we cannot allow her to stay in the Queen's living quarters, her fever may be contagious.'

'She will stay in my room until the doctor says otherwise,' Mairi was adamant.

'And what of Douglas?' Lucy asked quietly.

'Our meeting will have to wait,' Mairi answered curtly, turning to hide her disappointment.

Douglas dined at Holyrood for the first time since the hunting expedition that could have ended so tragically for the King and for Scotland. He was a hero and sat in the place of honour at the high table next to his monarch. Douglas noticed the lines of tense strain about the mouth and eyes of King James. The traumatic incident had taken its toll and in their conversation no mention was made of Douglas's accusations or of duels. There again, the King could well be troubled by rumours of fever breaking out in the town, Douglas thought edgily.

As the banquet wore on, he looked impatiently around for Mairi. Surely she had received his message via Lucy? He yearned to be out in the breezy night air. He had much to discuss with the young redhead who held his heart, the first of which was to ascertain her true feelings for him before he went ahead with any rash plans.

For a nightmare moment Douglas wondered if she could be ill. Reports of sickness in the burgh were growing as the hot spell gave way to heavy rain. No one dared think that the smattering of cases that had manifested themselves could be the herald of plague. To Douglas's dismay his father, only this morning, was making hasty plans to return to Duntorin, spurred on by the news that packmen from the outlying areas had been prevented from entering Edinburgh in case they brought fever with them. The Laird of Duntorin was adamant Mairi and Isabel should return with them; time was running out. All the more reason, Douglas thought, that he should act quickly. But where was Mairi?

When the chance materialised, he slipped across to Lucy, with all the appearance of someone greeting his intended. Isabel watched, not taken in by the courtly gestures. She would keep her ears and eyes alert to discover what rebellion her brother planned. Lucy and Douglas moved off as the minstrels played for the assembled guests.

'I will go to relieve Mairi,' Lucy assured Douglas, having explained about Margaret's sudden illness.

'Thank you, kind friend,' Douglas smiled at the willing fair face.

But when she had gone he gave way to black thoughts of plague. Had it struck in the very heart of the Palace? If so, the Duntorin maids would be swiftly packed off to their home to the north-west, just as his father intended them to be.

The deathly pestilence was the most feared retribution on any town and the Kirk was already denouncing the Danish visit and frivolity as the cause. There would be no visiting English players this summer and once news of Margaret's condition spread the Court would likely make plans to leave for Falkland Palace immediately. He would have to go with them.

Douglas left the false gaiety of the hall and headed for the Pavilion to wait for Mairi. Isabel saw Boswell shifting uneasily at the sight of his rival's disappearance. If he tried to follow she must forestall him and use this chance to make a play for Boswell. Manoeuvring herself towards him she greeted the young courtier with a smile.

'What a pity your betrothed is not well tonight,' she sounded sympathetic, 'but perhaps you will dance with me, sir?'

Boswell threw her a considering look. A shame her stepsister was not so obliging, he thought callously. Still, he could have some sport while he waited for the greater prize that was to be his.

'It would be a delight,' Boswell flashed a gleaming smile, the new pearl ear-ring catching in the candlelight. Isabel had a stab of unease to think Douglas's wild suspicions of this man might have held a grain of truth, then dismissed them as she warmed to his leading hand.

Lucy found Mairi in Margaret's own box-like room. The physician had given her a draft to help her sleep comfortably, but he would report her sickness to the Queen tomorrow. Whatever happened, Margaret must not be abandoned by all like a blighted animal.

'Go to Douglas,' Lucy urged, 'I'll sit with Margaret.'

Mairi hesitated, touched by her friend's unselfish offer. She would risk infection to allow her a brief moment with Douglas.

'You won't have long,' Lucy pushed her towards the door.

Mairi quickly kissed her cheek and then hurried to keep her tryst.

The wind whipped bitingly about her face, the half-groomed hair flying out of its cap. How swiftly the weather had changed to these cold easterly blasts. Then the hunched outline of the Pavilion rose out of the night and Mairi forgot her chill thoughts of impending doom at the realisation of whom she was about to meet.

Cautiously she waited by the entrance, sudden thoughts of the treacherous Boswell preventing her from rushing in.

'Mairi?' a deep voice questioned from the dark shadows. The thrill of recognition sent waves of pleasure through her. She heard him step forward and at that moment, the brawling winds tore the night clouds apart, the moon spilling briefly into the doorway. Douglas stood like a tall Norse god, dark face chiselled by the silvery light, his broad body triggered to move, watching her with dark forbidding eyes.

'I thought you would not come,' his voice was stony to her ears.

For a moment Mairi feared she had mistaken his reasons for arranging a meeting. He was not pleased to see her.

'I have come because you asked for me,' Mairi answered woodenly.

Douglas sensed her guardedness. She had come out of a sense of duty, he thought with annoyance. Did she really relish the prospect of being Boswell's bride? He held himself in check.

The moon disappeared again and neither could read the expression on the other's face. They felt only the nearness of one another.

'Mairi,' Douglas at last broke the tense silence between them. 'I need to know if you yourself wish for this match with Boswell, before I say what I wish to say.'

Mairi winced at the mention of the hated man's name. 'I wish for it as I wish for the fires of Hell!' she rapped out an indignant response that took them both by surprise. Mairi heard a deep chuckle released from the dark and then she felt Douglas step nearer, so near she could feel the warmth of his body beside her. Yet they did not touch.

'Neither do I wish to marry your fair friend,' his voice rumbled deep and soft and her pulse thudded at his next words. 'I want to marry you, Mairi, and only you.'

It was she who reached out in response to slip her arms impulsively around his waist. She felt him flinch as she brushed his wound and quickly withdrew. But Douglas caught her arms and pressed her to him.

'You cannot hurt me, my wildcat,' he laughed, 'only if your answer is no.'

'Oh it is yes, Douglas,' Mairi answered fervently, 'I never want to be parted from you again.'

Tears of relief spilled on to her cheeks as Douglas bent and kissed her tenderly on the lips. It lasted so long she was light-headed and breathless when he finally released her.

'We shall not be separated by anyone,' Douglas's voice rasped fiercely and he kissed the tendrils of hair about her brow. 'My father wants you to return at once to Duntorin and I cannot allow that to happen. Once he does we will be powerless to act.'

'But what of our parents' arrangements?' Mairi's fears began to drag down the soaring of her heart. 'The Braes are a powerful family, as are the Setons.'

'There will be other more willing suitors for them,' Douglas said harshly, 'like your proud brother, for instance.'

Mairi remembered with a chill, Boswell's threats to the Lismore lands and began to tell Douglas of her fears. He interrupted her.

'If I had had my way, Boswell would have his thieving hands only on the dirt that buried him,' the young Duntorin's temper rose. 'But don't worry my love,' his tone softened as he glimpsed her troubled look, 'I have already sent Sam with armed protection to warn Alexander. The King himself told me of the despicable plot. Rory, the piper, goes as guide and translator and I trust them to deliver the message swiftly.'

Mairi thought fondly of the grizzled old musician who travelled the Highlands freely.

'He will ward off unfriendly strangers with his quick wit and a tune of his pipes,' she smiled. 'You have acted generously towards my brother.'

'He is not my enemy,' Douglas answered stiffly, 'although Lismore may think differently.'

'And us?' Mairi asked shyly, the dark hiding her furious blushing. Douglas gripped her more tightly.

'We shall elope to Denmark,' he said with calm conviction, as if the suggestion was no more momentous than a trip to the fair. 'Today I arranged a passage on one of Bailie Greeves's ships. By luck it leaves the day after tomorrow from the Port of Leith for the Low Countries and then on to Denmark.'

Mairi gasped in amazement. 'You would risk your inheritance and everything dear to you for me, Douglas?' Mairi was full of wonder.

'It counts for nothing if I cannot share it with you,' Douglas replied without hesitation.

'And the Bailie knows of our elopement? Am I the last to be told your plans?' she questioned with amusement. Douglas gave a deep throated laugh and kissed the tip of her nose.

'The Bailie is a remarkable man. He thinks my father is wrong to insist on these loveless political marriages. He says if more people married for love, they would spend less time fighting others and more time at home! He does not fear my father's wrath; they have been friends too long.' Douglas stroked her cheek. 'The captain will marry us on board and we will have a church ceremony when we reach Copenhagen.'

Mairi's cheeks scalded at the thought that she and Douglas would soon be as one; it was hard to comprehend.

'You were very sure I would agree?' she teased gently.

'I've never been sure of your feelings, Mairi. I hardly dared hope you would love me enough to turn your back on Scotland and come with me,' Douglas raised her chin with his hand. The touch sent a shiver of delight through her. 'Are you that brave wild woman that I have loved since the Beltane dance?'

'Do not doubt the courage of a Lismore,' Mairi answered with spirit, then added lowly, 'the Beltane fires have burnt within me since that night too, Douglas.'

Douglas came to her.

'Let us pledge ourselves to each other now, Mairi, before God,' Douglas's voice was cracked with emotion. They stood clasping each others hands and swore solemnly to love and honour each other for ever, to the exclusion of all others. Douglas fumbled in his jerkin and pulled out a ring which he slipped on to Mairi's finger in the darkness and held it there.

'It was my mothers,' Douglas's words vibrated low.

'I cannot.' Mairi protested, a sore lump in her throat, 'it should go to Isabel.'

'Father gave it to mc to present to the woman I cherished above all others,' Douglas squeezed her hand, 'and that's who you are, Mairi, my dearest one.'

'Oh Douglas, I love you,' Mairi was choked with happy tears.

Then, charged with an unchecked passion, he consumed her in a burning kiss, his hands crushing her body to his. Mairi wanted to cry out in the dark blustery starless night as her whole being responded to his desire. She returned his embraces with equal ferocity, so that he could never again doubt the way she felt about him.

'I want you now, Mairi,' he breathed in her ear and her head reeled with longing. He felt his way down her silken skin with his lips.

'Douglas,' she moaned in protest, 'we will be husband and wife in a matter of days.'

Douglas swallowed hard, clutching her the stronger. 'We are promised to each other now in a hand-fast marriage, no one can take that away from us,' he answered. She could feel the intensity of his gaze and trembled from the urgency of their contact. 'I will never break that promise to you, my love,' Douglas hugged her and stroked her hair.

'I know,' Mairi could only manage a hoarse whisper.

'Do you want this too, Mairi?' Douglas held her away, trying to read the deep green lustrous eyes. 'I would die rather than make you do something against your will,' he rasped.

Mairi slid her arms up about his neck in reply. She wanted him with a sweet desperation. Knowing the cruelty of fate, this might be their only time to express the deep love they felt for one another. It must be now.

In a strong protective hold, Douglas brought Mairi to the ground with him, laying her on his warm cloak. They kissed again gently and then the quick-fire of passion lit as they explored each other.

She responded freely to his touch, replying to his sweet whisperings, her words thrown away on the wind.

Outside the lovers' trysting place, the black stormy night raged on unheeded.

CHAPTER 12

Later Mairi lay in Douglas's arms, bathed in his warmth. She ran a finger down the bunched muscles of his upper body, blushing to think of her fierce response to Douglas's loving. He stirred again, but gently removed her exploring hand.

'We must not be caught now, my wildcat,' Douglas kissed her fingers.

'Tell me I do not dream,' she murmured up to him, 'that soon we will be together for ever.'

'It's no dream, I promise,' he stroked her hair, 'but we must move quickly. Your mother and my father wish to take you and Isabel back with them to Duntorin and they must not guess of our plan.'

'Why are they so insistent?' Mairi asked in dismay.

'Because of the fear of plague in Edinburgh,' Douglas's voice hardened. 'My own mother was taken in such a way, when her time with her third child was upon her. Father is terrified of losing anyone else to the sweating sickness.'

'Oh Douglas, I never knew,' Mairi was shocked. 'Did it happen in Edinburgh?'

'Yes. In spite of the Bailie's help there was little anyone could do, it happened so quickly. The contagion took mother and baby,' Douglas answered bleakly, saddened by the memory.

'Margaret,' Mairi whispered in growing dread, 'has a fever.'

Douglas pulled her round savagely.

'From Lucy's description she may well be a plague-carrier,' he said sternly, 'you must not go near her, Mairi.'

'But she is my friend,' Mairi replied in astonishment, 'I cannot leave her alone, Douglas.'

'I will not lose you to the filthy pestilence, damn it!' Douglas's outburst shocked her and Mairi drew away.

'God will protect me if I am worthy of saving,' her reply was disdainful.

'And Duntorin will have you back home tomorrow when word of this gets out,' Douglas barked. 'I want you to go to a hiding place in Leith and wait for me there, Mairi. It belongs to the Bailie, it's little more than a warehouse but you will not be recognised and it is safer than the Palace. We will spend the night there and then slip to the ship before dawn.'

'You expect me to scamper like a fearful mouse while my dear maid dies of neglect and the fever?' Mairi was contemptuous. 'I will not run from my duty to her.'

Douglas seized her arm painfully and she was acutely aware of her undress.

'Your duty is to me now,' he said with a clenched jaw, 'I will not let your stubborn Highland pride stand in the way of our happiness. You have made a solemn promise.'

155

Mairi struggled to throw him off and pull her gown about her.

'I belong to no man,' she flung the words at him. 'I will see that Margaret is taken care of before I set sail anywhere.'

Douglas released an oath under his breath. Her sense of honour to the simple servant was infuriating, but he could tell nothing would change her mind, not even the thought of missing the sailing. At that moment he doubted they would ever elope together; fate seemed determined against it.

Mairi knew she hurt him by her stand, but she would never forgive herself if Margaret died far from home, an outcast from the Court in some fever hut on the moor outside the town.

'I am no more stubborn than you, who chose to risk your life in a duel,' Mairi reminded him.

'That was different,' Douglas growled, 'I was defending the King's honour as well as my own.'

'And settling a few old schoolboy scores into the bargain, no doubt,' Mairi pouted.

Douglas acceded with a sigh. 'I will tell Florence of your worries for Margaret; say you want her taken back to Duntorin too,' he agreed. 'She will not be left alone.'

Mairi felt sudden tears spring to her eyes and grasped his arm. 'Thank you, Douglas,' she whispered gratefully.

Douglas enfolded her in his warm hold. 'Let us not quarrel, my love,' he brushed her hair with his lips. 'Promise me you will be at Leith tomorrow?'

She nodded and kissed his mouth in reconciliation.

As they walked back, Douglas described to Mairi where she would find the Bailie's warehouse. A servant called Elliot would let her in.

'Tell no one of our plans,' Douglas warned her. 'After I have dealt with our parents I will come. I have agreed with Bailie Greeves that I will pretend to go away for two days on business of his in Dundee.'

Mairi nodded and kissed Douglas with a sweet desperation before they reached the Palace again. The taste of his lips lingered long after he had melted into the night, reminding Mairi that there had been such an exquisite meeting.

She found Lucy preparing for bed. Her friend assured her that Margaret slept peacefully; she would just have to sweat the fever out and hope that they had caught it in time. Mairi was bursting with her news but she knew she must not tell a soul, to do so could jeopardise everything. Instead she told Lucy that Douglas was sending immediately for her brother to return and fight Boswell's attempts to acquire Lismore lands.

'There is no fear of it,' Mairi said confidently to the worried face beside her, 'For I shall not be marrying Boswell anyway. He can have no legitimate claim to Lismore.'

Lucy observed the sparkle in her friend's eyes and the translucence of her face. An inner warmth suffused it and betrayed that something had happened.

'Oh, tell me what Douglas has planned,' Lucy cried eagerly.

'I have promised to tell no one,' Mairi blushed at her companion's appraising look, unable to deny what she already guessed.

'But Mairi, it affects me too,' Lucy remonstrated, 'and I'll explode if you don't tell me!'

Mairi hesitated, reluctant to say anything. Yet Lucy was her greatest confidant, she could not disappear abroad without letting her know. She would hear eventually, but it would not be the same as being entrusted by a best friend with the secret. Mairi succumbed to the pleading looks and told of the proposed elopement. Lucy hugged her in congratulation.

'But you must not breathe a word, Lucy,' Mairi looked severe, 'or tell where Douglas and I are to meet, no matter who asks.'

'Of course not,' Lucy giggled with delight. 'Only when you are far away and your handsome brother returned, will I break the scandalous news to him!'

Mairi felt a twinge of guilt at the thought of Alexander. What would he think of her running away with their father's enemy, nay worse, their father's killer? She tried to banish the unsettling thought, though it nagged away like a warning bell in her head.

As she passed Isabel's room on her way to bed, she saw the flicker of candlelight under the door. How glad she would be if she knew Mairi was no longer to be Boswell's wife.

Pressing her ear to the door she heard Isabel moaning strangely in her sleep. She felt a prick of pity for her tormented stepsister who never appeared able to find happiness.

Funnily, now Mairi knew she might never see Isabel again after tomorrow, she experienced regret. They could have been friends if Isabel's jealousy and her temper had not rubbed together like dry sticks to send the sparks of rivalry flying. It was her own fault too, that their sistership had failed, but it was too late to dwell on past mistakes and Mairi resisted the temptation to enter and speak to her dark stepsibling.

Passing on, the gust of her movement swept draughtily under the door and blew out Isabel's candle before the wax female form in her hands could melt. Isabel shivered in the dark room but, without knowing why, did not relight the ritual flame. Now she knew Mairi's secret; her stepsister's vanity had made her tell all to her silly friend. Well, let her go ahead, Isabel thought, she would have Boswell for herself. She was sure by the way he had danced with her tonight and made bold his intentions in the shadows of the antechamber that he would happily take her instead of

Mairi.

As Mairi bumped uncomfortably in the cart out of the town gates to the Port of Leith, she was dumbstruck by the half empty streets. The usual markets were disbanded and the high buildings rang with an eerie quiet. Panic had cleared the streets as quickly as the fever had struck. Her eyes stung with tears at the thought of the scene she had just left.

Bringing Margaret a morning draught, Mairi had found her maid dead. It had stunned her to see the white staring face and clutch at the cold hands; a life snuffed out as a candle. Servants had ushered her quickly away with damp cloths over their mouths.

Margaret would never again sing within the walls of Duntorin in her sweet way, or bustle encouragingly about her and Isabel as they dressed for a special occasion. Her maid's kitchen friend had revealed the reason for the disappearance of the suitor brewer; he lay tormented on a sick-bed and had been forbidden to leave his dwelling. He would die, not knowing why Margaret did not send word to comfort him.

Mairi had watched frozen as Margaret's things were bundled up for burning and the room was fumigated with an acrid mixture of resin and pitch, no trace of the girl to be left. Then Lucy had come to counsel Mairi, urging her privately to go at once to Leith. Mairi had sat, unable to take in what was happening, until Lucy shook her hard.

'Mairi, this is your one chance. The fever is spreading and at any moment your mother will come to take you back to Duntorin.' Lucy's pleading eyes had held her own. 'It is said the Court will remove to Falkland and so I will go with it. Go now to Douglas for my sake as well as your own, Mairi, else you will be Boswell's and I Douglas's.'

The hard truth had stung Mairi out of her numbness and they had clung to each other in emotion, neither knowing if they might see each other again.

'Take care of my brother, Lucy,' she had tried to smile. 'Tell him one day we will all be reunited in a time of peace.'

Her friend had laughed through her tears and helped Mairi to her feet.

'Tomorrow is your wedding day,' Lucy had kissed her cheek, 'you must go smiling and not in tears.'

The thought made her stomach lurch like a plunger. Had Douglas really been able to arrange it? By the smell of sea-salt and pitch she was near the port. There were the reassuring cries of busy commerce as Mairi emerged from under the sacking belonging to the carter who had agreed to take her. At least the harbour activities had not yet been paralysed by fear of the plague and that meant ships were still allowed to leave.

Mairi trusted Lucy would be able to pretend her ignorance as to her whereabouts until after tomorrow. If her parents suspected an elopement with Douglas they would probably first search Dundee where Douglas had allegedly gone on the Bailie's business. Her mother might even conspire to delay the pursuit, she felt sure she understood her daughter's feelings more than most. In time Mairi was certain her mother would forgive her disobedience. If she was fortunate, the Lady of Duntorin would still have Lucy for a sweet daughter-in-law, though in alliance with her lost son Alexander rather than to a reluctant Douglas.

Following the instructions, Mairi found the warehouse at the end of a row of creaking houses and wharves that made up the Leith quayside. A thin-faced man, answering sullenly to the name of Elliot, let her in.

'The gentleman is not here yet?' Mairi asked awkwardly, unnerved by his pointed expressionless features.

Elliot replied in the negative but offered to bring her a cup of ale. Mairi thanked him, thinking any comfort in this dark dusty upper chamber in which she waited, was welcome. A flutter of apprehension seized her. What if Douglas did not come? What if the ship was prevented from sailing? Thoughts of her dear mother and Alexander and Lucy filled her mind and she wondered if she was ever destined to see them again.

A creeping fear mocked her that she had been foolish to give way to her feelings for Douglas. It may all have been an elaborate trick of his to take advantage of her. The ultimate joke would be for him to have his enjoyment of her only to abandon her to disgrace and scandal. But she could not believe the tender, loving, sensuous man of last night could be such a monster. Yet how could she reconcile this image of Douglas with the callous, blood-thirsty youth who had hastened her father's death?

The ale did not cheer her and Mairi sat shaking with foreboding as Douglas did not come.

Isabel had seen Mairi leaving and had said nothing. She secretly glowed at her stepsister's stupidity. It was impossible that Douglas would actually flee to Denmark with her. He had too much to lose and the brother she knew would never risk his father's fury or the forfeiture of his beloved Duntorin. No, not for any reckless, impetuous Highland minx would he do so. Douglas had had his sport with Mairi and would now realise his foolishness. However, she could take advantage of their mistake.

It was with interest that Isabel listened to the conversation between a worried Florence and a tight-lipped Lucy.

'She must have given you some indication where she was going?' her stepmother began to lose patience.

'She was upset by Margaret's death,' Lucy looked pained, 'perhaps she went to pray for her soul? She wanted to be alone, that I know.'

'It is very worrying,' Florence twisted her gloves agitatedly in her hands. 'We wished to leave today for Duntorin. You will send her immediately to the mansion house when she reappears, Miss Seton.' Florence sounded unusually stern and the young friend's heart went out to this distracted woman, although she could not reassure her.

'As soon as I can,' Lucy rested an encouraging hand on Florence's arm that made the older woman look eagerly into the pretty face. But nothing was betrayed in the vacant blue eyes and Lady Duntorin thought she must have misheard the intonation.

'Isabel, you will come with me now,' Florence turned to her stepdaughter, 'your father awaits us.'

Isabel was taken aback by the attention suddenly swinging to her.

'Yes stepmother,' she agreed hastily, 'but I need time to gather my possessions and say my farewells, please.' Isabel smiled sweetly. 'Let me follow you in an hour or so.'

Florence was too preoccupied to see the veiled look of panic in Isabel's eyes. She had not expected to be removed so soon. Her hopes of being allowed to go with the Court to Falkland had been firmly quashed by her father who believed they would all be safer in the north. But at least she must endeavour to see Boswell before she left. The way was clear now to declare her love for him and she would tell Boswell how Mairi had insulted him by running away with Douglas. That would make him lose interest in her provocative fiery looks.

Isabel began a frantic search for the elusive courtier. She had so little time to say all that she wanted. The servants had not seen Boswell; they were too busy in preparation for the Court's move to Falkland Palace. By rights, Isabel should have been helping Lucy arrange the Queen's affairs, but her errand was too important.

In desperation she went to the stables and found Boswell preparing to leave with his entourage of retainers. He was surprised to see her.

'Sir, may I speak with you alone?' Isabel asked with a dry tight throat. He nodded impatiently and steered her behind a stall.

'Speak quickly, fair maid, I have a long journey ahead,' he managed a forced smile.

'You are leaving for Falkland with the King?' Isabel questioned nervously.

'No, Miss Roskill, I ride for Brae,' he answered curtly. 'I do not wish to dally where plague is likely to follow and I must see to my estates.'

'Then take me with you, please Boswell!' Isabel cried impulsively, her pale face dropping its accustomed guarded look. She could not bear the thought of being parted from him now.

She looked vulnerable and unsure of herself, Boswell thought as he watched impassively, her black eyes pleading with him. This outburst was indeed a surprise. He had thought that Isabel was as manipulative as him and that they understood each other. Last night's embrace in the antechamber was surely of mutual enjoyment and nothing more. But had not Mairi once told him that Isabel was lovestruck for him?

'You must realise that cannot be,' he laughed to cover his confusion, 'it would be quite improper.'

'When has that ever worried you?' Isabel flashed a rebuke at his amused face.

Boswell fixed her with narrowed eyes like cracks of blue lightning, his look cold and disdainful. 'You forget yourself, madam, I am betrothed to your stepsister. I could not insult her by flaunting you like a whore.'

The words whiplashed Isabel as if he had used his belt on her. Her eyes pricked with stinging hurt. This was not the charming man who had promised her a night of lovemaking when the opportunity arose. She could not bear his rebuff. The familiar pounding in her ears began as her panic surged. He did not love her, the demons shouted in her head.

'Mairi despises you,' Isabel's voice rose to a shriek, 'she is beyond your reach now, Boswell. It is she who has insulted you!'

She clung to his gauntleted arm like a falcon refusing to move. 'It is I who loves you. Marry me and you will inherit Duntorin, I promise. Marry me Boswell!'

The lean courtier grabbed her savagely by the shoulders.

'What are you saying, you mad wench?' he hissed in her face. 'Where is Mairi?'

'She's eloped with Douglas,' Isabel trembled at the bruising fingers about her upper arms, 'she went this morning, you cannot stop her. Take me with you, Robert!'

He raised a heavily gloved hand and struck her across the cheek. The jewelled studs caught her delicate skin and tore thin lines into it like a cat's claws. It froze the hysteria in Isabel's throat and she gasped in pained shock as traces of fresh blood oozed to the surface. Boswell seemed not to notice.

'Tell me where she has gone,' he rapped out, his face distorted cruelly, 'tell me before I strike you again.'

Isabel sobbed out the lovers' place of rendezvous, terrified by the violence in Boswell's face. It had come from nowhere to disfigure his handsome features. In that moment, she realised all too well, this man was capable of the treason and attempted murder of which Douglas had accused him.

He threw her out of the way and Isabel fell against the wall, knocking her head. Her mind drummed fit to bursting with the devils that screamed inside. She had brought this on herself, upon all of them. She was hateful and evil; she did not deserve to live.

Crawling forward in the straw, she was vaguely aware of shouting and horses stamping. Not only had she betrayed Mairi but her brother too. She dared not contemplate what Boswell intended to do. Perhaps he would be too late and Douglas and Mairi were already man and wife? A small voice inside prayed that they were.

But she, Isabel, was a witch who had made black magic and cursed that Mairi would die in flames. She had also sought vengeance on the man she hated most, the black-hearted minister who had abandoned her after making her a mistress and slave to his lust.

Isabel never imagined this malignant hate and jealousy could ever have poisoned her spirit so much towards others. She had closed her heart to real feeling the day her mother had deserted her and since then had forgotten how to love. She would go mad thinking about it. The thin prostrate figure buried her head in the dirty straw and wept in distress.

Douglas was on the point of departure when the message came. The Bailie had promised to keep his father occupied while Florence was at the Palace. The way was clear. Douglas was mounting with the pretend documents of business when a runner appeared breathless in the close.

'Douglas Roskill?' he shouted to the tall man on the mounting block. Douglas nodded with annoyance, eager to be away. 'I bring an urgent message,' the boy replied, 'please will you follow me quickly?'

Douglas resented the boy's confident demand, but what if it were a message from Mairi?

'Who asks for me?' he called down sharply.

'Reverend Zechariah Black.'

Douglas's face flashed with anger, he would not go to this man's bidding if his life depended on it and he would not be delayed by the despicable dog who called himself God's servant.

'Get out of my way before I knock you down,' Douglas proceeded to mount from the block, 'and tell your master to go to the Devil!'

To the young Roskill's incredulity the boy stood his ground.

'It is a matter of utmost urgency, sir. Please come. It will not take long.'

Something about the lad's steady gaze and courageous obstinacy made Douglas hesitate. He had no idea what Black was up to, but maybe he should go. He would not delay more than a few minutes, Douglas determined, being frantic with impatience to be with Mairi once more after the unspeakable pleasure of the previous evening.

Douglas dismounted and led his horse after the messenger. They wended their way through the narrow wynds and closes of the town, cleared of middens. Refuse now had to be taken out to the fields beyond the walls in a desperate attempt to stem the fever. They arrived at the meagre lodgings of the minister below the stair of a merchant's house. The upstairs rooms were shuttered and deserted and no sound of servants echoed around the courtyard.

The room Douglas entered was dark and stank of fetid air. Douglas retched as his eyes tried to pick out the occupant. Zechariah Black lay on a truckle bed in the corner. The boy, standing guard by the door, appeared to be the only person left to attend the sick minister. It must have been he who had mingled sweet herbs in the straw to try and overcome the foul stench.

As his eyes grew accustomed to the gloom, Douglas saw the drenched, haggard face of Black, no trace of the supercilious sneer he usually wore. The man was shaking uncontrollably, his jaw chattering as if frozen by his own sweat.

'I knew you would come, Roskill,' he groaned, clutching his stomach in a spasm of pain. Douglas felt sick at the sight of the pathetic skeletal figure and wished to be gone quickly.

'Come to the point,' he answered tersely, trying not to show his disgust. The place was plague-ridden.

'I can help you,' Black wheezed, gasping for air as he spoke, 'to convict Boswell.'

Douglas's eyes were suddenly keen. 'Explain,' he demanded.

'I was in a tavern one evening,' his dark glazed eyes looked self-mocking for an instant. 'I overheard Boswell plotting with the Ruthvens.' He paused as his body convulsed in a fit of retching and he gripped his stomach again.

'So I was right,' Douglas said more to himself, 'even then.'

'Better than that,' Black fixed him with his half-dead gaze, 'I was on a mission in Perth the time of the Gowrie incident.' Douglas drew nearer to make out the failing voice.

'Go on,' he encouraged.

'I saw Boswell with Ruthven the night before the kidnap. They were toasting each other in the street, drinking to their success, thinking they were alone, but I was - in a nearby alley.' Black broke off in a spluttering cough. Douglas waited. 'They both returned to Gowrie's house. The next night Boswell returned to the same tavern to lie low and left behind a coat of chain-mail. With encouragement, the maid and innkeeper would testify.'

'Why are you telling me this now?' Douglas was cautious, unable to trust the viper who had once turned his venom on Mairi.

Black crumpled with the searing agony wracking his body. The young noble came forward, helping him to drink from the mazer at his side. His lips and tongue were cracked like parched soil but the rough wine eased the pain.

'I know I am dying,' the words rattled in Black's throat, 'God wreaks his revenge on the wicked.' He gave a dry breathless laugh. 'You despise me Roskill, but by telling you this now, I may atone for some of my sins, don't you think?'

Douglas did not answer at first, looking at the emaciated, heaving body. 'You are no good to me dead,' he said dryly.

A thin ghostly smile flickered across the tortured face.

'Peter, my servant, heard their boastings too,' Black croaked, 'he will be your witness, he is a good boy, one of God's own.' He broke off, exhausted by the exertion of talking and sunk back on the bed.

Douglas looked quickly at the youth at the door, who nodded in agreement. The boy was brave indeed, Douglas thought.

Black began to mutter deliriously. 'My head, oh, the pain.' He grabbed Douglas's hand, his eyes staring wildly without recognition. 'You stab me with knives!' he cried. 'Knives in my head and belly -'

Douglas watched in horror as Black went into a fit, screaming like an animal in the throes of dying. He turned and strode from the death chamber. Stopping at the door, Douglas pressed a silver bottle into Peter's hand.

'Give him this whisky to numb the pain,' Douglas ordered curtly. 'When he is dead, come to me at the Palace. I go immediately to break the news to the King; Boswell may be a danger to his life even now.'

As Douglas rode swiftly through the town, breathing in gulps of fresher air, he felt the stirrings of victory. This changed everything. He had the proof he needed; Peter, the tavern-keeper and maid at Perth were his witnesses. Boswell would be clapped in irons for the King would not spare his 'favourite' if it threatened his life or the peace of the realm. Mairi and he need not run like guilty lovers; they would stay and confront their parents with their hand-fast marriage and Mairi would have the Duntorin blessing she deserved.

He found the Palace in a confusion of packing and haste. No sooner had Douglas entered the royal apartments than Lucy hurried to greet him.

'Douglas, what are you doing here?' she gasped.

Douglas explained as quickly as he could his reason for coming to the Palace before the Court removed to Falkland. Lucy paled at his words.

'Oh Douglas,' Lucy clutched his arm, 'I knew Boswell was an evil man, he has sent your sister Isabel nearly mad. I've just found her wandering in the courtyard, she's hysterical. Thank goodness Mairi is at least safe with you, safe from Boswell.'

Douglas's face darkened at Lucy's baffling words.

'Mairi is not with me,' his voice was hard as lead, 'I came straight to the Palace to warn the King of the adder that curls in his nest. What do you know of Mairi's whereabouts?'

Terror filled the dark blue eyes and Lucy shook as she spoke.

'I know she has gone to Leith to await you.' She saw Douglas flush. 'Isabel must have overheard Mairi telling me in secrecy. Oh Douglas,' she cried, 'I fear Boswell may have gone to try and stop your elopement, he forced your sister to tell your plan. I assumed you would have been in hiding with Mairi by now.'

'Mairi!' Douglas wheeled round his face a rigid mask. 'She is at the mercy of that devil.'

He strode to the door, cursing himself for allowing his triumph over

Boswell to distract him from his beloved. Boswell was unaware that Douglas had the power to expose his treason and he could at this very moment be abducting Mairi, snatching her out of his reach.

Turning to the frightened Lucy he ordered, 'Take Isabel and go at once to my father and tell him where I hasten. I will take two of the royal guards. Ask Duntorin to follow with his retainers. If that is where Boswell has gone, no doubt he travels with a pack of unruly curs to protect him.'

'Of course,' Lucy rushed after him.

Mairi jumped up at the sound of footsteps on the wooden stairs. The dim lamp flickered to reveal the morose face of Elliot.

'There is a gentleman to see you,' he announced without expression. Her heart fluttered like a nervous fledgling to think of Douglas so near.

'Show him up please,' she urged.

Elliot showed a hint of hesitation but Mairi assumed this was part of the man's cautious nature. He turned and descended. She listened to the unbarring of the outer door.

There was a sound of scuffling and a muffled groan. Mairi called out to Elliot but no reply came. Rapid footsteps beat on the ladder and then a figure appeared head and shoulders first up the make-shift stairway. Mairi's whole body turned to jelly at the sight of the loathsome Boswell in his riding clothes.

'So I come in time,' he sneered as Mairi backed away from him, 'my betrothed has not yet flown with her lover.'

'Get away from me,' Mairi hissed at him, clutching a bolt of cloth behind her that stopped her retreat. 'Douglas will be here any moment, you cannot stop us.'

Boswell laughed viciously and came towards her.

'My rival will never set eyes on you again, sweet wench,' he crowed, the blue eyes raking her like dagger blades. 'You are mine to do with as I please, with your own parent's blessing.' He lunged forward and gripped her wrist, pulling her to him roughly. 'First I will take my pleasure of you.' His scented chin brushed her half-turned face. 'I have waited too long for you, you sorceress. Then I will lock you up in Brae.'

As he tried to force his mouth on hers, Mairi bit his bottom lip savagely. Boswell yelped in pain, momentarily loosening his hold on her. Quick as a cat, she sprang from his grasp and threw herself towards the ladder. Lurching after Mairi, he knocked the oil lamp on to the bails of dusty cloth as he moved.

In an instant, flames leapt up and licked around the bundles. The fire flared, lighting the ugly lust on Boswell's ghastly countenance as he crushed Mairi to the floor. She began to scream and tear at his face like a frenzied animal. A spark jumped from the kindled cloth on to his hat and the

165

feather caught alight.

'You're on fire!' Mairi shrieked to distract him and Boswell cursed as he felt the hat and burnt his hand. He rolled away, beating his hat on the floor. Mairi moved crab-like towards the ladder, hurling herself down its steep steps. Her head crashed against a post and she slumped winded in the straw. Closing her eyes, Mairi could hear Boswell's screaming as he toppled down the steps after her.

She pressed deeper into the prickly hay, vaguely aware of a distant commotion at the door. Shouts rang in her ears like church bells, yet all she cared about was that Boswell did not come for her. She was safe in her bed, there was a blazing fire to warm her like at home in Duntorin Castle. Strange, Mairi thought dreamily, to think of Duntorin as home . . .

Boswell jumped the last four steps, spotting the crumpled shape of Mairi half buried in the straw. He hesitated, coughing on the thickening smoke as a roll of burning cloth drop to the floor near her. It cut off his path towards the slumped unconscious form; to reach Mairi now would put his own life at risk.

Boswell turned his back quickly and rushed for the door. For a moment he was stunned by the sight of the fierce fighting outside. The wharf rang with the clash of sword blades and shouts of men. In dazed panic, the escaping courtier realised it was his own retainers who struggled to beat off Duntorin's host. He briefly glimpsed the tall lunging figure of his despised rival, Douglas Roskill, delivering the death blow to one of his guards and then Boswell broke from the warehouse.

With the cover of the bloody confusion, he crouched down and ran along the quayside to where his horse stamped in fright. Driven with the speed of fear he reached his terrified animal and jumped on to its back. As it reared up at its master's vicious tug, a voice bellowed behind.

'You'll not escape now you traitorous coward!' Douglas shouted in fury and seized the bridle.

Boswell drew his pistol and fired wildly at his assailant, but Douglas wheeled the horse about, avoiding the point-blank fire and toppled his enemy from the saddle. Boswell crashed to the ground and Douglas leapt upon him, gripping his throat.

In a tight hold they rolled to the edge of the quay, a frantic strength coming to Boswell's aid. He jerked up his knee and punched into Douglas's wounded side. Young Duntorin loosened his hold as the old pain seared through him, giving Boswell a moment to topple him over the wharf. Douglas, his face contorted in agony, pulled the struggling Brae after him into the dark chill waters of Leith.

They went under, Boswell surfacing first and thrashing frantically for the shore. Douglas swam after him, catching hold of the courtier's sodden doublet, his energy sapping with each stroke. Boswell grabbed on to the wooden staithe and drew out his dagger with his free hand. Douglas saw the blade swipe at his face and plunged under water to avoid its attack. He seemed to submerge for an age, until his lungs would burst for air, aware only that he clung to his writhing opponent.

Suddenly a dull noise cracked above the water and Douglas felt Boswell go limp. Bursting to the water's surface, he saw his father standing on the quay, pistol in hand. Boswell rolled over in the water, face upwards, eyes staring and struggled no more.

Hands seized Douglas from above and hauled him gasping to safety.

'Mairi?' he rasped, coughing up water. He turned to see the stocky figure of Alexander Lismore disappearing into the burning warehouse.

'We may be too late.' Duntorin's face looked haggard.

Douglas did not stop to question how Mairi's brother had arrived to support him. He took one look at the crumbling warehouse roof and with a supreme effort, mustered a last reserve of strength. He threw himself after Alexander, his father following. In seconds the Chief of Lismore was beaten back by the heat. But ignoring the warning of his father to 'in God's name take care!' Douglas fought his way through the blackening smoke.

Suffocating fumes filtered into the pocket of safety in the hay where Mairi had crawled. At the point of choking he spotted the red hair trailing out from the nest of straw. Douglas dived for Mairi and pulled her from the inferno, saving them both from the flames with his drenched body. A moment later the floor above broke up and crashed in a fireball to the ground floor. As flying debris rained from above, hands grabbed them both and heaved them to safely.

Someone threw a pail of water over Douglas to douse his singeing hair and beard. He caught sight of Boswell's bulging eyes staring up from the murky water where his dead body bobbed. At least Mairi was spared such a gruesome spectacle, Douglas thought faintly. Brae's supporters were routed. In a silent throat-choking victory, Duntorin and Alexander Lismore clasped each other in a bear-hug. Their feud was over.

Mairi gradually became conscious that she lay in soft sheets. Her eyes flickered wide as the horror of the burning warehouse leapt to her mind. Douglas sat beside her. He was holding her hand, yet she could not feel it through the bandage that swathed it. His eyes were darkly tender and glistening.

'Douglas,' she whispered his name and smiled. He smiled back; his generous, sensuous, dear smile, that set his black eyes alive with mischief. Mairi gasped as she noticed his half melted beard, stubble hugging the strong chin. 'You came in the end, I knew you would.' Her green eyes filled with grateful tears.

'I should have come much sooner, my love,' he leaned towards her and kissed her cracked lips lovingly. 'I would have died in the flames rather than have come out without you.'

Mairi's face streamed with tears as he lifted her gently to him and held her close in his strong arms.

'And Boswell?' she whispered, almost dreading to hear.

'He is dead, Mairi, and will trouble us no more,' he rocked her reassuringly.

'Oh, Douglas, never let me go again, promise me,' Mairi's voice quavered as she hugged him weakly.

'I promise,' Douglas replied huskily, feeling the emotion towards her squeeze his throat. 'Duntorin and your mother plan a great wedding for us at Duntorin Castle.'

Mairi could hardly believe her ears. She buried her face into his warm chest, too overcome to speak. 'And it may not be the only one,' Douglas sounded wry, 'judging by the healing of the past few days.'

Mairi looked up puzzled and Douglas kissed her forehead. 'The Bailie seems to have taken a liking to my strange sister, Isabel. We are here in his Leith house while the fever abates. Isabel is learning to live again under his attention, perhaps even to feel love.'

'I'm glad,' Mairi said simply, smiling into his dark eyes.

'Now I will not be forgiven if I do not allow someone else to share in your recovery - two people in fact.'

Mairi smiled quizzically, not wanting this happy dream-like state to end. Douglas stood and went to the door. At his beckoning, a familiar figure entered.

'Sandy?' Mairi croaked with delighted amazement. 'And Lucy!' She felt tears welling up again. Her friend rushed to the bed and planted a kiss on her cheek, laughing with joy to see Mairi reviving. Alexander bent to kiss her too.

'When did you arrive back?' Mairi gulped emotionally.

'In time to beat off the Boswell boys,' Douglas intercepted quickly. Mairi noticed the spark of admiration light her lover's eyes. Could it be that they were friends at last?

'I was on my way back to Edinburgh when Sam met me,' Alexander explained. 'Certain things that needed attention drew me back more quickly than expected.' The fair Chief and Lucy swapped bashful looks.

Mairi smiled in understanding. 'I had just arrived with Sam at Duntorin's house, hoping to see you and Mother, when Lucy came with Douglas's message.'

'Then you will not stand in the way of my happiness, Sandy,' she asked quietly, wanting his approval, 'even though I have fallen for our father's enemy?'

The men exchanged quick glances and Douglas nodded.

'No enemy, Mairi,' Alexander reproved her gently. 'Douglas told me of your suspicions of him as our father's slayer.' Mairi felt herself blushing under his green-eyed gaze. 'They were unfounded - I heard the confession from the murderer's own lips before I killed him.'

Mairi caught her breath sharply, wondering if she could withstand anymore shocks. 'Admittedly he was drunk and boasting,' Lismore's mouth curled in disgust.

'Who?' Mairi asked, holding onto her brother's hand with her unbound one.

'Our cousin Cailean,' Alexander sighed. 'He could not bear the thought of the Lismores living side by side in peace with the Roskills. After all his father had died on one of his thieving skirmishes at Roskill hands.'

Mairi gave Douglas a wary look, but he did not gainsay her brother's words. 'Father was on his way to make a treaty with Duntorin,' Alexander continued. 'You and mother were invited as guests too. But Cailean sent his assassins to betray father and cut him down within sight of Duntorin Castle to make it appear like Roskill treachery.'

Mairi's eyes pricked with tears at the thought of the desolate bothy and her father bleeding to death on a stranger's soil. 'Douglas arrived too late to capture the Garroch murderers, but at least he gave father a shred of comfort as he lay dying,' Alexander's voice was proudly lilting, 'promising to look after his wife and daughter.'

Mairi's eyes met Douglas's and he shimmered before her as she blinked away the tears of thankful love.

'I always suspected the treacherous fox, but could not be sure,' Douglas spoke quietly and added, 'your brother now inherits Cailean's lands. The King has ratified his claim.'

She held out a hand to Douglas and he came swiftly to her side. Alexander stood by Lucy, quietly happy. In a tender clasp, Mairi and Douglas had thoughts only for each other.

'I love you so very much, Douglas,' Mairi whispered, her green eyes dancing with their old sparkle.

'And I you,' Douglas's dark eyes shone with happiness, 'my Queen of the Beltane.'

Lightning Source UK Ltd.
Milton Keynes UK
UKOW050608050713

213257UK00001B/23/P